PLAYBACK EFFECT

KAREN A. WYLE

Published in the United States of America
Oblique Angles Press

Cover design by Kit Foster

Photographs in cover art by
Olga_Anourina, mik ulyannikov,
ostill, Inga Dudkina

Author photo by Alissa Lise Wyle

Interior layout by Livali Wyle

DEDICATION

To my family.

And to the man on the plane who raised an eyebrow
when I told him I couldn't tell stories.

CHAPTER 1

WYNNE CANTRELL PATTED the lightweight helmet, switched the setting from Record to Play, and prepared to inspect her dream. Already, remembering, her excitement began to build. This one should make her agent grin his evil grin and rub his fingers together in the ageless gesture for counting money.

It was always strange, though, to relive her own dream without the specifics she had included. The helmets could record the ebb and flow of emotion with exquisite delicacy, but the capacity to capture full sensory detail remained out of reach. Instead of seeing her ex-lover, her customers would encounter a mysterious Other, imbued with the aura of forbidden fruit; they would find themselves in luxurious surroundings, but not necessarily the scarlet leather and shining dark wood of her dream decor. Where she had recreated specific implements and their various impacts, she could only be sure of conveying the surge of pain and pleasure intertwined, arousal and fulfillment.

How disappointed the researchers must have been at the limits of the technology! Wynne herself would no doubt be a good deal wealthier if she could market her visions more fully. But she was just as glad that she did not have to fine-tune the line between profit and privacy. The customers would fill in the blanks with their own subconscious imaginations—particularly if, as was recommended, they set the playback to begin when they entered their own REM sleep.

Even without that assistance, by the time the playback ended she was panting and twisting in her chair. She turned off the helmet, took two deep breaths, and stood up to stretch, the smile on her face fading as she turned her mind to the business of the day.

It was a good thing she could dream in this lucrative direction. All lucid dreamers had their strengths and weaknesses, scenes they could easily generate and others that would dissolve away despite their best efforts. Dreamers who could handle any kind of kink had a clear advantage.

If Hal and her lover had ever met, there was a chance Hal would sense familiarity in the man's dream analogue—but the issue was unlikely to arise. Twice a month, at most, he condescended to "see what she'd been up to." And it had been some time since she attempted to interest him in any dream of intimacy.

What did it say about their marriage, that she could more easily share herself with strangers than with her husband?

She shook off the question and glanced at the latest industry news summary. She was engaged in an entirely new form of competition. On the one hand, performers of various kinds, from athletes to dancers to porn stars, were busily recording their actual experiences. On the other team: the few dreamers like her, striving to outdo mere reality with the vigor and creativity of their imaginations.

(And then there were those other recordings, with their grimmer purpose. Justified, cruel, or both? Well, no one was asking her.)

She had better get dressed. It didn't much matter what she wore to meet with her agent, so she could concentrate on how she wanted to appear at lunch with Hal. She would not aim at an obviously enticing look: Hal responded poorly to the obvious, let alone the desperate. But she knew well enough, by now, what colors and shapes would spark his interest.

Luck was with her: she finished with her agent in plenty of time, and the subway came roaring up almost as soon as she reached the platform. Wynne reached Cardinem Square almost ten minutes before Hal was supposed to show. It was a perfect day for relaxing by the fountain: the water catching the sunlight, with the occasional fleeting rainbow in the spray, and just enough breeze that a few errant drops touched her, but not enough to be a bother. She sat on the low stone wall surrounding the fountain with her legs crossed, facing the sculpture from which the water leapt in a nested series of arcs. Nearby, a woman her age, or perhaps younger, held a toddler around the waist while the child reached out to feel the spray, squealing in delight whenever the water reached him.

The fountain was one of her favorites of Hal's pieces. When his submission won the contest, she'd been over the moon, not only because it meant money and recognition for Hal, but because she knew that she'd be able to see the work in situ, often and easily.

The week after the sculpture was installed and the water turned on, she had had a dream—a spontaneous one, not controlled—that the fountain's long, branching arms had grown long, graceful hands, their bronze fingers reaching out to her and beckoning her in. She had held hands with the sculpture, then climbed to the top of the fountain, with the water—sparkling like champagne, refreshing but not cold—dancing over and around her. She had dreamed it again, on purpose, quite a few times since then—and had offered to record it for Hal, despite the lesser level of detail he'd be able to experience. Predictably, Hal had shown little interest.

She had time to relax for a bit, and enjoy the warmth of the early May sunshine. She stretched her legs out on the wall, leaned back on her hands, and closed her eyes.

Some while later, the ache in her arms roused her from her almost meditative state and reminded her of the time that must have passed. She checked, then sighed. Hal was late again. But only a few minutes. She would wait a little longer before trying to reach him. The restaurant was a few blocks away—would they have time to get there and eat before Hal would want to return to his studio?

She checked the time again. She had better call. She reached for her phone, rolling her eyes.

And then the world exploded.

Chapter 2

Hal Wakeman looked at the model on the table and grinned. He loved this idea. He had always marveled at the unexpected beauty of buildings in mid-demolition, the ever-shifting shapes as the rubble descended. But it had never occurred to him before that he could hearken back, in his art, to the days when he had destroyed—carefully, expertly, benignly—instead of created.

Would strangers, those who neither knew nor cared about his background, perceive the origin of these straight and curving lines, this towering and crumbling structure? Well, he had revealed as much in an interview or two, if anyone bothered to read them. Hal glanced at his monitor, still displaying the latest story. Of course they'd eaten up the father/son angle: the father builds skyscrapers, the son used to obliterate them. He hadn't tried to convince them it was coincidence. (And Wynne had never accepted that it really was a coincidence. She kept hinting that he'd been trying to goad his father in some way, or even hurt him. Why did women see drama wherever they looked?)

The photographer had taken the theme and run with it: the portrait of Hal had an intense, wild-eyed look. (Maybe he'd spooked the fellow by commenting that he sometimes missed the noise: the first explosions, then the even louder second series, then the anticlimactic but sensuous hissing as the building collapsed....)

If only the structure could be larger, towering over the observer, almost as a building would have done. Perhaps he could sell the committee on an expansion.

Damn! He'd lost track of the time again. If he didn't hurry, or even if he did, he would be late meeting Wynne.

She was used to it, but in the barely patient manner of long-suffering spouses.

Hal checked his pockets for keys and phone and ran out the door, thundering down the stairs rather than waiting for the elevator. Hitting the street, he raced toward the subway entrance, taking deep breaths of the crisp spring air as he ran. It had turned out a splendid day, a gift of a day. Maybe after lunch, he and Wynne would take a walk around the city. He would listen to her describing her latest dreams, and she would indulge him as he imagined how long it would take to bring this or that proud building tumbling down.

As he ran up the steps toward the subway exit, a phalanx of police—riot police or something of the sort, with shiny plastic body armor and tall transparent shields—converged on the exit. Unless he moved quickly, they would prevent his leaving. Wynne had been kept waiting long enough without that. But there could be some dangerous situation in the street, from which these officious Myrmidons genuinely sought to protect him.

As he neared the top of the stairs, one of the officers reached out an arm to block him. "Where do you think *you're* going?"

Well, that didn't sound like someone especially concerned for his safety. To hell with that attitude! He ducked around the fellow and darted out into the street, ignoring the shouts behind him.

But in a moment, he skidded to a stop, mouth frozen open in a gape of disbelief.

***

The bomb must have been hidden inside the fountain.

The van rounded the corner, wheels screeching, throwing the rookie against the window, and he caught his first glimpse of the devastation. The bronze sculpture at the center, always abstract, had become a nightmare vision of itself, twisting off in every direction, reaching jagged claws toward the chaos around it. The debris of the fountain was littered with an incongruously colorful array of other objects—water bottles, bits of clothing, toys—that had been sucked back toward the center by the vacuum after the blast.

The van pulled up and the driver flung open the door. The rookie shrank back as the wailing and screaming hit him at full volume. A moment later came the odors: the sharp bite of explosive mingled with a stench that might be burnt hair and clothing, and a smell like roasted meat that could only be burnt flesh. And all around lay sprawled and writhing bodies, pools of blood, severed limbs.

For a moment the rookie stood paralyzed, as all around him the more experienced record techs spilled out of the van and got to work. Then, just as they had told him would happen, his training kicked in. He grabbed a case of helmets and looked around. Right away he noticed and tried to ignore the explosive ordnance disposal techs, sweeping the scene for additional bombs. They would do their job; he had his own.

Highest priority were those victims still conscious, yet grievously wounded. The most potent experiences would occur before the emergency medical personnel reached the victim, and he was not allowed to apply the helmet without an EMT or paramedic present—but if he acted quickly, he could get a helmet on before any pain medication kicked in. And the new helmets were supposed to be able to grab a few minutes' worth of short-term memory.

He needed someone to follow. There were dozens of EMT's and paramedics on the scene, some doing triage, some tending to those victims already tagged as most urgently in need of help. Close to him lay a woman whose shoulder bore the painted symbol for Second Tier: seriously injured, but likely to survive a few minutes while the First Tier received stabilizing treatment. She would have been given pain medication a while ago. That would not do for his purpose. He trotted over to one of the workers. "Recording team, here and ready. I'm—."

The woman snorted and turned away, the sound and movement eloquently conveying both anger and contempt. "Vulture squad. Just what we needed."

"I'll try to stay out of your way."

"The hell you will. You'll be grabbing at the victims over my shoulder, shoving helmets on their heads."

He should have expected this attitude. The police were used to working with recording techs, who hung back until a path to the victim was secure and then rushed in. EMT's most often dealt with trauma that had no human cause. Unlike the police, they did not normally view themselves as adjuncts to the criminal justice system.

The rookie's supervisor chose that moment to appear. The rookie wasn't sure whether to be relieved: he could use the backup, but he doubted he cut an impressive and competent figure just now.

"Any problems?"

The EMT glared at the new arrival with impressive scorn. "You know exactly what the problem is, but let's stop wasting time." She hurried toward a man—well, more of a boy—lying a few yards away, clutching his leg. His thigh. It wasn't a leg any more, not all of one. The boy seemed to be in the process of regaining consciousness.

The supervisor dug his elbow into the rookie's ribs and hissed in his ear. "Get on it! He's about to realize what's happened to him."

The rookie gaped. "But when they're conscious, we're supposed to try to get consent first—"

"There's no time! We've got to catch the moment when he knows his leg is gone! A memory won't be as vivid—*move!*"

The rookie jumped, then scurried over to the boy, approaching him from the side opposite where the EMT was kneeling. He looked quickly at the helmets, grabbed one the right size, then made himself stop and breathe. It was a good thing the helmets were shaped as they were—he could apply one without taking the risk of lifting the boy's head. As gently as he could, he seated the helmet across the boy's forehead and hit "Record". Then he clambered to his feet and stepped back. The EMT's jaw dropped in shock. "What the hell are you doing?"

The boy reclaimed the EMT's attention by moaning and muttering something the rookie couldn't hear. Then came the moment the supervisor had anticipated. The boy struggled up onto one elbow and looked down at himself. Even from the distance to which the rookie had retreated, he could see the boy go pale. "What—did—my leg! My *leg!*" He turned and gripped the tech hard with one shaking hand. "Can you—is it here, can you find it, can you *fix* it?"

The rookie turned toward his supervisor, who was almost rubbing his hands in satisfaction. Of course, it wasn't what it might seem to an ignorant observer. Neither of them was some kind of sadist. They were here to ensure that when the police caught the son of a bitch who had planted the bomb, the bomber could be made to live through something close to the agony he'd caused.

And knowing you'd lost a leg—that was horrible. The victim was just a kid, the age the rookie had been when he was playing high school football. And now? If he was lucky, maybe they'd be able to grow him a new leg, but legs took years, even when everything went well. The kid wouldn't be whole until long after his football, or whatever, days were over.

Suddenly the supervisor's expression changed. "What the—get over there and switch it off!"

The rookie's head whipped back toward the boy. He had collapsed, and the EMT was cursing under her breath, unpacking a portable defibrillator, checking around the boy, applying the device. The rookie froze. If he followed that order, if he went anywhere near the boy, he might somehow be responsible for what was about to happen.

In a few minutes, it was over. He might not have known, even watching the boy shudder, and shudder again, and then slump in final relaxation; but the EMT's body language told the story. The boy had died.

Had died, with the helmet on "record."

The rookie looked back at his supervisor. The older man was shaking his head heavily from side to side. "Well, now, don't we have the hot potato on our hands."

***

At police headquarters, all was chaos. Crackling radios, phones buzzing or ringing, screens muttering on multiple channels, people constantly in and out with more and more information: the growing list of identified casualties, the status of clearing buildings which might be structurally compromised, sightings of suspicious persons, sightings of suspicious planes and spacecraft....

Arthur Kellic granted himself a moment to rest his face in his hands. It was a mistake: now he could tell just how exhausted he was, how his shoulders ached from immobility and tension. And there, waiting, were the feelings he had no time for: horror, rage, grief.

What had they done to his city? Who had done it, and how would he catch them?

Arthur straightened up and looked around to see who might be awaiting his attention. His assistant Hannah hovered in the doorway; he waved her over.

"Boss, something's come up with the vultures. They've picked up something they weren't supposed to."

Arthur frowned. "You know I don't like that label." The recording technicians might be a nuisance for police and medical, but Arthur thoroughly approved of the idea. What better punishment than inflicting the very same suffering that the perp had caused? Without the barbarity of an eye for an eye, the criminal could learn firsthand how it felt to be blinded.

Hannah shrugged. "Whatever. One of them recorded a death."

Arthur whistled. "Hoo, boy. Are the press on it yet?"

"Not yet. But you know they'll get hold of it soon enough."

"Where's the recording? I want it locked up tight. No one makes a copy, no one gets near it, until we have instructions."

Hannah nodded and threaded her way back through the desks and people toward her own station. A phone buzzed while she was still en route; Arthur looked for anyone likely to answer it, shrugged, and picked it up. "Senior Detective Kellic here."

"Sir, we've detained someone who tried to evade the patrol near the subway."

"Trying to get out, or get in?"

"Out. Should we hold onto him or cut him loose?"

"Anyone we know? Does he have a sheet?"

"No, but I ran him through the database, and I came up with something. He's some sort of artist now, but he used to bring down buildings. With explosives."

Arthur found he was clutching the phone so hard that the edges hurt his hand. "Harold Wakeman."

"Yeah, that's the guy! What's the story?"

"Just hang onto him. I'll be there as soon as I can." Arthur hung up and put the phone down, carefully, so as not to drop it. He looked around. "Who's got the latest casualty list? Send it to me."

He opened the file, willing his hands not to shake, and scrolled down. The names were going by too fast; he made himself slow down. Had she been at the site?

And there it was. Status critical, traumatic amputation of one hand, extensive reconstruction necessary.

Wynne.

And Hal—the rival, the victor—caught in the thick of it, trying to get away from the police.

What had that bastard done?

Arthur sat in the Director's office as the Director studied images of the wreckage, trying not to fidget. He could just as easily have made this report by phone, but the Director sometimes preferred, according to no rule or pattern that Arthur could identify, to have his subordinates appear in person. He would lean slightly forward in his expensive office chair, his hands just barely resting on the desk, and peer at one as if examining a bacterium through a microscope; or he might inhale, slowly and deliberately, and then sit back and smile. But however eccentric, the man was more competent and efficient than many a superior with whom Arthur had had to cope in his career.

"So you already have a suspect?"

"A person of interest, at least." Arthur handed his tablet to the Director, pointing toward the top. "Harold Wakeman, the husband of one of the victims."

The Director raised both eyebrows. "Looking first to the victim's nearest and dearest seems somewhat less appropriate when the victim is one of many. Where the others merely thrown in for good measure? How very heartless."

Arthur couldn't help but frown. "Fourteen people dead. Dozens more burned or maimed or both. Heartless enough, whatever the motive."

The Director scrolled through Arthur's notes, nodding a few times. Then he put down the tablet, picked up a marble paperweight, and stroked its smooth surface. "And what motive do you propose for Mr. Wakeman? Was the bombing an artistic exercise of some kind? An experiment in the aesthetics of destruction?"

It sounded so implausible, stated like that. But to his surprise, the Director gave him back the tablet and gestured toward the door. "One never knows how the artistic temperament will express itself, Mr. Kellic. Carry on."

INTERLUDE

THE POP-UP ad read:

"YOUNG—FOREVER

"Nothing feels like youth.
"You who are young cannot yet appreciate your youth. The humming in the blood, the tautness of skin, the spring in the step, the sharpness of perception are bestowed on us for far too short a time. In later years, only a wisp of scent or a scrap of song can revive for a moment the sensation of youth—and then it passes, beyond recall.
"But now, you can capture these sensations forever!
"Our studios provide a wide variety of activities to ensure your full enjoyment of your youthful vigor and vitality.* (*Parental consent required for customers under eighteen.) Record any or all, for a single one-time fee! Then, take your recording with you—or entrust it to our secure storage facility, where we will keep it safe, through the years, for you to enjoy again and again.
"Helmets available for an additional charge.
"Parents, what better graduation present could you possibly give your proud young graduates? Special rates available through May 31st. Helmets available in all local school colors. Call now!"

Chapter 3

The lawyer—what was his name? Pavel something—stared at Hal as if Hal were an exotic and dangerous creature. God knows what the man had been told. The tale must have been hair-raising indeed to overcome the well-earned sangfroid of someone who dealt with criminals for a living.

It was a discouraging beginning, but he had no one else to ask. The police and jailers had all refused to acknowledge his questions, let alone answer them. "My wife—*she was in the plaza!* Is she all right?"

The lawyer's eyebrow twitched, as if he had expected some other initial question. He brought out his tablet and poked at it, then scrolled down some document. "She's on the list of those you're charged with killing and injuring—"

Hal's head swam. He clutched the side of the hard metal chair, willing himself not to vomit. "*And?* Which? Is she—is she alive?"

"I'll have to check, and that may take a while. Let's talk a bit about your defense first—"

"I'm not talking about anything until I know what's happened to Wynne!"

The lawyer heaved an aggrieved sigh, then retreated into a corner and made a phone call, muttering almost inaudibly. Hal did not try to follow the half-heard conversation. He felt somehow detached from his own terror, observing it with interest as he experienced it. What medium, what forms, would translate this emotion into tangible art? How could he make the observer share some dim reflection of it?

Finally the lawyer hung up and turned to him. "She's alive, but she's in pretty bad shape. Assuming she pulls through, she—"

"Assuming? What kind of—" Hal did not finish. If his lawyer thought him guilty of mass slaughter and mayhem, he could hardly expect him to have tender sensibilities.

But something in Hal's tone or body language seemed to have gotten through to the man: his face, for the first time, showed something like sympathy. "I think she's expected to make it."

Hal slumped backward, the relief leaving him almost as nauseated as the initial suspense.

The lawyer went on. "She'll need a lot of reconstructive surgery. And—I'm sorry, but she's lost a hand."

Hal was seized with a sensory memory of Wynne's hand lightly tracing the contours of his face. Her hand. Was that the hand that someone had blown into pulp? And they thought he'd done it. Who, why, how could they think that? "Why did they arrest me?"

The lawyer consulted his files again. "Well, you were there. Sort of. And you evaded the police. And then they found out about your background—explosives and all that." He paused. "There's a note in the file from some higher-up. Arthur Kellic. He seems to have taken charge of your case personally."

Of course. Arthur. The man must be delighted—oh, horrified, of course, but delighted as well—to have some excuse for hating Hal's guts, after all this time.

Hal was well and truly fucked.

The lawyer looked as if he agreed with that assessment. He shifted uneasily in his own chair. "Look, Mr. Wakeman. I'm not a complete novice, but I haven't handled very many serious felony cases, and only one murder case. I'm not sure why you chose to call me—"

"I needed someone in a hurry. And they wouldn't let me look up any names." The anger welled up again, a welcome respite from panic and grief. "They have an old wall phone for the prisoners to use, and someone scratched your name and number on the wall—so I figured I'd start with you and see how we got on."

"Mr. Wakeman, I'm not saying I won't take the case, but I'm not sure you should hire me. You're kind of famous, right? Couldn't you afford some big-name private lawyer, someone who's got staff and backup and a bunch of major trials under his belt? It might not make that much difference, the way these cases go. Still, you'd have a better shot."

Hal tried to remember the details of his latest bank statement. He had been planning to rent a larger, better equipped studio, and had been saving for the deposit. But—"Wynne lost a hand."

"I'm afraid so."

Their health coverage would cover most of the cost of a prosthetic, nothing more. Regeneration cost much more—"an arm and a leg," as some wit had put it. If he used his savings and bonds and retirement account, and hocked his propane furnace, Wynne could maybe get her hand back. But not if he blew all their money on legal fees.

If he'd met Wynne on schedule, if he hadn't figured keeping her waiting was no big deal, then Wynne—both of them—might well have been safely away by the time the bomb went off. She would have been safe.

"If I'd been there on time, she'd still have her hand. I'm damned if I'm going to keep her from getting it back."

He did not realize he had spoken aloud, until the attorney responded with a long, whistling sigh. "Damned? That's not too far from what may happen to you. You may get a chance to visit hell."

"I want to see Wynne." Having said as much, Hal realized how intensely, how frantically, he needed to see her, to hold her hand—oh, my God, which hand?—and tell her he loved her, whether or not she could hear.

"No way they're going to allow that."

Finally, belatedly, Hal found that he was crying. "Please. Please check. I'll talk to them; I'll do whatever they want. Please try."

The lawyer shook his head vigorously. "No, you won't." Then his disapproving expression turned sly. "But I might be able to hint at some sort of cooperation and see if it gets us anywhere. You're already in enough trouble that it can't make things much worse if we disappoint them afterward."

Hal finally did laugh, a short bark. "Good enough."

As they rode to the hospital, the lawyer kept muttering. "There's something going on. I don't think I fooled anyone, but they're letting you see her anyway. They want something."

Hal looked over at the guards accompanying them. "Should we be talking?"

The lawyer shrugged. "I haven't said anything that matters. Don't you."

Wynne still looked tall.

It was an absurd thought, to be sure. But weren't patients in hospital beds, surrounded by machinery, supposed to seem smaller? Wynne still came near to meeting the ends of the bed. He felt a stirring of pride in her.

She was unconscious. The lighting had an odd purplish cast—Hal vaguely remembered something about lighting with antibacterial properties—that gave Wynne's face a cold, lifeless quality. Even her dark red hair, the locks that showed, looked maroon. But a reassuring steady beep came from the monitor, as various incomprehensible jagged or wavy lines scrolled continually from left to right.

There was no one by the bed. Why was she all alone? Her parents might not be able to afford the trip, even in this extremity: they would be keeping track of her progress and waiting in desperate hope for the chance to communicate long-distance. But Wynne's sister should be there. Or did she even know? He had had no chance to call her.

Hal could smell nothing but the aggressive reek of cleaning chemicals. A craving for Wynne's own scent, her natural blend of musk, lemon and cinnamon, swept over him. He tried to approach the bed, but a nurse and one of the guards converged, the nurse blocking the way, the guard grabbing his shoulder and yanking him back. He tensed, then backed up in the direction of the guard's pull, waiting with clenched teeth until the guard released him.

Hal turned to his lawyer. "How long can I stay?"

A voice came from the doorway. "That depends."

Hal turned to see Arthur Kellic lounging against the door frame, inspecting him as if were some poisonous but intriguing specimen.

"If you really want to stay a while, that can be arranged. If you cooperate."

Hal opened his mouth; his lawyer dug an elbow into his ribs, presumably to silence him. "My client has no statement to make at this time."

Arthur sneered. "Of course. But he doesn't need to say a thing. We just want to put a helmet on him. With his wife's activities, surely he's accustomed to helmets."

Hal kept staring at Wynne. "I want to stay. If I let you, will you let me stay? And get closer to her? Touch her?"

The lawyer interposed himself between Arthur and Hal, herding Hal into the far corner of the room. "No way, no how. We don't know what those recordings can be made to yield. A week or a month or a year from now, they may turn out to have all sorts of information no one can read today."

"But—"

"That thing records feelings! Can you tell me you don't have any feelings someone could use against you? Or could twist into damaging evidence? Hell, they could find someone to lie about what they recorded, and who'd be able to contradict it? Some 'expert' who doesn't know any more than the cop's tame scientist?"

Hal cast a despairing glance toward Wynne's motionless form. The nurse, who had been hovering protectively by the bed, saw his face; her glare softened into a sort of wary sympathy. Quietly, as though Wynne were capable of being disturbed by louder speech, she said, "I don't think she'll be conscious for some hours yet."

Hal slumped, fighting to stand at all, utterly drained. His lawyer came and took his arm. "We'll be going now."

"Please—can I kiss her?"

No one even bothered to answer him. He swallowed tears once again as the lawyer, flanked by the alert and suspicious guards, led him away.

* * *

Tertius Shaw pondered the latest news as he squeezed his morning orange juice. Naturally, in the absence of the actual perpetrator it was necessary to produce a scapegoat—and it seemed one had already been found. Mr. Wakeman should be flattered to be named the author of so dramatic an event.

Tertius finished squeezing the juice and carried the glass to his breakfast nook. The sunlight streaming in backlit the juice; he relished its intense orange color. The toaster oven pinged as he set down the glass. Tertius extracted the bagel, slathered on a liberal portion of truffle-infused cream cheese, and settled in to enjoy himself.

Was it too soon to plan his next project? He may as well begin. He could stretch out the early phases as much as he liked, let the populace relax somewhat before jerking the chain once again.

Tertius took a judiciously sized bite of his bagel and washed it down with the tart, tangy juice.

What a very lovely morning it was!

***

"The problem is, you could have set it up ahead of time—even way ahead, when you installed the sculpture. So it doesn't matter how many alibis you have: you're bound to have some time unaccounted for...."

Hal listened to his lawyer tell him all the ways he was up the proverbial creek. It didn't sound as if they had many paddles available.

"You haven't been spending much time with people as a couple, so we're short on current character witnesses—at least, favorable ones. The prosecution seems to have dug up a couple of their own. And we're stuck with the new anti-terrorism procedures, so we can't file a motion for change of venue to a different county, or get a continuance until Wynne is able to testify."

Somehow, despite the noose contracting around him, he found time to mourn the destruction of the fountain. It had been his biggest public contract, at the time—a real game-changer, a paradigm shift for his career as an artist. And Wynne liked it so much.... That dream of hers, the one she tried to describe to him: he had the thoroughly irrational conviction that if only he had shown interest in the dream and let her try to share it with him, then maybe they could have joined together somehow to protect the sculpture. He had abandoned it spiritually, and Wynne was too weak to protect it on her own....

Was Bitsy feeling abandoned? They had never boarded her before. He had forgotten about her for hours after his arrest: she must have been horribly bewildered, with dinnertime passing unheeded, her water bowl empty, no one heeding her whines.... When he finally remembered, only the luck of a dog-loving jailer had allowed Hal to arrange for his father to go and fetch her. (Fetch. Ha ha.) Was his father up to taking care of her? What havoc might she wreak, without walks and games to exhaust her energy, and how would his father respond?...

"From their witness list, it's hard to tell whether they're saying you tried to kill your wife, or whether you were making some twisted artistic statement, or both."

The first few times the idea had been mentioned, he had erupted, turning his fury on the hapless messenger, even lunging toward the lawyer on one occasion. But now, the accusation that he had meant to cripple or kill his wife could barely rouse him from dazed lethargy.

He had to stop drifting like this. He had to do something to help his lawyer, to help himself. But only this strange detachment, like a ringing in his ears blocking out unwelcome noises, kept him from unendurable terror.

* * *

Nothing made sense; nothing was as it should be. Wynne kept trying to awaken from dreams, only to find she had been awake already; or she believed she was awake, and proved to be dreaming. Waking and dreaming were more alike than they had ever been: in this place, she could control neither.

She had seen a child, a child with its mother, and everything around them had been bright and joyful, and then something terrible had happened. What had happened? Where was the child, and where the mother?

She closed her eyes and tried to dream that she was well and whole; without pain, with Hal. She almost achieved it, but it all fell apart again, swept away in dust and noise and fire.

Could she possibly have used her hands in dreaming? It seemed so unlikely; but a part of her was missing, and at the same time, another essential part of her was gone or broken.

She worried about Hal. Something must be wrong. If not, he would be here. He might, perhaps, have found some way to suggest that this was really her fault, at least a little; but he would be here. She had a dim sort of notion that he had been, at least once, but it might have been just another muddled dream.

Could he have been caught in the explosion, perhaps hurrying up to meet her just as the bomb went off? Was he somewhere in this hospital, alone like her, needing her as she was needing him?

Wynne became aware that she was awake, and that not far away, people were talking. She could feel the pain waking as well, and if she had some way to summon a nurse, she could not find it. Were those nurses talking, and how far away were they, and could she find the strength to make a noise?

Then she caught a fragment of what one of them was saying—or had she misheard? Had the nurse said Hal's name? She strained to hear more, even as the buzzing of an electric wheelchair in the hall, and then the rattling of a cart, intermittently obscured the words.

"...believe he would... his own..."

"...what's coming to him... know what it feels..."

She managed to force an ugly, honking call of distress. The gossiping ended abruptly; a nurse came hurrying over. "You poor dear! It's time for your medication again, isn't it? Here, I'll run and get it." She moved away again before Wynne could begin to form a question; but as she passed the other nurse, she murmured something and shook her head.

Wynne must have misunderstood. It had sounded as if they were blaming Hal for the explosion. No one could have thought such a thing! Or maybe none of this was happening. Maybe it was a nightmare. But she never had nightmares.

And then the nurse was back with an injector, and sleep flooded over Wynne again, a blanket of sleep too thick for dreams.

Chapter 4

"For better or worse, it is beyond my power to decree the ending of your life, as you ended the lives of fourteen of your fellows. Our civilization has chosen to hold itself to standards far higher than the standards of those who come before such tribunals as this.

"But technological progress has made it possible, without the brutality of ages past, to impose a punishment that in some respects fits the heinous offenses of which you have been found guilty. With a precision unavailable to the Medieval sheriff or beadle, we can ensure that you suffer the full measure of the anguish you inflicted on others. And while you may deserve more, this is most assuredly suffering that you deserve."

Hal found that he was nodding. The judge must have noticed: his face seemed to swell, and turned so red that Hal feared for the man's health. No doubt he interpreted Hal's gesture as mockery; but if only the judge had been describing some other man's crimes and deserts, Hal would have wholeheartedly agreed.

* * *

They had strapped Hal down, binding every limb and every part of him that could conceivably be used to struggle. Efficient technicians glued electrodes all over him, while chatting to each other as if manning an assembly line or washing a car. Every once in a while, though, one of them would take a quick glance at him. When he was writhing — or trying to writhe, twisting against the restraints — and howling in borrowed agony, would they finally look at him, in licentious enjoyment of his suffering, or even in reluctant sympathy?

His lawyer could have been there, but he could not have brought his tablet or other devices—and Hal needed him to be spending every remaining second trying to get a pardon, a stay, any possible kind of reprieve.

In some bizarre gesture of counterfeit consideration, they had asked Hal whose suffering he wished to experience first. That had been a simple enough choice. There would be no redeeming value, no conceivable silver lining, to any vicarious experience but one.

At least, in this delayed and useless manner, he could share Wynne's pain.

* * *

Pavel Medved tried not to fidget. The governor's receptionist was no doubt tasked with reporting the behavior of those who were waiting to see him. He would have tried not to sweat, as well, but as that was beyond his powers, he had doubled his antiperspirant and dressed to conceal any failures of the same.

They could be hooking Hal up any time now. He had a contact on the "medical" staff —now there was a misnomer— who might slow things down a little, if he could do so with no risk of detection, but they could hardly count on much help from that quarter. Especially since that contact was happily married, and probably thought Hal deserved everything that was coming to him.

Ten victims. That was the maximum sentence, and that's what Hal had received. Ten separate plunges into the sensory and emotional experience of agonized, terrified, possibly despairing victims—victims, quite likely, of someone else's crime. If this is what it felt like to have a possibly innocent client, he was just as glad he had so few of them.

Most of the media had happily gone along with the prosecution narrative. If Hal had any projects in progress, they would no doubt be canceled. It would be quite a task to rehabilitate his image, even if Pavel could rescue him from the most immediate peril. He knew a publicist or two who might take on the job, if Hal would only cooperate. Hal did not strike Pavel as the cooperative type—but an ordeal like this one would change any man.

Anyway, Pavel had worked harder than he had ever worked in his life, and the tide was starting to turn. Hal's father had been an enormous help, once Hal had grudgingly agreed to bring him into the loop. It was thanks to Harold Wakeman Sr. that Pavel was sitting here sweating in the governor's antechamber, and that a few reporters had started to listen to his side of things. He had the advance copy with him of a story about the miscarriage of justice in Hal's case, and another about serial killers who had gone free for years or decades because others were falsely accused. The governor had a nose for shifting winds. He might just come through.

Pavel walked slowly out of the governor's office, barely able to pick up his feet as he went. He had succeeded beyond his expectations, and failed miserably.

The governor had stayed the execution of Hal's sentence, pending resolution of Pavel's motions to vacate Hal's conviction and obtain a new trial. But all the wheedling, flattering, and understated threatening had taken time. Just a little too much time.

***

Hal had wondered, in morbid moments of waiting, just when the recording had begun. How soon had the technicians reached Wynne? Would she still have been in shock, her body too stunned for the nerves to deliver their first urgent messages? A fellow prisoner had claimed the recording could reach back into short-term memory, starting before any rescue personnel had arrived. Was it true?

Now he had his answer.

BURNING BURNING BURNING my arm (whose arm who am I) my arm my arm my arm burning burning

throbbing back something threw me to the ground my back something wrong broken?? MyARM MYARM BURNING

somethingwrongwiththeair trytobreathe can'tbreathe

smoke alltheairissmoke

Something wet on my face smell kitchensmell blood ohgodblood allovermyface inmynose smellingmyownblood

I can't move THE AIR SO HOT Is a fire coming?? AM I GOING TO DIE HERE OH GOD ooohhhh my head my ARM MY ARM MY ARM

Hal, Hal, where is Hal Hal come find me Hal makeitstop HALMAKEITSTOP HAL HELPMEHAL HELPMEHAL PLEASE PLEASE

One of the two technicians standing by to ensure the prisoner's survival dug his elbow into the other one's ribs. The prisoner had stopped screaming. Instead, he was lying very still, moaning, tears streaming down his face.

The emergency phone buzzed. The technician went to answer it, and came back to his companion shaking his head.

"Well, what do you know? It really does happen! A call from the Governor's office! I thought that only happened in the movies."

"What, they're stopping it?"

"Yup. Where's the off button? Does it even have one? It's all programmed ahead of time."

"Hmmm—I think this is it."

The button must have done something: the prisoner kept moaning, but more softly, and he seemed to slump even as he lay prone on the cot.

"Left it a little late, didn't they? Think they'll give him a big kiss and say they're sorry?"

"And the recovery team won't be ready yet. Somebody better get 'em down here on the double."

***

"You've got to be kidding me."

Hannah moved her hand toward his shoulder, then evidently reconsidered and instead hit a button to print the email. Arthur picked it up, glanced at it, and put it down before he could do anything so melodramatic as crumple it up and throw it across the room.

"Now they say he didn't do it? That son of a bitch could always talk his way out of anything. Did Wynne get him off somehow? And who the hell do they think planted the bomb?"

Hannah smiled a crooked smile. "That's what we're supposed to figure out. Again."

***

Tertius Shaw read the account of Harold Wakeman's reprieve and chuckled. At least Wakeman had been subjected to playback before that happened. In effect, it increased Tertius' tally for the incident by one.

Had anyone thought to record the experience of a prisoner enduring playback? Such a recording might provide fascinating subtleties for the discerning to appreciate; and more prosaically, it would provide an additional level of deterrence. He would assign a subordinate to write up the recommendation.

His thoughts returned to the released prisoner, the hapless Harold Wakeman (Hapless Harold!). Tertius had done insufficient research last time, or he would have predicted Wakeman's arrest. Next time he would be thoroughly on top of the situation, in more perfect control.

INTERLUDE

THE CHAIR OF the Corrections and Criminal Law Committee called the next bill, and its sponsor rose to speak. The bluish light reflected dimly from his bald pate as he stood at attention behind the podium.

"House Bill 322 would add, as a Class D felony, the possession—with certain authorized exceptions—of any recording of experiences resulting from ingestion or exposure to any controlled or prohibited substance listed in the designated sections of our Criminal Code. Distribution and possession with intent to distribute would constitute C or B felonies, depending on the number of recordings and the specific substance ingested by the subject of the recordings...."

The junior member of the committee listened to the sponsor drone on, waiting for her undoubtedly futile opportunity to question or comment. When it came, she rose in place and addressed the committee.

"I wonder if anyone here besides myself feels as if he or she is re-enacting history. Not so many years before, committees like this one gathered in self-righteous assembly and decreed—"

The Chair tapped once with his gavel. "Kindly take care to observe this body's rules of decorum, with which I'm sure you've had a chance to become acquainted."

The junior member nodded, but could not bring herself to apologize before she continued. "Committees like this one, with comparable responsibilities to act based on evidence rather than emotion, passed the substantial restrictions now in place on smokeless electronic cigarettes. They did so despite the relatively minor health detriment involved in the sort of nicotine use those devices made possible, and the far greater harm inflicted on the user and others by burning tobacco and breathing its byproducts. They acted based on the essentially Puritanical view that only abjuring the despised act of smoking—preferably with some penitential suffering in the process—was societally acceptable."

Looking at the increasingly indignant faces around her, the junior member knew she had little time left to speak. She hurried on, trying not to trip on her words. "Now, once again, we are poised to prohibit a more benign alternative to the use of various proscribed substances. The psychological effects of drug use may be obtained, for those who seek them, without *any* of the pharmacological impacts of using the drugs themselves. How can this lead to anything but an improvement in public health?"

The sponsor replied before the junior member's lips had closed. "Even if we accepted your premise that nicotine delivery systems were benign enough to tolerate, the present case is completely different. These recordings cannot exist without someone taking the drug! By allowing continued sale of these recordings, we would enable that drug use. Indeed, we would be responsible for it."

The junior member, still standing, straightened her spine and stared defiantly at the sponsor. "Are we all, then, to pretend to believe that deprived of the recordings, those who had purchased them would 'go, and sin no more'—rather than procuring the drugs themselves?"

The sponsor turned to the Chair. "Are there other questions?"

There were none. The bill passed out of committee by a vote of 7 to 2.

Chapter 5

"I need to see my wife."

"Mr. Wakeman, we just need to complete the release process. Then you'll be free to go to the hospital, or anywhere else you want to go. So let's try to get through this quickly, shall we?"

This cheerful, sympathetic, superficial young person was not his enemy; she had not been his judge or his torturer; nor even, directly, his jailer. It would be worse than pointless to subject her to any of his rage: it might delay or prevent his release, and keep him away from Wynne.

But without the rage, he was left feeling bewildered and adrift.

The young woman was talking again, rattling off details in a well-practiced manner. "There are some after-effects you can expect, and you may be able to cope with them better if you know ahead of time. Over the next few weeks or months, you may experience insomnia, difficulty concentrating, emotional instability, flashbacks, nightmares...."

In his dreams, he was Wynne, burned, bleeding, lying helpless in the midst of chaos and death, needing him.... Or sometimes he was the fountain, torn apart and flung in every direction, piercing hapless bystanders with the limbs torn from him by the explosion; and then Wynne again, crying for the fountain she had loved.

"There's some paperwork, of course. Mr. Enderton will answer any questions you may have about it, but you can start reviewing it while I go tell him you're ready for him." She slid the tablet toward him, then got up and headed toward the door.

Hal tried to focus on the text. It seemed to pulse, going in and out of focus. He covered his face with his hands and massaged his temples.

The footsteps heading away from him had stopped. He looked up to see the woman standing in the doorway, gazing at him with a new and unsettling blend of sympathy and curiosity. She seemed on the verge of speech.

"Is there something else?"

The woman opened her mouth, then hesitated before she answered him. "If you experience any other, ah, symptoms, effects.... The process isn't completely...."

"If you're quite finished?"

The woman jumped at the sudden question. A man in a suit, with neatly trimmed salt-and-pepper hair, had appeared just outside the door.

"Oh, no, Mr. Enderton—I mean yes, we've finished up here. Excuse me. Mr. Wakeman—best of luck." She scurried away.

Enderton took the woman's place in the chair opposite Hal. "I see my young associate has given you the release paperwork."

Hal forced himself to read the first few lines, then looked up at the man and found himself laughing, almost hysterical. "Release. Here I thought this was about you releasing me. You release me, if I release you. Forth and back! Do-si-do!"

"Please keep reading, Mr. Wakeman."

Hal tried, using his finger to keep track of what he had already scanned. If he released the prison, the prosecutor, this and that and the other office and lackey and functionary, he would receive, as full and entire consideration—

He could not help showing his surprise. "Did my lawyer negotiate this?"

Enderton did not deign to answer.

"I'm impressed. Do they let lawyers accept bonuses from grateful clients? I could almost afford it. That is, if I let bygones be bygones…. Speaking of my lawyer, I'd like to talk to him before I sign anything."

Enderton showed his teeth in a smile. "Of course. We should be able to get him in here tomorrow afternoon."

Hal sneered back. "Whereas, if I damn you all to hell and sign your form and take your money, I can get out of here and be with my wife."

Hal used his finger to scrawl a signature—not his usual signature, just in case that might make some difference later—and shoved the tablet back at Enderton. Then he stood up and moved toward the door, staring at the other man, daring him to interfere.

Enderton made no move to stop him. Hal was able to turn a corner and get out of the fellow's sight before stopping to ask for directions. He needed to pick up his phone and his keys. And possibly, if it was ready, his bribe.

Hal shivered in the overly air-conditioned air of the ward. Once again, he was seeing Wynne in her hospital bed. But this time, she was awake.

The bed had been cranked up to an almost-sitting position. Wynne was eating breakfast. Hal offered up a rare and fervent prayer of thanks that the explosion had spared her right hand. From the doorway, he could not see what bandages or apparatus might be covering the stump of the left.

He was not surprised to find himself crying again.

Whatever noise he made caught Wynne's attention: she looked up and dropped her spoon. Her face lit with joy, followed by the profound relief of a lost child or marooned traveler who has finally been found. And yet, somehow, there was also the faintest trace of uncertainty. It looked familiar, at the same time as he realized he had generally failed to notice it.

She called out to him. "Darling! You're here! Are you all right?"

He stumbled over to her, seized her hand—her one hand—and kissed it. He used his second hand to fumble for a tissue and wipe his eyes.

This was no time to try to assess or summarize his own condition. "I'm here. Thank God, I'm here." Suddenly he found it possible to smile, for the first time in weeks. "Now finish your breakfast."

Many a visitor had preceded him. Every ledge and corner bore its burden of flowers, from modest carnations and baby's breath to a gigantic, tasteless basket that he guessed had come from Wynne's richest and most demonstrative fan. Stuffed animals peeked out between vases and flowerpots. Most were the usual hospital teddy bears and puppies, but those who knew Wynne best had brought or sent giraffes. Wynne loved giraffes (and swans, though he saw none of those), probably because of her own long neck, that elegant dancer's neck that made her seem even taller than five foot eight.

When Wynne had swallowed her last bite of breakfast, he presented his own offering, a tiny plush giraffe pendant with blue pseudosapphire eyes on a long gold chain. She could wear it without—he clenched his jaw and swallowed hard—without having to fasten or unfasten it with her remaining hand.

Wynne laughed in delight, beaming at him. Hal carefully draped the necklace around her neck. As he bent over her, she grabbed his arm, grinning, and pulled him in for a loud, smacking kiss.

"I've been trying to dream. You know, to get ready for going back to work."

He, on the other hand, was ready to try any desperate means, every potion or mantra or position anyone could proffer, to keep the dreams away. But of course, Wynne had a power he had not. Or she had, until now.

"Can you—can you decide whether or not to dream about it?"

Tears filled her eyes as she shook her head. "Sometimes— not all the time, but I can't predict it—it keeps turning into the accident."

"*Accident?*" He must not shout at her. He must not make her the target for any of his anger, even if she spoke foolishly. "That wasn't any damn—it was no accident. You know that."

She shrank back just a bit against the mattress. "I know, Hal. Of course I know. But it seems easier, somehow, to think about it that way. And whoever did it, whatever made them want to do such a thing—that could be some sort of accident, in a cosmic sense: a gene here and a gene there going wrong. Or maybe someone made a mistake, years ago, that changed or twisted someone's life."

"I wish I could see it that way." It took a fundamental decency even to try for such a viewpoint. He kissed her hand again. "I'm glad you can."

Had he even said it, since he entered the room? "Wynne, I love you. And I'm so grateful for you. For your still being with me."

Wynne beamed again. "I love you, sweetheart—so much." Her face fell into sadness. "And I'm so sorry that you had to—I would never have wanted you to feel what I felt. It's so unfair—I hardly even remember it, and it must be so much more vivid for you."

Hal looked around for a chair, spotted one, and dragged it to the bed. "Yeah, 'vivid' is a good word for it—if a little underpowered." He almost smiled again. "But you don't know how glad I am that you don't remember it well." But if she was dreaming about it, her claim not to remember must be a falsehood meant to spare him. He was about to say that he knew how terrible the dreams could be; just in time, he realized it would only hurt her more. "Is there anything you can do, any exercises or suchlike, to strengthen your control?"

Wynne shrugged, then winced. How many bruised and strained places, how many half-healed cuts and abrasions must be lying in wait for her every move? "I'm trying some things. It's too soon to say if they're helping. It's humbling, in a way—to be at the mercy of dreams, like most people." She smiled wryly. "I'm not so special any more."

That was angling for reassurance, of course. He answered her by leaning over her, placing an arm very carefully across her shoulders, and giving her a kiss. He should have expected the wave of passion that swept over him, but he fought it back and kept his touch gentle.

She might still want the words. "You're as special as special gets. Don't forget it."

Wynne was peering at him, her pale forehead wrinkled in concentration. "You're being—different today, somehow. Especially sweet, or something." Then she looked apprehensive. "Not that you aren't always, but—"

"My love, I'm not very sweet, as a rule. We both know that. If I'm finally learning how, it's about damned time."

She reached up and stroked his hair, and said again, "I'm so sorry, sweetheart. So sorry they did that to you."

At that moment he was not, exactly, sorry—not completely—that it had happened. Something had changed, or was changing—a change they both had needed, even if he had failed to realize it. Was it her sympathy for his ordeal that had brought them this new closeness? Or had sharing her pain jolted him into awareness of what else she might feel?

***

"You can forget about that disgusting excuse for orange juice." Wynne's sister Sara opened her oversized handbag and winked. "I smuggled in a bottle of iced chai!"

Wynne laughed—she was just getting strong enough to laugh again—and shook her head, one quick flop to each side of the pillow. "I'd better stick to the rules. Drug interactions and all that. Crank me up so I can drink my disgusting juice?"

Sara cranked the bed and handed Wynne the juice, grimacing. "You and rules! I thought you were learning to cut loose and do what you *want.*"

Wynne closed her eyes and looked away. Sara knew all too well about the rule Wynne had broken. With her innate intuition and a bit of bad timing, Sara had stumbled upon the knowledge of Wynne's lover, and she had been all too willing to accept that transgression.

Wynne looked back at Sara. "I can do what I want in my dreams—without getting myself or anyone else in trouble."

Or at least, she always could before.... She must have winced: Sara leaned forward. "Does something hurt? Should I call the nurse?"

Wynne held out the juice for Sara to take and leaned back, closing her eyes again. "It's nothing." She would have to keep trying, that was all. "But I think I'll rest for a while."

Chapter 6

Martin Prujack, Chief of Security for Holdark Correctional Facility, knocked hesitantly on the warden's open door. He had been telling himself for weeks that the pattern was not that clear; that he need not open Pandora's box, or a can of worms, or whatever metaphor occurred to him at three in the morning. But he had a limited capacity for self-deception, and he had reached that limit.

Warden Edward Heath looked up from his screen, pushing a button with a fleeting furtive expression. The chief did not bother to speculate, this time, about which illicit website or supposedly prohibited game had been thus concealed.

"Sir, we have a peculiar situation."

The warden donned an indulgent, avuncular air, resting his interlaced fingers on his large belly and drumming them in what was probably an unconscious gesture. "Do we, really? What is it this time?"

"We've had a marked increase in the number of prisoners trying to contact their victims."

"Marked increase, you say? Don't these things fluctuate? We can hardly expect some sort of constant prisoner output. They're not an assembly line, you know." The warden smiled at his wit. Martin gritted his back teeth, hoping the gesture escaped the warden's notice.

"We have records going back for decades. No one was trying to track the number, you understand, but all the mail the prisoners submit has been logged in. And once email and the like came along, we've done the same for that. Well, I happened to notice a discrepancy, and I've gone through and added things up. There's been a pretty steady increase over the last six years. By now, we're at something like thirty-five percent greater volume than before the trend began."

Heath lowered his eyebrows. "All that going through records and adding up numbers must have taken a good deal of time. I do hope you haven't been neglecting your more—established duties."

He had better spit out the rest, before he lost heart or lost his temper. "Sir, there's more."

The warden heaved a deliberate sigh. "Well, go on, then."

"The increase isn't coming from a random selection of prisoners, or from all of them. It traces back to prisoners who've gotten the helmet."

The warden jerked upright in his chair. "What's that?"

"Sir, for some reason, prisoners who've been subjected to experiential playback are a lot more likely to try to contact the victims whose experiences they were made to share."

The warden worked at his lower lip with his teeth for a moment. "What the devil are they saying?"

Martin struggled briefly, then succumbed to temptation. "Sir, I didn't see how I could invest the time to review the messages for content. Not with my established duties to perform."

Heath stared at Martin for a moment, and then, to the chief's utter astonishment, laughed out loud. "Touché." The warden's expression shifted quickly back toward worry. "But we've got to get on this right away. Is there something in those playbacks that we don't know about? Are the prisoners getting some sort of background information on the victims? Have we got a goddamned blackmail racket going on at this prison?" The warden lowered his voice to a confidential tone. "This could go two ways, you know. Move fast enough, we're the heroes who caught this thing early. Too slow, and it'll all be our fault, if the people who really fucked up can spin it that way. Now get moving!"

Interlude

The new operative was sweating, and knew the others could see it. To compensate, he tried harder to keep his voice from shaking. "But what's the point? We can't learn any useful details from the recording."

The old hand just smirked. "You might know if they were telling the truth. That's worth something. And besides, we've all been through it. It's a rite of passage." He gestured toward a wiry and petite woman in her forties, who had been with the unit longer than most. "She's done it. Is she tougher'n you?"

The recruit would have gulped if his mouth had not been so dry.

"Well? Are you going to go crying to the boys in suits? Tell him the big bad old-timers are hazing you?"

The recruit knew, at some level, that to refuse the hazing and report it, to put an end to the game, would require more courage—or a more important kind of courage—than enduring the playback. But that level of courage was more than he could summon. He gritted his teeth and stuck out his hand. "Give me the damn helmet already."

"That's our boy!" The old hand slapped him on the back. The blow jarred him so that his clenched teeth slipped, and he bit his tongue.

Now the helmet was in his hand. He took a deep breath, and knew that in a moment he would give anything for another. He would have flipped the switch himself, he was sure, but the older woman had joined the circle by now, and reached out to set the helmet to "play."

And then he was drowning, gasping, water cascading down his face, his chest exploding for lack of air.

Chapter 7

Hal shifted from foot to foot on the doorstep. His father moved slowly these days. The wait gave Hal a little more time to think. How do you thank someone for saving your sanity, when you had hoped never to owe him anything again?

The sound of halting footsteps was almost drowned out by high-pitched barking. Hal slipped in quickly when the door began to open: his father had had no occasion to develop quick door-closing reflexes.

Bitsy bounced up and down, tail wagging madly. Hal was proud to see that even in this moment of intense excitement, she remembered her training enough to keep from planting her paws on his trousers. He leaned over and scooped her up, letting her wriggle in his arms and lick him all over his face, lapping up the tears that had begun to trickle down.

As discreetly as possible, he dried his face on Bitsy's coat, and then put her down with a pat. Finally, he turned to face his father.

"Come in, boy, come in. Come sit down. You look—you must be tired." His father put a hand on Hal's shoulder and steered them toward the living room. Bitsy scampered ahead of them.

"Want a drink?"

Hal had not touched any alcohol in weeks. It was probably the last thing he needed, but the thought of a beer, golden and crowned with foam, in a tall glass mug, had him salivating.

"Heineken, if you have it. Thanks."

His father brought him the bottle. "I'm sorry—I haven't washed up in a while."

"It's fine, Dad. It's great." Hal took a swig, letting the liquid bathe his mouth before he swallowed. "Aaaaaahhhhhhhhh....

That's good." He leaned back into the too-soft embrace of the well-remembered couch, resting his head on the back.

Harold Senior fetched himself iced tea, and took a careful sip before setting it down on the coffee table. "Son, I'm so sorry I couldn't do more, or do it faster. I would have done anything to save you—that."

Hal stared. "Are you kidding? You did save me. Do you know what they had lined up for me? Ten recordings. Ten! Fatal burns, flayed faces, shattered legs. Ten." He found his hand was shaking, the beer sloshing out; he put the bottle down and folded his arms, his hands clenched under his elbows. "And then I'd have rotted in prison for decades."

"But even one playback—that must have been terrible."

"Could we not talk about it? Except—thank you. You were amazing. I didn't think anyone could do what you got done."

"Well, that lawyer of yours was pretty damn helpful. He's got a future, that young man."

"I hope so. If you hadn't been so effective with the press and all, he'd be a pariah for even trying."

Hal untucked his hands and held one out, testing it. It seemed steady. He picked up his beer again and took another glorious swallow.

"How's Wynne doing?"

"Mending. She's having some plastic surgery on her cheek today. They've had her in physical therapy for a few other problems. But of course, the hand is the most serious." He was still negotiating with the hospital. The settlement would pay for perhaps half of the regeneration fees, and before all this, his credit would have more than sufficed for the remainder. But no one, Hal included, could predict his future credit status.

Hal's father looked worried. He loved Wynne, of course. Wynne made that easy. Hal had never seen his father happier than the day Hal announced their engagement. He could tell that his father had not entirely trusted him to persuade Wynne, to secure her. Well, Hal had been equally uncertain.

He was woolgathering again. How long would it take him to regain some mental discipline? But his father was speaking. "You need to let me help with that."

Hal gritted his teeth. Was this another dig at the financial uncertainty he had embraced when he allowed the world of art to seduce him? But—he did need it. Wynne needed it. Hal could not afford pride, not this time. "Are you sure you can manage?"

Harold Senior sat up straighter. "I'll be fine. I live simply, these days. You tell the hospital administrators to call me. Don't worry, son—we'll get Wynne fixed up, and bring her home." He turned to Bitsy, who had come over to thrust her nose against his leg. Bitsy did that with Wynne, begging for attention; she must sense a similar soft touch in Hal's father. "That's right, girl. Your mama will be home very soon."

People always lied to dogs and children. At least the dogs would never know it. Wynne would not be home so soon. Not soon enough for him.

Change the subject. Though what occurred to him was little less painful. "How's Mom?"

"The same. You know. The treatment they have, she doesn't get worse. By the time they had it, she couldn't get better. The same."

"Did she know anything was wrong? Did she notice I wasn't there?"

His father gave a small, sad smile. "One day, she thought you were. She thought I was you. She asked me, why did I look so tired and move so slow?... She did ask where you were once or twice recently. I said you were busy."

Hal watched his father decide not to say, as he might well have done, that his mother would be used to that excuse.

"Wynne will want to visit Mom as soon as she can."

"Your mother will like that. She's always a little more lively when Wynne stops by."

Wynne was the missing piece, for all of them. But they would all have to wait a little longer.

Hal yawned, then stretched mightily, his left arm and leg reaching over into what was usually Wynne's territory. It was a freedom he could never count on, as Wynne was often still in bed when he awoke. He generally cherished the mornings when he could stretch completely. Now, the pleasure was a hollow one.

He swung out of bed and stumbled to the bathroom, still groggy. Approaching the toilet, he felt suddenly disoriented. What was he supposed to do? Should he stand or sit? He looked down at the tube of flesh emerging from his pajamas, and recoiled. What was *that* doing there?

And then, everything shifted, and there was nothing more natural than his penis ready for his morning piss. But the memory of that momentary horror was itself horrifying.

Chapter 8

THE PLAY DEALER scanned the line of bottles in his medicine cabinet, trying to make up his mind. He should probably take something that would help him think clearly: the news had given him plenty to think about. But he would rather, so much rather, take something to smooth him out.

All the talk about a sort-of-legitimate death recording might be good for business. People who'd never heard of snuff product would be hearing about it now, and many of the reports mentioned the availability of black market versions. It wasn't as if the curious could just wait for a legal product—no way would the powers that be let folks buy those recordings just for fun.

On the other hand, all the publicity would make it trickier for the cops to keep looking the other way. The percentage he could afford to pay might not be enough when a cop faced a serious possibility of getting canned or worse.

Maybe this was a sign. Maybe he should just get out of the snuff end of the business. The dudes who provided the product were pretty damn scary.

Of course, they might not care that his end of the business was getting riskier. The only time he'd even hinted that he might drop that product line, the supplier had hinted back about how they were always looking for new source material. As in new people to snuff.

The dealer shivered and reached for the blue and white capsules. To hell with thinking clearly! He needed to get smooth.

***

A decision, Tertius Shaw realized, had been thrust upon him.

Of course he had considered incorporating helmet technology into some of his projects; but the unpredictable, unquantifiable aspects of that technology, those known only to him, had made him cautious. He had suppressed the necessary files and constructed false trails to divert the other researchers from his discoveries, but he had taken no further action.

Now, however, the death recording would undoubtedly trigger a new wave of helmet research. His private reserve of information would not only be invaded, but possibly rendered obsolete, his expertise eclipsed.

How offensive a prospect! Time to seize the opportunity—and to put it out of reach of his former underlings, with their banal and pedestrian outlook. He would bring to the exploration of this recording not only the intellect of a scientist, but the aesthetic refinement of an epicure.

And if all went well, this serendipitous recording would be only the first of many.

***

"Hey, did you hear about Maury?"

"Hoo, boy. Security escort and then some. He must have hit the pavement with a bounce. And the helmet right after him."

"It's not like he was the first one to sneak someone in and record 'em. I guess he was clumsy about it. Too bad—he's probably ruined it for the rest of us. Before, they thought only the researchers had the brains to flip a few switches."

"He was sure acting funny the day before he got canned. He kept saying that now he understood. And that he was going to propose."

"You've gotta be kidding. Maury?? I never thought anyone'd tie him down."

"Wasn't he trying to find out if she was lying to him about being knocked up? Maybe she wasn't. But you're right—I wouldn'a thought a baby'd be enough. I hope she'll still marry him now that he's unemployed. If that's really what he wants."

"Crazy. Been a crazy week. Did you hear they got a death recording?"

"What, the cops busted another snuff ring?"

"No, I mean the legit folks, the techs that go out with the EMT's, one of *them* got one!"

"Got one how? By accident, or on purpose?"

"By accident. Kind of funny—all the talk about whether to go that far, and it happens by accident. What are they going to do with it?"

"That's rich. Like anyone knows! But I guess we'll be finding out what it's really like. Instead of listening to those death-heads and not knowing if they're full of it."

"They could try it on an animal. Maybe a dog."

"Don't let Linda hear you say that! You'll blow it for sure. She loves dogs. Besides, it wouldn't work. Now, if you killed a dog and recorded it...."

"That's cold. That's a lot worse than what I said! Huh. I wonder if they did that, early on, maybe."

"If Shaw still worked here, you could ask him. He was there at the beginning, wasn't he?"

"Noooo thanks. Shaw gives me the creeps."

"You're kidding! He always seemed pretty friendly to me. You know, for such a high-up guy and all. Even-tempered, like, and cheerful."

"Whatever. You ask him, if you want to and can track him down. He's some high-up official somewhere. Think we should throw a bachelor party for Maury? If he really goes through with it?"

"Suits me. I could use a good drunk."

***

The Deputy Director had hoped the rumors would prove false. No such luck. She stood before the Director's desk (she disliked sitting in that office) and concentrated on suppressing any expression or movement of dismay.

"So, as we already have secure storage for pieces of evidence, we've been asked to store this valuable recording as well, at least for the time being. Feel free to keep Mr. Kellic in the loop, but I'm putting you in charge of the arrangements."

If she ground her teeth, the Director would notice. She had never met anyone more observant. Later, once she left his office, she would take a break and walk off her chagrin. "Sir, I'd like to limit the knowledge of the recording's presence and its nature as much as possible."

The Director nodded, with a quick and surprisingly amiable smile. "That seems reasonable. We don't want to tempt our personnel to ponder the uses that could potentially be made of such an item."

That was a subject she had no wish to ponder—and what sort of uses did he have in mind?... But that would be pondering. She nodded at the Director, as if dismissing herself, and hurried out.

<h1 style="text-align:center">Chapter 9</h1>

"They're kicking you out? You mean my exciting career as a smuggler is almost over?" Sara looked around with exaggerated stealth, then handed over the iced frappuccino.

"That's right! You'll have to turn to industrial espionage or something like that." Wynne sat forward in bed, reached for the drink, and slurped it with noisy vigor. A nurse passing by the door paused, then shrugged and kept walking. The sisters laughed together, and Wynne raised her cup in salute to the empty doorway.

"Mom and Dad saved up enough to come see you. They might feel kind of bad that they didn't manage it before you got out."

Wynne shook her head, a little cautiously—but the movement no longer caused as much as a twinge. "You'll just have to talk them out of that feeling. I'd much rather see them at home than in this place." She could imagine her mother's face, no doubt already pale, in the weird purple lighting; she shuddered at the image.

"Sis? There's something I was wondering. It's none of my business—except, if by any chance what I thought of was true, you might need someone to talk to about it." Sara bit her lip, with a nervous expression Wynne had rarely seen.

"What is it? It's all right to ask. I won't get huffy." Wynne tried to make her smile reassuring.

"It's just that I was wondering. When the explosion happened, when you got hurt—you weren't, by any chance... expecting?"

Wynne's jaw dropped; quickly she closed her mouth again and shook her head. "No, I wasn't. At least—I don't think so. I wasn't aware of anything like that, and I think they would have told me…. Wouldn't they?" She stiffened. "They didn't tell you or Hal that I was, did they?"

"Oh, no! I don't know why I thought of it, really. It's just that—you always wanted children someday. And Hal's new career has been—was going well. So I thought maybe…."

Wynne sagged back against the bed. "I'd thought of it. It did seem more, well, more feasible than it had earlier. But I hadn't found the right time to mention it."

Sara slumped in the visitor chair. "I'm sorry. I didn't mean to bring you down."

Wynne sat up again and gestured imperiously for Sara to come closer. "Nonsense! You cared, and I need that, and I'm grateful for it. Now come get a hug. And then tell me all the gossip you've been saving."

* * *

He had had to wait so long, or so it seemed. But at last Wynne was coming home.

Hal guided Wynne toward the waiting taxi. She seemed steady on her feet, but he kept a firm grip on her upper arm. He was on her left: she had insisted on carrying her travel case, and there was only the right hand available for the task. He took care not to jostle the stump, covered in its flexible casing.

As the driver came round to take Wynne's bag, Hal heard a familiar jingling tune and turned to see an ice cream truck drawing near. The truck pulled up a few yards in front of the taxi. It seemed an odd spot for the truck to choose—there were no residences or schools or parks nearby. But workers began converging on the truck from nearby buildings, faces alight with the pleasure of escaping the concerns and habits of everyday adulthood.

Hal chuckled; Wynne echoed him with her silvery giggle, and moved as if to clap her hands. Of course, she did not complete the movement. A sickening cocktail of rage and pain swelled up in Hal's chest. He turned to the driver. "Start your meter—please. I'll be right back." He ran to the truck, joining the queue and shifting impatiently from foot to foot as the patrons ahead of him made their slow choices. Several placed multiple orders, presumably for office-mates. Finally he reached the counter. He was going to order two chocolate eclair bars, as he had done on the rare occasions when they had encountered such trucks together; but some impulse he could not identify led him to change his mind.

"One chocolate eclair bar and one raspberry ice, please."

He hurried back to the taxi. Wynne had taken a seat in the back, and was watching his approach, a fond smile adorning her face. He made a sweeping bow and presented her with the treat. "One raspberry ice, milady."

Her eyes grew wide. "When I went to visit my gran by the shore, every summer, I used to have these! The taste was just as refreshing as the breeze blowing in off the ocean. It was like sparkles on my tongue."

Hal's head swam with confusion. He did not answer, but slid into the seat beside Wynne, reached for her right hand, and placed it on his thigh, stroking it gently as the driver pulled away from the curb. He took one quick look back at the ice cream truck as they drove off down the street.

INTERLUDE

THE HOSPITAL'S DIRECTOR of Human Resources sat stiff and uncomfortable in the alcove outside the CEO's office, despite the relatively luxurious couch on which she perched. While she waited, she rehearsed once again how she would introduce, and then try to explain, the unwelcome news.

They should not be needing more psychiatrists. She had finally managed to obtain approval for three new hires, just last fall—new hires with particularly impressive credentials. She had been so pleased to be bringing in young and forward-thinking doctors trained in cutting-edge advances, willing to try new techniques and approaches. The hospital would benefit as much as her own reputation.

Her phone tinkled the incongruously cheery tone for texts from unidentified sources. She would have to change it. Something orchestral and ominous would do nicely. She heaved a sigh and checked the contents: an update on the first of the new doctors to become a patient on his own ward. He had been followed within two weeks by the second. She was still trying to develop discreet methods for monitoring the mental status of the third.

Could the helmet technology be used to find out just what had gone wrong? Probably not: helmets had been approved only for monitoring the status of medications and other treatments, not for primary diagnosis, and there was no gossip about fruitful off-label uses. She could, she supposed, ask Doctor Number Three, who surely knew more about helmets than she did—more than anyone else who remained on the professional side of the doctor-patient divide.

But there was the CEO's secretary waving her into the office. She made a quick note to consider the matter further, stood up, squared her shoulders, and marched on in.

Chapter 10

OF COURSE she was lucky the accident had taken her left hand rather than her right. But until it happened, she had never noticed just how many everyday tasks required—or at least, were much easier using—two hands.

Parting her hair, for example. In order to get by with one hand, she had to wet her hair down first. And putting toothpaste on her toothbrush. Even with a pump, she had to lie the brush down underneath and tap the pump in just the right way. And when she missed, cleaning up the mess involved more steps.

As for putting her hair in a ponytail—not a chance.

Of course, she could ask Hal to help. She was trying to keep such requests to a minimum. But Hal was being positively sweet about it, volunteering, asking whether she needed assistance with this or that or anything at all.

This morning, it was makeup. She'd been doing without mascara or eyeliner or anything with a cap to be removed. But Hal had caught her looking in the mirror and sighing, and had somehow divined what was making her wistful. So now, all she had to do was help him identify the various tools.

In no time an array of products lay before her, lined up neatly and ready for use. She beamed, kissed him, and returned to her mirror. Hal lingered in the doorway, watching. From time to time, as she perfected her face for the first time in months, she paused and smiled at him via his reflection.

As she was filling in the curve of her left eyebrow, a movement in the mirror drew her attention. What was Hal doing? She tried to observe, surreptitiously, as she continued her work. His right hand was moving, twitching in time with the larger movements of her own, flicking upward just a little as she applied mascara, drifting in a curve as she drew the liner along her eyelid.

She focused once again on her own reflection and muttered a curse. In her distraction, she had strayed from the proper path. And the makeup removing wipes were still in their sealed package! Reluctantly, she turned to Hal. "Sweetie, I'm sorry—I messed up. Would you open those?" She pointed.

"Of course. It's no trouble." He pulled open the package, extracted a wipe, and laid it across her palm.

An unexpected wave of frustration and impatience swept over her. She bit her lip and turned away. But Hal stepped closer and put an arm around her shoulders, drawing her close and kissing her hair. Then he let go and retreated to the doorway again, leaning there, watching as she started over.

Hal had taken Bitsy out for a run, so Wynne used the single-serving filter for her morning coffee. As she poured the boiling water over the coffee grounds and put the kettle back on the stove, she caught movement in the corner of her eye and turned back toward the counter.

Steam was rising from the filter, illuminated in the morning sun. She had never noticed that steam rose from coffee grounds; she had never known steam could look like this, curling and rising, ribbons twining up and away. She watched until the ribbons finally faded to few and then to none.

She stood in the warmth of the sunlight, gazing out the window behind the counter, words repeating over and over in her mind: *I'm alive. I'm still alive. I survived.*

Wynne hummed happily as she emptied the dishwasher. It was so nice to be a hostess again, serving Sara lunch in her own home, instead of a patient in a hospital with her sister hovering and worrying. Hal had been perfectly companionable, eating lunch at a leisurely pace and chatting with them both, instead of bolting the food down and hurrying back to his studio. And now she and Sara could enjoy some just-sister time before Sara left to pick up their parents at the station.

Though Sara seemed a bit preoccupied. It might be problems at work. Those engineer/inventor types were much like artists: they could be difficult. Sara, as an entry-level design tech, would end up on the receiving end of many a temperamental display.

Which reminded her: "Have you heard about anything new coming down the pike, helmet-wise? Any new features I should prepare for?" (Once she could work again.)

"Naah. They've been tweaking the amplitude controls for the designers and offering more comfort features, but no one's made any breakthroughs lately. There's some kind of scandal they're keeping hushed up—but that isn't what you were asking about."

Wynne paused between plates to pat Sara's hand. "Is it tense in the office, with all that going on?"

Sara shrugged. "I don't fret just because the higher-ups are fretting." She paused, then visibly gathered her courage. "Wynne—Don't you ever wonder who *did* it?"

Wynne almost dropped the dish she was holding. She clutched it tighter and swiveled to stare at her sister. "Where did that come from?"

"Well, don't you? Nobody knows, do they? And if they don't figure out who did it, he might do something *else!*"

"It might be a she. Or a they."

"That's not the point!" Sara glowered, then looked thoughtful. "Anyway, I don't think so. When they find him, it'll be a he. Him. Whatever."

Wynne bit back a pert response. Sara did have quite the track record where intuition was concerned. Interestingly, her dreams often contributed to her insights. Wynne suspected that Sara's tendency to synthesize data in her sleep, to dream her way to creative solutions, was in some way akin to Wynne's own talent.

And it would certainly be good to know who had done this awful thing to her, and to so many others—and to Hal. And she could clear Hal's name!

"Sis—I'd be grateful if you slept on it."

Sara looked a bit startled for a moment, then nodded. "I'll see what I can do. Now let's leave the dishes and go walk off our worries."

Chapter 11

"In other news, hearings will be held next week on a bill to subject memory erasure procedures to federal regulation...."

Hal had not actually been listening to (let alone watching) the broadcast: he merely wanted some background noise. The flashbacks came more often when he was left alone. Wynne's parents had reluctantly returned home, after four days of hovering over Wynne and peeking timidly at Hal, and Sara was taking Wynne for her weekly regeneration checkup. Human voices, even the monotonous and unemotional babble of the news, might keep the memories at bay.

But what was that coming from the screen—something about memory? Had he heard the words "memory erasure"?

He pivoted toward the wall screen, but he had been too slow in paying attention. The well-coifed reporter with the artificial half-smile was now chirping about tomorrow's celebrity dodge ball tournament.

Hal seized his tablet and muttered a search about memory erasure, setting the feedback for text. Yes, there really was a way to erase specific memories, using some sort of electric shocks. Apparently it had been discovered decades ago, and had gradually become a treatment operation for PTSD.

The young woman had talked about PTSD before they let Hal go. Why hadn't she said anything about uprooting the trauma?

The tablet was shaking in his hand. No, his hand was shaking. He dropped the tablet on the sofa next to him and tried to take a deep, calming breath. It took him several tries, but he managed it. Two more deep breaths, and he was able to pick the tablet back up again and find the copy of his release papers. They had arrived the day after he got out. He had almost deleted them, then saved them without looking at them. Now, he searched them for any form of the word "memory."

He scanned every highlighted word and phrase, then went back and did it again. Nothing about erasure, or removal, or any other way of describing it.

Why the hell not? How could they offer him money, "compensation," when they had the power to undo the damage—to cleanse him? He could be himself again, whole, free of the nightmares from which he woke screaming, the flashbacks that brought him to his knees on the street....

He looked at the paperwork again. Who had signed on the state's behalf? Damnation! It was that fellow Enderton. He could not imagine that any encounter with Enderton would end well. But the man must have an assistant, who might conceivably be more approachable or humane.

Even with fumbling fingers, it did not take long to find the necessary contact information. He punched the numbers and settled in for a siege.

"If you wish to report suspicious behavior, press 1. To respond to a summons, press 2...." And on and on. Finally, he pressed 9 for "further options"; and then 5, for "other"; and then, when connected with an interactive program, simply barked "human" at it until it gave up and sent him further into the labyrinth, where the actual people lurked.

Neither the first nor the second would confirm that Enderton even existed, let alone worked at the agency or had an assistant.

He knew his anger and frustration were starting to show, and to call forth increasingly indignant reactions. Finally he was passed on to some sort of supervisor. The supervisor did not show himself, the screen displaying only the appropriate logo.

"Mr. Wakeman." (Had he stated his name? He could not remember. But of course they had their ways of knowing who was calling.) The voice was low, smooth. "This is an unexpected pleasure. Is there, perhaps, anything of which you wish to inform us?"

Hal's heart raced. His fingers seemed to be going numb: he could hardly maintain his grip on the phone. He knew the man could hear him gasping for breath.

"Well, Mr. Wakeman?"

He had to speak, before this chance evaporated. He clutched the phone and fought for control, expecting any moment to hear the click and hum of a severed connection. But it did not come. Perhaps, after all, they wanted to know what he had to say. He tried to summon the ghost of his former self, that self so arrogantly certain that he could control his fate.

He had nothing with which to threaten or to make them respond. He would have to bluff.

"I have a question for Mr. Enderton—though perhaps his assistant could answer it. I've just noticed some interesting language in the release paperwork he signed. I wanted to review it with someone before I—before I proceed. Before I act on it."

In the pause before the voice replied, Hal had time to imagine a car streaking toward his home, bringing some instant retribution. He strained to hear any sound of a siren.

"You will be contacted by the appropriate party."

Hal paced back and forth, waiting, even though he knew it might be hours or days before the call—if it ever came. Bitsy had jumped to her feet the first few times Hal approached, hoping to play; now she simply tracked Hal's movements, ears alert and twitching.

How would it work? Would he know just what horrors he no longer carried in his memory? Or would even the bare facts be gone?

Maybe he could go back to that hole-in-the-wall restaurant, where the fans filled the street with an odor that used to make their mouths water. He and Wynne had tried just once to go back. The smell of meat on the grill had sent both of them reeling and retching. And Wynne liked that restaurant even more than he did.

Wynne!

He had not even thought about Wynne, about what the process could do for her. Wynne, who had suffered every bit as much as he, for even less reason.

He was the most selfish bastard, the worst husband, the poorest excuse for a human being....

Enough of that! He would find a way to help her. Somehow, he would free them both.

The call, when it finally came, was audio only, as the last encounter had been. The caller did not introduce herself. She might be Enderton's assistant, or his superior, or anyone else.

He had been afraid that as soon as he revealed the purpose of his call, the call might end. But the woman seemed willing to assist him.

"Sir, the process is mentioned in the agreement. Look at Section 10, paragraph (c), subparagraph (i)(E)(4)."

Hal enlarged the print and enlarged it again. "I don't see anything about memory—"

"That isn't the term used, of course. Look on the seventh line. 'The recipient agrees not to request or receive any form of suppression services without prior written authorization from the Department.'"

"Suppression services. All right. But what's this about prior authorization? How do I apply for it? And does 'authorize' mean agreeing to pay for it?"

The unseen woman cleared her throat. "Authorization for the suppression procedure would not be available to you at this time."

"At this time? What *is* this time? Is there some—" (he barely bit back an expletive) "waiting period?"

The faint hint of discomfort, even embarrassment, he had sensed seemed to have vanished. Now the voice was businesslike. "If, at some point following your release, the crimes of which you were convicted are satisfactorily explained and the resulting process concluded, you may then apply for the authorization in question."

Hal stared at the logo on the screen. "Would... you... please... repeat... that."

The woman did so, slowing her delivery, perhaps unconsciously, to match his own. But before she could finish, Hal hung up and called his lawyer.

"It's not just about getting my memory cleaned up, is it? I'm still in some sort of danger from them, aren't I? But how? What about double jeopardy?"

On the screen, Medved's head and shoulders moved as if the lawyer were wriggling in his chair. "Hal, I tried to explain this to you when you were released. I guess you weren't in any shape to absorb it."

Hal gritted his teeth. "Evidently not."

"Double jeopardy protects people who've been acquitted. Plus there are some mistrials—but that's not at issue here. Anyway, you weren't actually acquitted. Your status is sort of in limbo. The conviction was vacated and the charges dismissed—but dismissed without prejudice. That means they could charge you again, if they got more evidence. And in the meantime, just in case they do, they're not going to take some action that makes it more awkward—like, ah, un-punishing you."

Hal tried to fight back the nausea long enough to think of questions to ask. "Do they have—is there any time limit? Or can they just keep me hanging for years? For the rest of my life? What?"

There were times that Medved looked rather like a spaniel, and this was one. He shook his head, his hair flopping, his eyes large and sad. "It's murder, Hal—multiple murder. There's no statute of limitations on murder. No limit."

* * *

Wynne stared at Hal, slumped in one of the kitchen chairs, Bitsy crouched shivering at his feet. He seemed to have grown more haggard in the two hours she had been gone. But what he was saying sounded like good news—wonderful news. How could it have made him look like that?

"We can have those horrible memories just—taken away? Is it dangerous? How dangerous?"

Hal furrowed his brow, then let his face sag again. "I don't know about any risks. I'm not sure. I guess I didn't get to asking."

"But—"

He put up a hand to stop her. "You didn't hear me right. I didn't say we. I said you. We can get this for you." He bit his lip, then released it. "It's sure to be expensive. But we can do it. Raise money. Lots of people would contribute."

"But why not for you? If it's expensive, we can flip a coin or generate random numbers to see who should go first."

He shook his head without looking at her. "I can't. They won't let me." He made a choking sound like a stillborn chuckle. "Turns out I promised not to. When they let me go."

Wynne sat down with a thud in the chair opposite Hal. Her approach appeared to comfort Bitsy, who stood up, stretched, and lay down between the chairs, looking up at Wynne as Hal reached for his tablet and called up a document. "There. That's what this part means."

"But *why?*"

Hal looked up and bared his teeth in a bitter imitation of a grin, his eyes wide. "In case they're not done with me yet. In case they build a better case against me, and drag me back in, and find me guilty. Again. In case they sentence me to playback. Again. Why waste time putting me through ten recordings? Why not just start with the second, instead of repeating the first? It's more efficient, don't you see?" Abruptly, his face contorted and he spun the chair to face away from her, his body racked with sobs.

Wynne jumped up and ran to him, but he started out of the chair and stumbled away from her. *"Don't!"*

She leaned against the cabinet, biting her lip helplessly, waiting for her chance to speak and be heard.

Finally, he grew quiet, so quiet that the hum of the refrigerator seemed loud.

"Hal. My dear one." She spoke just over a whisper. "We'll do it together. We will. I promise. Somehow, we will." She stopped and drew a slow, deep breath. "I won't until you can."

His head jerked up, and he glared at her. "Don't you do that! Don't make it worse! Do you imagine it'll be better for me, knowing you're still suffering? When I *made it happen*?"

For a horrible, chilling moment, she thought it was some sort of confession. But no, of course not! All he meant was— "Because you were late? Late for lunch? That's hardly a crime! Whoever did this—" She lifted her stump, throbbing from the doctor's latest ministrations. "Someone else made this happen to me, to us, and to all the others. You can't forget that!" She tried desperately to relax her face enough to smile. "And I think I remember being late once, a few years ago. Yes, I'm sure of it. Five years ago next April!"

She shouldn't have tried to be funny. For just a moment, she saw contempt flicker across his face.

If she let him find a way to procure for her this relief, this exorcism, he would end up resenting her for it. Blaming himself for her pain, he would, when she was free of it, find it impossible not to blame her for his. It was not only the survivor who could inflict survivor's guilt.

And then he would hate himself that much more.

They would have to find some other way to get through.

***

"Oh, no!"

Hal looked up, startled, at Wynne's exclamation and the simultaneous clatter of her tablet hitting the kitchen table. He jumped to his feet and came to stand beside her, his hands on her shoulders. "Should I look, or do you want to tell me?"

Wynne looked up at him, surprise briefly erasing her shocked expression. She reached up and placed her right hand over his. "There was another bomb—in a playground! But they found it before it could go off." She shuddered. "A *playground*! It would have been so horrible…. I guess you'd better read the rest."

He would have to let go of her in order to reach the tablet. He kissed her hand and extricated his own, moving to retrieve the tablet. It had reverted to its welcome screen; he suppressed his impatience and found the site where Wynne had been reading the news.

He scanned the story once quickly and then reread it, hoping he had missed something. No: the police had not caught the bomber. The security video had shown only a dimly lit figure dressed in black, face masked.

When had that image been captured? The story said nothing more precise than "last night." He started hunting for other accounts, then remembered and slid the tablet back over to Wynne. He retrieved his own tablet and started over.

The fourth story in the list had the information he needed so badly. A photo of the security footage showed that the bomb had been planted at 8:43 p.m.

Hal slumped against the back of his chair, the sudden shift of weight almost toppling the chair backward. "I was at the pharmacy. And I think I can prove it."

He had almost forgotten Wynne's presence during his frantic search. Now her audible exhalation of breath reminded him that she must have understood and shared his fear. He looked up at her and attempted a reassuring smile, an attempt that faltered when he saw her tears.

"Oh, darling!" It was her turn to come and stand beside him, stooping to put her right arm around him as she kissed his cheek.

Wynne's arm—the other arm—had hurt more than usual yesterday evening. He had gotten her settled with the heated rice pad and rushed off, cursing his thoughtlessness, to the pharmacy where the refill of her medication had been awaiting his convenience.

The electronic pad where he had scrawled his signature: didn't it show the date and time?

He would call the pharmacy. With luck, they would answer his question without asking too many questions of their own.

* * *

If Tertius Shaw were less conscientious in his dental care, he might well have ground his teeth. Why must clumsy oafs insist on copying his work—and do it so poorly?

Of course, such false trails reduced the chance that Tertius himself would become a suspect. But he had already protected himself against exposure. He did not need the public's attention diverted, and his own previous work possibly attributed to some proletarian bottom-feeder.

Well, if he had had any doubts, this episode removed them. He would refocus his efforts from wholesale to retail, as it were, obtaining carefully chosen subjects and exploring all the refinements that helmet technology made possible.

* * *

Wynne awoke with a scream frozen in her throat.

Some people still insisted that one couldn't feel pain in dreams. Wynne could, when she chose—and it was often a profitable choice. She had wondered if the claim might possibly be true for those whose dreams were uncontrolled. It seemed unlikely: why should untamed dreams be so benign?

Now she knew. The untamed dream was anything but kind. The untamed dream could burn.

She lay in bed shaking, stroking her healed skin with one trembling hand, feeling its reassuring smoothness. All over, over and done with.

But there was a faint throbbing in her right shoulder, as though from some recent impact. What could it—of course! She had not managed to free herself from her nightmare: something had awakened her. Hal must have rolled over in his sleep, or stretched out, and accidentally poked her with his elbow. She turned toward his side of the bed, but it stretched empty beside her. Where was he?

Wynne slid out of bed, careful not to jar the tender bud of her new hand,then slipped on a robe and went in search.

She found Hal slumped in his armchair in the living room, hair a chaos of tangles, eyes closed. She started to tiptoe away, but he opened his eyes and turned toward her. "Couldn't you sleep either?"

She perched on the arm of the chair and stroked his cheek. "I wish I could help, love. I know it's awful."

A brief wry smile twisted his mouth. "Yes, you do." He closed his eyes again, and she saw his throat moving in a swallow. "I wish I could help, too."

"Shhhh, baby. Hush, now." She stroked his cheek again, then his hair, pressing his head gently toward her thigh. If she could send him back to sleep, then maybe she could sleep herself.

***

Wakeman appeared to have an alibi for the playground bomb. And somehow, that was supposed to make it less likely that he'd blown up his fountain. Arthur thrust his chair back from his desk with a sudden shove that almost sent the chair toppling backwards. Couldn't the fools see the difference between the two incidents?

Hannah, at least, acknowledged that the latest bomb might have nothing to do with the earlier explosion; but then, she seemed ready to exonerate Wakeman of both. She would be just as difficult to convince as any of the others. Not that he needed to convince his assistant that he was on the right track: she would serve him with her usual competence in any case. But he had learned, over the years, to respect her judgment. If he could overcome her doubts, it would give him the confidence he needed to go head to head with the top brass. Then, perhaps, he could try again to take Wakeman down.

Chapter 12

Warden Heath's secretary covered the receiver and turned toward her boss, rolling her eyes. "It's another blushing bride, wanting permission to hold the ceremony here. Are you in?"

The warden waved his hands in a frantic negative, backing away and bumping into Chief of Security Prujack, who had been trying to enter the office. They untangled themselves and scurried away, leaving the secretary to temporize, evade, and perhaps even reason with the caller. When they had reached a safe distance, the warden stopped and looked back. "I will never understand these women."

The security chief shrugged. "They're not so different from other women, really. Women want to believe that a bad boy can change—especially if they think they're changing him. The men here are just a little more deliberate and calculating about playing along."

"Excuse *me*." The secretary had followed them and stood tapping her foot. "I thought you might want to know. That lady—she's the prisoner's victim."

Prujack whirled to face her. "The caller? The would-be bride?"

"That's right. She's wanting to marry the man who broke into her home, threw her across the room, and held her hostage while he ransacked the place."

The warden wrinkled his nose in disgust. "Well, *that's* worse than the usual."

Prujack fiddled with his belt buckle. "As a matter of fact, sir, she's not the first. There've been three this year. And all of them—do you remember what I told you about the pattern with the playbacks?"

The warden closed his eyes for a moment, as if it would make the security chief and the secretary and the prisoners and the bride go away. "You're telling me that three different female victims want to marry the perps who got the helmet for attacking them."

"Yes, sir."

The warden turned toward his secretary. "This woman. The latest one. What did she say? How did she sound?"

The secretary frowned. "She didn't sound as—well, as brainless, or naive—as they usually do. She even said she knew what I must be thinking, that she'd been conned, that she was some lonely, desperate woman begging to be taken advantage of. She said it wasn't like that. They've been writing—"

Prujack snorted. "Oh, that's altogether different, that is."

"She said he understood her like no one ever has."

"Chief." The warden spoke through gritted teeth. "Expedite that research. This is getting out of hand way too fast."

Prujack seemed to take up most of the room in the cell as he loomed over Prisoner 1624, crowding the warden into the background.

"Why'd you start writing this lady? You didn't find the good stuff before the boys in blue showed up, so you thought you'd make nice, soften her up and get a few good hints?"

The prisoner shook his head. "Naah. It was more like—she was so scared. I got to wonderin', was she okay? Worrying. So I finally figured I'd write and ask her."

The security chief spat into the corner of the cell. "You do smash and grab for a living, you punk! You never figured people get scared?"

"It was just part of the job, ya know? I didn't think about it." The prisoner looked the warden in the eye. "You guys, you made me think about it this time. Feel it."

Prujack played an imaginary violin. "So, you sensitive lug, you, why'd you keep writing her?"

The prisoner sat as upright as his position on the bottom bunk would allow. "Turned out she's a real special lady. There's no one like her."

"Riiight. And why did she keep writing to *you*?"

The prisoner lifted an impudent eyebrow. "Just lucky, I guess." The chief twitched forward; the prisoner flinched. "You should ask her, okay? No, f'get that—I don't want you botherin' her. I dunno, I guess she liked that I appreciated her. When she said stuff, I asked her questions so she could tell me more. I can't exactly be a good listener from in here, can I? But I tried."

"What do you make of him, Chief?"

Prujack made as if to spit again, then apparently thought better of it now that they were back in the administrative wing. "I've always thought of him as just another thug, without the skills to be a con artist. If the playback gave him some kind of leverage or power over the victim, I'm not sure he's got the brains to take advantage of it. But maybe he thinks he does."

Chapter 13

SOMEHOW, HAL and his father rarely visited Hal's mother together. It was perhaps not so surprising: Hal spent little enough time with his father, for any purpose. Nor had Harold Senior been much in the habit of asking favors from his son. But this time, he had asked. "I really should visit your mother. I've been putting it off. It's hard to think of anything new to say—not that she'd know I was saying the same things as before.... If we're both there, it'll be a treat for her, and easier for me."

The request was, in fact, so uncharacteristic that Hal suspected an ulterior motive of some kind. Curiosity as to what it might be had something to do with his assent.

His suspicions were hardly allayed by his father's suggestion that they travel together in Harold Senior's large and old-fashioned car. Did his father have some lecture in store for him, to be delivered en route, with his mother's presence afterward to prevent him from sulking? But nothing of the sort transpired, though Hal's father did seem preoccupied and disinclined to chat.

They made a point of walking in side by side, to reduce the chance that his mother would mistake one for the other. And indeed, she greeted them both immediately by name, her face lighting up with a pleasure that banished for the moment any sign of confusion. Hal gave her a hug and a kiss, then sat back and let his father take the lead.

It was a painful enough encounter to observe. Hal's father made dutiful efforts to start and carry conversation. Hal's mother, he saw with surprise and pain, made a visible effort as well. She reminded him of a visitor to—or from?—some foreign country, uncertain of language and custom, halting and hesitant.

They stayed about half an hour and left exhausted. The ride home began as even more silent than the trip to the nursing home. Hal had by now forgotten his search for a hidden agenda; he had, therefore, no sense of vindication when his father cleared his throat and spoke.

"You know how much I was away, working, when you were growing up."

Hal bit his tongue. Yes, he knew. He could hardly fail to notice that even though his parents, unlike those of many of his friends, remained married and purported to live together, he could go weeks or even months without seeing his father in the flesh. He might well have seen him more often, and had gone on more exciting excursions with him, if the two had been divorced.

"It wasn't that I wanted to leave you and your mother alone so much. It seemed—I thought it was what I needed to do. My work called me away, and my work gave us all the things you needed. Your mother—well, she loved her drawing and painting so much, but it never brought much money in."

Hal had never really thought that much about his mother's art, either its importance or its economic aspects. He had managed to appreciate its quality, from time to time, but he had been more conscious of how her attention to it sometimes delayed her attention to his own needs. What a self-absorbed child he had been. And his own artistic gifts: he must have inherited them from her.

But his father was talking again. "She wanted us to travel, or at least go on day trips—picnics in the country, or theater and dinner in the city. It didn't happen very often. I was the one who traveled. And when you and she went on that ski vacation, and I was supposed to meet you...."

Hal remembered all too well. The lodge in the mountains, the air colder than he had ever felt or breathed; the long, gleaming skis propped up against his shorter ones; his gleeful anticipation of showing his father what he had learned in his first lessons—and then, his mother's downcast face, soon forced into a determined smile, as she told him that it would be just the two of them, all cozy, after all.

"When you and your mother came home, something was different about you. I apologized, and I told you we'd go together, some day soon; and you just shrugged. In those few days, you'd gotten harder."

That was one way to put it. He had learned how to shield himself. No, not a shield: a wall, a wall as high and strong as any his father would ever build. He would never again leave his feelings so unprotected.

Not even with Wynne. He had gotten so used to living with the wall that he no longer noticed the absence of a gate.

"I always told myself the day would come. I'd feel secure in my work, and I'd have enough saved, and then we'd all travel together; or your mother and I would go off on a second honeymoon. And then, her symptoms started. I wasn't home even for that. And it was too late."

Listening, Hal thought he heard tears, but when he turned to look, his father's face was drawn and dry.

"Son, I don't want you to make my mistakes. You almost lost Wynne, the way I—even more than the way I've lost your mother. You have another chance, one I'll never have. I know I'm probably saying too much, and you can be angry if you like—but please, Hal, don't waste it."

He could not go so far as to absolve his father, let alone to thank him. But he said no word of blame, and he nodded.

A young and bubbly attendant led Hal and Wynne through the corridors, pointing out doorways to the left and right. "Here's the water garden. There are hot springs and cool pools—" (the woman giggled) "—and waterfalls, small enough to sit in and big enough to slide down. And here's what we call the Bakery Window. You can get all sorts of breads and muffins and cakes and pastries. Of course they smell wonderful, but we also pipe in extra baking smells, and we keep changing them so your brain doesn't start to ignore them. Oh, and here's the butterfly garden. It's full of aromatics that attract butterflies, and the scents are also pleasing to people. You'll find flowers and flowering trees and vines everywhere you look. We don't need to depend on the actual season, so we can choose whatever we—and the butterflies—like. And the lighting is just like late afternoon sun. It's gorgeous!"

Wynne tugged just a little on Hal's left hand. "Honey, could we go there first? It sounds lovely. Soothing."

"Sure thing." Hal turned to their escort. "When we're ready to move on, can we just find our own way?"

"Oh, sure! There's a plaque outside each room with a description, if you want to try one we haven't seen yet." She paused. "Did someone already explain to you about the discount we offer?"

Wynne glanced nervously at Hal; Hal stiffened, and clenched his teeth to hold back an angry response. Wynne squeezed his hand as if to reinforce his self-restraint, and answered the girl herself. "Yes, thank you. We would rather not."

That should win some sort of award for understatement. The spa gave a substantial price break to anyone who would take in their various luxurious indulgences with a helmet in place. The spa made much of its income from selling the recordings to those who could afford neither the time nor the fees to come in person. A pale shadow, indeed, of these carefully designed surroundings—but some vestige of the environment, along with the relaxation, pleasure, or even euphoria it induced, was apparently worth peddling.

But nothing would induce Hal to don a helmet, ever again.

* * *

Wynne wondered whether it would violate some intellectual property law for her to use any of these rooms in her dreams. With the limited level of detail transmitted, it might be hard for them to prove the source of her inspiration.

She sighed. Even if the idea had not felt like cheating, she might not be able to implement it. She had been trying ever since she got home, almost every night. She could not hold her dreams together: she never knew when they would veer toward pain and lostness and terror. When that happened, it took all her strength to drag them back toward bland blankness, the equivalent of a holding pattern.

If she did not regain control soon, she might have no business to return to. She had many loyal customers—but they would only go on asking about her, sending her encouraging messages and waiting for her return, for so long. Soon they would find other dreamers to follow.

It had been such a welcome surprise when Hal suggested this place. He could hardly have known how much she needed the refreshment of peace and beauty and innocent stimulation, now that she could no longer count on creating her own oases.

* * *

Hal drove their little carlet home from the spa. It was not really meant for a couple as tall as they. Wynne, climbing in, often remarked cheerfully, "Snug in a bug!" But it would give them privacy, and take them home.

The visit had done Wynne good. She had color in her face, and the premature lines that had creased her forehead were almost smoothed away. But as they drove, Wynne seemed to be getting more fidgety, glancing at Hal and away again, scanning the road as if searching for something. Finally she pointed to an exit sign. "Could we stop for a bite to eat?

There's a sign for a diner. I've got a craving for scrambled eggs."

A craving—that was an interesting choice of words, one Wynne rarely used. It made him think of stereotypical pregnant women, sending hapless husbands out into the snow for a bucket of pickles. He grinned. "By all means, let's stop. Can't let those cravings get out of hand!"

They found the diner after only one wrong turn. The dinner rush, if any, had ended, and there were few other customers. He could see only one waitress. Wynne looked around and headed for a corner booth in the back; he followed her, hoping the booth was in the waitress' area of service.

Wynne's restlessness increased as they waited for menus, waited to order, waited for their food. Wynne's scrambled eggs and his own bacon sandwich finally arrived; the waitress moved away and sat down with what might have been a crossword puzzle. Wynne picked up her fork and twiddled it about for a moment before starting to eat. As Hal was crunching up his first mouthful, Wynne swallowed and laid down her fork again. "There was something I asked the doctor before I was released."

He raised his eyebrows in inquiry as he took another bite of sandwich.

"The blast sort of shoved me around some, internally. I had bruised this and distended that. I started to worry that I might have trouble, later, if we...."

Hal put down his sandwich and reached over to take her hand. "Hon, what is it?"

"It's okay, it turned out. It'll be all right, we shouldn't have any trouble, if we decide—" Wynne took a deep breath. "—If we decide to have a baby."

A baby! All he could think of, at first, is that his vision of pickles must have been psychic. A baby!

They had talked about children once or twice before their marriage, perhaps two or three times since. When Hal decided to leave the lucrative implosion work and make his way as an artist, starting a family had seemed impractical. Then, when he was becoming successful, he had so little time! And Wynne, even when she gave up the last of her series of day jobs, still seemed to have plenty to keep her busy.

"It wouldn't be right away. The doctor said that while my hand is still, um, growing, that with everything they use to stimulate the cells, it wouldn't be a good time. But when my hand is all right again, then we could... I know money may be tight for a while, after all that's happened, so we could wait, but...." She was faltering, needing some response to help her continue.

How often had she wanted to talk to him about this? Had she felt something fundamentally missing in their lives, as full as he had thought their lives to be?

Hal thought of Wynne's protective concern for her clients, an interest and curiosity he had found somewhat silly and had teased her about from time to time. She was so warm, so eager to help. Of course! How could he have missed it? She was fundamentally, constitutionally maternal. She was made to be a mother.

And now, when his prospects were reduced, his ability to provide so uncertain, now she was finally showing him her need.

They would find a way. He would not deprive her any longer.

"When you're well again, we'll do it. We'll make you a mommy."

Wynne's jaw dropped, and her eyes went wide as joy dawned in them. "Oh, darling—really? Are you sure we can manage it?"

Hal released her hand and placed the fork in it. "Now eat up, mother-to-be. You're going to need your strength."

*　*　*

Wynne got up to see Hal off as he headed to the dentist, trying not to flinch at his parting comment: "Well, at least I don't think twice any more about what the dentist might put me through." She closed the door and turned, yawning, toward the bedroom. This would be a good opportunity to work on her dreaming.

She paused at the drawer where she kept her helmet. It was hardly likely that she would produce a salable dream. But it would probably be best to record in any case, for what she could call diagnostic purposes. She could review the dream later, wide awake, to assess her degree of control.

Since she would not need a coherent story, she would simply indulge in one lovely scene or snippet after another. She could feel her face, and then her neck and shoulders, relax as she planned the journey....

She was sitting in a wide wooden swing, hanging from some unseen tree, watching the butterflies flit from flower to flower. It was rather like the butterfly garden at the spa, but the butterflies were just a little larger, so that one could see the words written on their wings. One butterfly the color of lilacs lighted close by and spread its wings, "breathe" in flowing calligraphy on the left wing, "deep" on the right. Wisps of every pastel color drifted on the air, the aqua and sky blue barely visible until they landed on some contrasting flower, the yellow and pale green showing more clearly in flight. There, brighter than the others, hovered a large orange butterfly, its wings proclaiming "love... lives." And now a pure white butterfly with blue script landed light on her knee, urging her to "hope" and "trust."

A misty dissolve and a new scene, a real place: the Wisteria Flower Tunnel in Japan, reality that resembled an Impressionist painting, with curtains of purple flowers hanging overhead and quiet paths beneath, and parents holding their children's hands as the children skipped along....

Another blooming tree, from a picture once seen and never forgotten: a large tree with pale pink blossoms, and fallen blossoms covering the ground, everything pink but the turquoise of distant trees and mist.... No one around, no one anywhere....

Too lonely. Too quiet. Not what she had intended, not what she had planned. Again, yet again, her dream had gone awry. Where would it take her?

She fled toward safety, toward a time before danger, before fear.

She was floating, floating in a golden, glowing place of perfect warmth, rocking, cradled. She had nothing to need, nothing to do; she could simply float, and wait, and be.

...But something was calling her. A voice, familiar and urgent. Somewhere out there was someone who needed her. Someone with a claim.

She said goodbye to the warmth and peace, and made herself dissolve that other world.

Hal was bending over her, his eyes wide, chewing on his lip. He straightened up and gasped as her eyes opened. "Wynne! I was so worried! You lay there, so still, and you wouldn't wake up!"

She reached up to stroke his arm. "I'm sorry, sweetheart. I'm all right. Really, I'm fine. I'll tell you about it later."

His glance shifted, and his jaw and his arm muscles went tight. He had seen the helmet.

"I'll get this right off. Why don't you wait for me in the living room? I'll be right there."

He started to turn toward the door, then stopped and turned back toward her instead. "No, it's okay. You take your time. I'll be right here."

* * *

Wynne had always seemed so upbeat, almost smug, as bedtime approached, with its opportunity for any dreams she chose. Like other aspects of her self-sufficiency, that attitude had sometimes engendered resentment in Hal, sometimes relief, as his own mood and needs had fluctuated. Now, seeing her nervous and forlorn, remembering his own fright at her condition that morning, he was filled with a fierce determination to give her back what she had lost.

"Wynne, I'd like to try something."

She looked up at him, curiosity mixed with the gratitude he had so often seen in her these past weeks. Had he really been so aloof, so self-involved, that any simple sign of caring came as unexpected?

"You can start out all right, can't you? With your dreams, I mean. It's only later that things go wrong."

She nodded, eyes wide.

"I know you don't sleep very well spooning, but still, where the dreams are concerned, it might help if I held you. And if you seem distressed, I could—I don't know, hold you tighter, or something."

"I'd love that." Wynne beamed. "Whether it works or not."

As they got ready for bed, Hal caught Wynne looking at him and frowning.

"What is it?"

She came close and stroked his arm with her hand. "I didn't think, before. If I'm wearing the helmet...."

He could not help but flinch.

She went on tiptoe to kiss his cheek. "Let's not bother with it tonight. If I can get over the—the problem, then I might be able to manage by myself when I record. This'll be a practice run."

He nodded, a lump in his throat.

He felt Wynne start to tremble and held her closer, kissing her hair. She relaxed, her breathing even again. Another minute, and she was smiling in her sleep.

He lay there holding her, pride warming his chest, watching her darting eye movements beneath her closed lids.

Wynne's shift of position, sitting up in bed, woke him, and he sat up as well, looking toward her expectantly. "Well?"

Her eyes shone. "I did it! *We* did it. I put myself in a lovely wood, with a picnic spread out on a blanket, and birds singing—and a few butterflies." She looked self-conscious for a moment, then went on. "And then it started to go wrong again—I smelled smoke, and the wind got hot, and I knew it was a forest fire. And then there *you* were! You waved your hand, and the prettiest sparkling rain started to fall, and I could smell that the fire was gone."

He forced himself not to show the shame that swept over him. There at her side, bandaged, was the proof that he had failed to protect her in the waking world.

But at least he had saved her dream.

"...And then—" Wynne blushed—"then we packed up all the food, very slowly, looking at each other; and then we lay down on the blanket. And we made love. Oh, it was splendid. It seemed like *hours.*"

He had little doubt that she was ready; but she was far from healed. How could he seize her, or thrust against her, without the risk of doing further harm? Instead, he put an arm around her, gently, and kissed her hair.

Interlude

The woman in the fashionable suit slammed the helmet on the conference room table. A less experienced attorney might have jumped, or feared for the table's finish; but this lawyer had seen many a passionate display, and knew that the table was appropriately durable.

"The bastard *tricked* me! He made up a letter about a free sample, and faked the packaging and everything—and it was *him!* The whole recording was *him,* moping and being all broken-hearted and whiny about my leaving him. He *tricked* me into listening to him *inside my head!*" She shoved the helmet and sent it sliding across the table like a shuffleboard disc. "So I want to sue him. I want to hang him out to *dry.*"

The lawyer looked at his notes. "He simulated a recording from...."

The woman looked down at her manicure. "He knew my favorite—*artists.* Because we'd been living together. I even offered to *share* the recordings with him. So we could liven things *up* a bit. I should have known, when he refused, that he could never offer me a truly *deep* relationship."

She looked up again, back on the attack. "Can you do it? I have a case, don't I? I know you people can sue anyone over anything—and this was an *assault.*"

The lawyer sat back in the leather swivel chair and considered. This potential client presented a novel situation, but there were existing frameworks into which he could incorporate it. Intentional infliction of emotional distress, for example: hardly a judge's favorite, but well established. In fact, the tort was tailor-made for this fellow's little prank. It might have been dreamed up precisely to accommodate it.

Not to mention—"He mailed this to you? As a parcel?"

The woman nodded. "I was *surprised*, of course. Who gets mail, these days? But it does happen now and then."

The bureaucratic staying power of the Postal Service had kept the largely useless organization from vanishing entirely. Its staff did not tend to be of the highest quality, and would be unlikely to ask questions about the implausible mailing of a single "sample" rather than batches of them.

And lingering along with the post office itself were certain federal statutes about its misuse.

"The gentleman might be subject to criminal prosecution for mail fraud. Of course, that wouldn't redound to your financial benefit—"

The woman sat forward with malice gleaming in her eyes. "I don't care. Do it. *Do it!* He wants me to suffer, because he's chosen to wallow in his hurt little feelings? I'll show *him!*"

Chapter 14

"Oh, she's standing by him, but if he's guilty, she's bound to have some idea."

Arthur's assistant Hannah theatrically threw up her hands and gazed heavenward. "How long, oh Lord, how long? Boss, you've got to let it go. We have to look at all the other possibilities now. There are tips to sort through, forensic pattern analyses to check—"

"All right. All right! Why don't you make me a list, or a stack, or something, and I'll dive in. I just have a few things to do first."

Hannah snorted and withdrew.

Arthur knew it was pointless. Even if his superiors would ever admit that he'd had the right man after all —that they'd been scared off by an aggressive lawyer and a little bad press—Wynne would never testify against her husband. And even if she would, Wakeman had spousal privilege to turn to. He could muzzle her.

Unless....

As she lay there, terribly wounded, afraid she was dying: if she had any suspicions, wouldn't she have thought about them? He dimly remembered some ruling that recordings weren't considered testamentary statements. And if Wynne's recording wasn't a statement, how could the privilege apply?

Of course, the recordings didn't pick up thoughts. Not exactly. But they did catch emotion. And a loving, tender woman like Wynne, whose husband might have set off the bomb that could be claiming her life, would feel betrayed. She would be horrified in quite a different way than the other victims.

Even if that were true, he couldn't use anything so vague as evidence. He'd be laughed out of the courtroom.

But at least *he* would know. He would have a reason to go on fighting, to stand up against all the pressure to move on. Or he would know it was time to find another culprit and forget about Harold Wakeman.

Was he really considering this?

Did he have the courage to flip a switch and follow Wynne into hell? Could he do it, for her?

"Boss, I'm onto you."

Arthur took a moment before turning toward Hannah with what he hoped was a bland and inquiring expression.

"You're trying to get hold of Wynne Cantrell's recording. And don't give me any of that guff about making sure it's preserved. Why wouldn't they hang onto it? After all, they think the perp is still out there. They'll want to make him or her or them get the playback."

"I don't trust the brass on this one. With what happened about Harold, that recording is a reminder of a political embarrassment. They've got lots of other recordings to use. This one might disappear if I don't safeguard it."

Hannah shook her head, her dark curls jiggling. "There's a limit, boss. Well, two limits: on how long you cling to a hopeless romance, and how far over the line you go before I have to notice. Please don't put me on the spot."

That was fair enough. If he succeeded, he would have to be extremely careful to keep Hannah out of the loop.

Later that week, Arthur approved Hannah's request for a personal day with some relief. Coincidence or not, it might give him just enough time to accomplish his mission.

Arthur sat in the conference room, the only room in their offices that had a window, and watched the sun go down behind the autumn leaves. The fall of night made no objective difference—all the day shift employees had left already, and the custodian would be gone any minute—but it might calm him to observe the gradual fading of the light. He needed calm. He needed anything that would slow the squirming of his gut, and dry the fear sweat that had already soaked through his shirt.

The custodian peeked through the doorway. "I cleaned here already, so I'll be going. Don't mess it up, now!" He guffawed, waved, and left, his heavy footsteps seeming to echo in the hallway.

Arthur waited until the echoes died away. He waited some more.

The building was empty. No one would be coming, not before morning.

He tried to imagine what he was about to experience. He had read the report; he knew the details of Wynne's injuries. Imagining might help.

Who was he fooling? Nothing would help.

He got up, went back to his office, and unlocked the drawer in which he had hidden the recording. Then he unlocked the other drawer, in which he had buried the helmet under piles of reports. He started to take the recording and the helmet back into the conference room, before he realized that was the last place he should go. He could not afford any chance of witnesses in another building. He returned to his office. If anything messy happened, it would be impolite to let it happen in someone else's domain. And if the result were somehow more extreme, he would be found at his desk, where he belonged.

When had he last been this frightened? Perhaps when he was six, and the bully down the street had targeted him, sending his message through this child and that, telling him what would happen when school let out. Or before his first parachute jump, two weeks after another recruit's parachute had failed.

He had cried, when he was six. He might have cried the other time, if he had not been surrounded by so many others who seemed to be conquering their fear. He cried now, a little, before wiping his eyes and his nose on his sleeve. Then he took out his phone, entered his password, and called up his picture of Wynne: Wynne on a sailboat, wind in her hair, laughing. Wynne, the month before Harold Wakeman had entered her life.

He kissed the hard surface of the phone, put it down, donned the helmet, and with a steady hand pushed the playback button.

He came to on the floor of his office, the helmet lying askew under his cheek. For a moment, he could not remember anything but the gut-wrenching maelstrom of terror and agony. Had he endured it for nothing? Or, worse, would he have to try again in order to find the clues he sought?

He barely managed to get up and stumble to the washroom before retching himself empty.

He grabbed the rim of the toilet and managed to hoist himself upright, then lowered the toilet lid and sat on it, forcing himself to breathe deeply and steadily. His head began to clear, and in a few minutes the memory began to assemble itself.

He ran through it, searching, searching again, before conceding that none of Wynne's feelings or impressions suggested any thought that her husband might be responsible.

Of course, she might not know. There was no particular reason for Hal to have been careless. And once Wynne had chosen him and cleaved to him, she would ignore any conduct that others might have found suspicious.

But whether or not he was guilty, she had needed him, and he had failed her.

Arthur would do whatever he had to do to keep from failing her as well.

It took him three tries to stand up and walk back into his office. He had drooled on the linoleum where he fell; he wiped it up with a tissue, the kind anyone could find on any day in his wastebasket. He hid the helmet again and put the recording in his briefcase. He would put it back where it belonged as soon as he could.

***

Hannah stood in the recessed doorway of the building next door and watched Arthur emerge; watched him stagger and catch himself, then head toward the subway, weaving a little as he walked.

The damned besotted idiot! She had known it. But of course she did not know, not really, not officially. He seemed determined to dig his own grave, and she obviously could not stop him, but she would do her best not to help him dig.

CHAPTER 15

DREAM DAEMON REVELED in the success of his latest attack. (He much preferred his chosen alias, with its appropriate double meaning, to his parents' utterly pedestrian choice of "Bert.") The principal was probably still stuttering and twitching after his Schoolgirl Spanking dream suddenly morphed from giver to receiver POV. Good thing some customers preferred the latter: Dream Daemon lacked the skills to create a version from scratch.

He was no fool—he confined his hacking to dreams whose purchasers would be reluctant to admit their original choices. "Officer, I was unable to complete my dream about putting students just like mine over my knee, buck naked...."

Who should be next?

Dream Daemon scanned the most popular vendor's registry of customers who took delivery of their dreams online. He hoped it would be a long time—months, maybe—before the vendors would commit enough resources to cut him off. He would have to make sure that they could do no more than exclude him (until he found a way around such future security), rather than tracking him down. If they found him, he had his doubts that they would confine their response to legal alternatives. He might find himself strapped down and dreaming of medieval torture chambers.

Here was a ripe one! His mother's slimeball boyfriend had just bought himself a night of leading a motorcycle gang. Now, what to substitute? Baby shower, church revival.... Yes! A rousing church revival as experienced by some sad sack of a sinner. Who knows—maybe the scumbag would hang onto some repentance in the morning. He'd have to call his mother next week, and see if she was any more cheerful.

***

The sales manager massaged his forehead just between his eyebrows, his eyes closed. He shook his head at the phone, despite the economy model's absence of a vision circuit. "This sort of claim comes with the territory. We do everything we can to prevent them."

The insurance agent huffed in apparent disapproval. "Not everything! You don't have to market these extreme sports experiences."

The sales manager bared his teeth at the phone. "We don't have to stay in business, either! Our customers *love* the sports products. How else can all the—" (he bit back the pejorative label that came to mind) "—people whose schedules don't permit the intensive training and conditioning of these athletes experience the thrill of racing down a Black Diamond slope at top speed, or free-diving off a cliff into raging surf?"

"They can use their imaginations, like all the generations before. Imagination doesn't put you in the emergency room."

"We warn them, repeatedly, not to attempt to duplicate these experiences. Some people just don't listen."

"Why don't you stick to the sex stuff? We hardly get any claims out of that."

The sales manager laughed, without amusement. "That's because you aren't our lawyer! Do you know how many of the erotic dreamers get stalked? Lately they've been insisting that we provide security as part of the contract. No, sports aren't our biggest problem. And if you don't want our business, I'll find someone who does."

***

The phone number was unfamiliar, but Wynne's screening program hadn't flagged the caller as a known solicitor or a convicted criminal, so she went ahead and answered.

The man rattled off a name she wouldn't try to remember. She could ask again if he proved worth remembering.

"Wynne, I'm so glad to reach you. I believe we have some exciting opportunities to discuss." Somehow, he made the commonplace use of her first name seem unpleasantly familiar, as if he had reached through the phone to pat her knee as he spoke.

"I do hope you're recovering from your ordeal. It would be such a shame if you were unable to produce new product for much longer."

He could be a particularly smarmy fan. Fans sometimes had their own agendas and proposals, often outlandish. She waited.

"You see, I distribute a particularly select inventory of special dreams. We specialize in the unusual, the difficult to obtain."

She did not have an exclusive contact with her usual agent, but it would be churlish as well as unwise to antagonize him, after he'd been so understanding about Wynne's unavoidable hiatus. "I'm sorry, but I don't think—"

"Please, Wynne, hear me out." She disliked the man more with each repetition of her name. "I'm guessing you don't want to complicate your relationship with your current distributor. Naturally not! But I believe the product we're hoping you could provide is not really within that distributor's market area. You see, our customers like to plumb the *boundaries* of human experience, to push the envelope. They relish *intensity*. And no other lucid dreamer in the modern era, the era of recording and playback, has had your unique exposure to, shall we say, the darker palette of that experience...."

Wynne unleashed a rolling barrage of profanity, the like of which she had never previously mastered. She wished she had more languages at her command so as to prolong it. When she had exhausted her material, she shrieked as loud as she could into the phone, just in case the caller was still listening and had his ear in a vulnerable spot.

Then she dropped into the nearest chair and curled herself into the tightest ball she could manage, shivering. It took some time for the shivers to stop.

Should she tell her agent about the call? It would be an awkward conversation—but she might not be the only one of his artists to be receiving such offers. If warned, he might be better prepared to repel the invader.

He heard her out, with less dismay than she would have liked him to express.

"I've been fending off those offers for weeks. I guess someone got tired of hearing me say 'no' and decided to go around me. And it's not just the private dream porn people calling—it's the government johnnys as well."

"The *what?*"

"The correctional folks. They don't have nearly as many recordings to use on convicts as they'd like to have. Lots of times, no one can record the victim in time. They've been getting less particular, using other victims with similar experiences—and now, they want to start using dreams. Naturally, they thought of you."

Wynne shuddered and twisted away from the phone.

"I did have a quite different idea, one I hope you wouldn't find nearly as, ah, as unpleasant. We've had a most positive response to the dream you brought me just before, um, er, your injury. Anyway, we've had a number of customer requests concerning the man you featured. You know I don't try to impinge on your, ah, your creative process, but if it proved convenient, that is, feasible, at some point...."

She evaded his inquiry and ended the call as soon as she could manage. The last thing she wanted to do now was to dwell on memories of, or spin fantasies about, her former lover. It was bad enough that her imperfectly controlled dreams were still, on occasion, landing her back in his embrace.

Just last night, she had stood, naked, at the foot of his bed, waiting to be coaxed, complimented, seduced. She had relived with perfect clarity the heady, stimulating uncertainty: where would he touch her? What would he ask of her?

But the novelty of ignorance wore off so soon.

***

The judge looked down her eagle's beak of a nose toward the group clustered at the counsel tables. "Next case. In re Experience Preservation Project. EPP present by administrative representative and counsel. Intervenors Metropolitan Ecumenical Counsel and Tri-Urban Regional Association of Defense Attorneys, present by counsel. You all registered your appearances on the way in—so let's get started. Please tell me that this is a practical joke, and I'll refrain from holding anyone in contempt."

The Project's attorney smiled broadly, acknowledging the judge's exceptional wit. "No, indeed, Your Honor. The creation of a death recording is a circumstance we could obviously not precipitate, but we have been preparing for some time to, ah—"

The judge's narrow lips twitched toward a smile. "To take advantage of it, I believe you began to say. Let's not waste time looking for a phrase with more public-spirited connotations. Go on."

"We have preliminary protocols already in place, to be adjusted to the current circumstances. Extensive precautions will be taken to minimize negative impacts on the test subjects. The recording will be edited to eliminate all sensations, impressions and events prior to the onset of systemic collapse.

The subjects will be extensively monitored, and the playback terminated at any sign of physiological distress—"

"I'll be most interested in how you intend to define such distress. If I allow this testing to proceed, I'll require frequent updates. Please continue."

The attorney ran his fingers through his expertly trimmed hair, then returned his hand to the lectern. "All staff are already bound by stringent nondisclosure agreements, whose language will be reviewed and expanded if necessary.... That's the basic outline, Your Honor."

The judge turned to the table on her right. "Intervenors: who wants to go first?"

A petite young woman stepped forward. "Your Honor, the Ecumenical Counsel believes this petition is premature, to say the least. We are discussing an unprecedented intrusion into the most sacred moment of human existence. Petitioner is proposing to expose the deceased's encounter with the Presence Beyond to multiple unrelated individuals—"

"If I may, Your Honor. The deceased's next of kin have agreed—"

"In exchange for what astronomical sum?"

The judge put up her hand to silence the squabbling attorneys, then peered at Project counsel. "Were these relatives represented by counsel?"

"Yes, Your Honor. We made sure of it."

"Prudent of you. And as for the inducement you may have offered, that is not the State's affair. Or the Ecumenical Counsel's. You were saying?"

"Thank you, Your Honor. In addition to the intrusion on this one individual's most personal experience, we have the potential for an unprecedented disruption of the religious practices and beliefs of our member institutions and many others besides."

The judge shook her head; her hair, in its tight bun, stirred not a whit. "It is also not the State's province to prevent new information from challenging the doctrines of any—or all—religious orders. Let's hear from the representative of the defense bar."

A muscular man of middle years stepped forward. "Your Honor, this is the first step on a diabolical slippery slope. Your Honor may well recall what occurred when this form of recording was first examined—the representations that no one was contemplating any use of the technology in the criminal justice system, either as an investigative aid or a punitive option. Only the limitations of the technology have for the most part prevented the former; the latter is by now well ensconced in our criminal code. If you allow investigation and development of this extreme variant, its use as a form of 'death penalty' is well-nigh inevitable."

The judge tilted her head and appeared amused. "Counselor, you appear to have pre-judged the nature of this recording. Unofficial reports, based on the illegal predecessors of this recording, conflict substantially on this subject. If this project is allowed to proceed, we may all discover that the experience reported is benign, or even blissful. Then we'll have a whole different set of problems.... Your concerns, if appropriate, can be raised when the facts have been adequately developed. Any last words from Project counsel?"

"Your Honor, all of human experience has shown that discoveries will not be suppressed for long. Knowledge will not be denied. The recording technology has already been disseminated into numerous private and public hands. This is not, in fact, the first known recording of the death experience, and it will not be the last. The genie has already begun to emerge from the bottle. Would it not be best, Your Honor, that she be provided with a carefully chosen scientific escort?"

***

"Looks like the hotshots'll be testing that recording after all."

"The death tape? You've got to be kidding me! What crazy son of a bitch is going to sit through it? One of those sickos that's been buying—"

"They're lining up! Everybody and his cousin, seems like, wants to see the Pearly Gates."

"Is that what the special meeting is about?"

"Indeed-y. They're all going to be busting their asses getting ready."

"What about government oversight? Isn't there anyone from the Hill screaming that we're going to end up killing people?"

"Most likely. But there's been some kind of a hearing. And I'm guessing they'll be writing up some really thick double-talk for the oversight folks, and some *really* solid waivers for the saps—excuse me, the public-spirited volunteers."

"Why'd the meeting get canceled?"

"It's missing!"

"The recording? How the hell could that happen?"

"Got me. There's a lot of whispering about an inside job."

"But they've got copies, don't they?"

"Corrupted."

"I've got a very, very bad feeling about this. They're going to be turning us all inside out trying to find it."

"You don't know how right you are. The police want us all recorded, to see who's twitchy."

"No way. No fucking way. I'll quit first."

"Suuure. Like that'll stop 'em."

* * *

Small as the record disc was, the hard edge seemed to be digging a hole through Arthur's shirt pocket and into his skin. As a smuggler, he showed little promise. It would be a relief to return Wynne's recording to the storage room.

Arthur turned the corner and stopped dead. The corridor leading to the storage room had never been guarded before, but it was guarded now.

He donned an expression of polite interest and approached the guard. "New procedures?"

"Yes, sir." Somehow the guard managed to combine blank stolidity and impersonal suspicion.

"What's involved, then?"

"Anyone who enters that room gets a pat-down and a scan"—the guard held up what must be a portable scanner—"when they come back out."

Well, that should pose no problem. By the time he emerged, there would be nothing for the scanner to detect. He nodded to the guard and walked past him toward the storage room. A shrill whine sounded behind him; he jumped and turned around. The guard stood facing him with the scanner in one hand and a phone in the other.

"We figured whoever made off with the death recording might copy and return it. So we set a little trap." The Deputy Director sat back in her chair and shook her head, laughing a little. "And we caught you carrying around an entirely different recording. What the blazes were you doing with the Cantrell disc?"

"I, uh, I've been investigating the bombing in which Ms. Cantrell was injured." Arthur tried to remember how he had explained his intentions to Hannah. He could all too easily imagine Hannah's reaction to hearing that her prophecies had been fulfilled.

"Never mind." The Deputy Director waved him to silence. "It really doesn't matter. Under the circumstances, we have to be strict about protocol. We can't let anything slide. As of now, you're on unpaid leave. I'll be speaking to the Director about what to do with you."

Arthur stood up and left the room with as close an approximation of dignity as he could manage.

* * *

Tertius Shaw sat back in the luxurious embrace of his black leather armchair, holding a snifter of brandy and watching the reflections of the firelight in its depths. From the stereo, in celebration of and ironic comment on his achievement, came the solemn strains of Mozart's *Requiem*.

Obtaining the recording had posed certain challenges, but of course he had surmounted them. How satisfying to once again outwit the unsuspecting! It had been well worth the touch of apprehension he had felt upon confronting the unknown.

He had now answered one threshold question: experiencing a death recording was not itself fatal. His expertise had suggested as much, or he would not have proceeded, but there had still been some element of risk.

The playback had been most interesting, if not as theatrical as some would have predicted. The recording, as edited, began after the most acute consciousness of pain, which gave him some dissatisfaction as a researcher, but there had been a most intriguing degree of lassitude. He had caught just the trailing edge of terror; much of the fear must have passed with the pain. While he had not seen what he personally would identify as a tunnel, there had certainly been some impression of light—bright light. The boy had not evinced any recognition of departed loved ones, but perhaps he was simply too young to have lost any.

The final moments, the dissolution into nothingness... extraordinary.

Tertius would have to choose his own subjects judiciously. It should not be difficult to ensure that some had been predeceased by family or spouses. Perhaps he could even collect some survivors of previous projects.

And of course, he would need to sample according to religious origin. Would the beliefs with which one approached the moment of transition significantly affect the nature of the experience?

There was also the question of whether to keep the project clandestine. He would have no trouble making his subjects simply disappear. But it might be more amusing, more piquant, to leave some hints. He would ponder the question, and decide in due course.

In the meantime, a massive search was underway. The near impossibility of an outsider getting access to the recording meant that everyone within the institution—or almost everyone—would be subject to scrutiny. How many extraneous sins would come to light!

Tertius put his feet up on the padded footstool and listened to the music, utterly content.

Interlude

The operative tossed and turned. The dream, so vividly recalling every horrible moment of his informal initiation, was slow to fade: he found himself conscious of each breath as if the water might come pouring down his throat at any moment.

How many of the agency's prisoners had been waterboarded since then? Was one of them choking and gasping at this very moment?

Before he actually joined the agency, he had spent nights like this imagining the presence of lithe and deadly female agents with uncertain loyalties, teasing and grappling and taunting and finally surrendering. He had not been such a fool as to expect fulfillment of these film-derived fantasies, but he had expected to find excitement and purpose in his new calling. Instead, it turned out to be just another desk job, albeit with more cumbersome restrictions on what he could say and do after hours. No matter what any of them did (and rarely did he know whether anything he did achieved anything at all), there would always be more jihadists, flooding the borders, burning with zeal, eager for self-sacrifice.

And no wonder. Just as he had hoped to serve a higher calling, these would-be warriors sought to serve Allah. How could he blame them, when he admired their passion? When he understood?

Yousef, for example. (When had someone told him the suspect's name? Well, no matter.) People might dismiss him as too young, indoctrinated from childhood onward—but he was his own person, afire with conviction, determined....

The operative looked furtively about to make sure no one was near, in case his disturbing thoughts could somehow be perceived. He had better head to the gym for an extra workout, and try to exhaust himself past thinking.

Chapter 16

Wynne awoke, sighed, and tried to look on the positive side. She had made it through two dreams, on her own, without interruption or incident. Only the third had veered out of control, back to the plaza. And then there had been the horrible fragment at the end, where she thought she had awakened, and found that her left hand was gone again, and then her right....

Beside her, Hal stirred, then rolled over to face her. "Hon, are you okay?"

Rather than answer, she scooted closer to him and waited to see if he would put his arms around her, sighing and relaxing when he did so.

They lay quietly for a moment, and she wondered if he were falling back asleep. Then he spoke, softly, in the slow, almost chanting cadence that meant he was barely awake. "How did it all start? The dreams. Knowing what you could do. Do you remember?"

Oh, yes. She had always remembered; and lately, since the accident, she had thought of it often.

She spoke as softly as he, so that her tale could be a story or a lullaby, whatever he needed it to be.

"I was about three years old...."

In her dream, she had been playing on the beach, her parents absorbed in conversation farther up on the sand. She was making a sand castle, concentrating with all her might, her tongue sticking out between her teeth. The chill salt breeze blew at her, sometimes catching the sand she was dumping and blowing it back in her face. Then she saw that the tide was coming in, closer, closer. It was lapping at the edge of her castle. Soon the water would swallow the castle, melting it, and all her work would be gone and wasted. She started to cry, but her parents could not hear.

She jumped up and stamped her foot. This should *not* be happening! If her castle were stronger than sand, a real castle, the waves could not harm it no matter how they tried!

Suddenly her castle doubled in size. It was still small, a toy castle, but made of gleaming golden stone, with carved archways at the windows and doors, and balconies at two large windows facing the sea. Delighted, she conjured dolls to put on the balconies, a king and a queen. She allowed the tide to flow into a moat around the castle, in which she placed a graceful, long-necked swan. Then, finally, she made the princess doll, a princess looking much like Wynne herself, in a shimmery sky-blue gown, and placed it on the balcony, between the king and queen.

She crowed in satisfaction and awoke.

"And that's how it began. I never had another real nightmare. If a dream started to go wrong, I could change it—fix it." She could not hold back the tears. "Until now."

Hal turned her around to face him and dried her face with the sleeve of his pajamas. "You'll get it back, Wynne. I know you will."

Of course he could not know that. Neither of them could know. But somehow, his show of confidence gave her courage. "Yes, sweetheart. I will. And now, I'm going back to sleep."

Not even in their courtship days had Wynne felt entirely welcome in Hal's studio. To be sure, he would show her his work from time to time, especially when it was about to be moved (with much trouble and suspense and care) from studio to destination. But Hal had nothing to show her today. The project that had consumed him before the accident had been canceled—or rather, his contract had been terminated and the job given to someone else. She had expected Hal to sue, but he wanted nothing more to do with lawyers and courtrooms. He was not even planning to work on the model for his own satisfaction. When she asked about it, he had muttered something about tainted memories.

So why had he invited her to come with him this morning, on his first day in the studio since everything had happened?

At least while she was here, she could do some cautious straightening up. She collected fossilized pizza crusts on abandoned paper plates and threw them in the oversized trash can. Then she glanced toward the tools that needed cleaning. She had performed that task, at times, when Hal was racing to meet a deadline or simply lost in creative frenzy. "Honey, shall I clean these?"

"Not just now. Come here and sit down. I wanted to see what you thought about something."

As she sat down beside him, he reached for her right hand. She had not consciously noticed, before the accident, that Hal more often held her left hand than her right. Now it would be months before she had a left hand. She tried not to think of what bizarre, pre-Cambrian shape the bud might have under the protective wrappings.

Hal lifted the hand he held, brushed it with a quick kiss, then grasped it more firmly. "There's going to be a memorial where the fountain used to be. It might be another fountain, or it might not. There's a competition for the design." He grinned, mischief in his eyes. She had not seen that look in too long. "I'm expecting Benedict Black to submit an entry."

Hal enjoyed the occasional use of pseudonyms, for anything from dinner reservations to competitions to phone messages. Benedict Black had several sculptures to his credit. After all the publicity, of so many sorts, it was hard to say how an entry from Hal under his own name would be received. Benedict Black could test the waters.

"Do you have any ideas yet?"

"I'm thinking of starting from the fountain. Of course, it can't look too similar, but I want some form that follows from it—some transformation of it. And I want to include a human figure."

"But—have you ever done that?"

"Not exactly—at least, not for anyone to see. I've waited long enough, don't you think?... And sweetheart, if you're willing, I'd like it to be you. Not like a portrait, naturally, but I'd like you to sit for it."

Her eyes filled with tears. "Hal, that's perfect. It's like—you'd be reuniting us, me and the fountain."

"That's what I was thinking." He leaned over and kissed her. She leaned into his embrace, marveling that the tribulations they had suffered had mellowed him so much.

Chapter 17

Now that Arthur had experienced the most intense experience Wynne would ever record, he felt fewer compunctions about exploring her more typical wares. The helmet he had used remained off-limits, perhaps still in the drawer in his unattainable office; he bought another.

He had not visited her website since soon after it appeared, but now he went online and browsed through the offerings. He avoided the erotica, grateful that it was honestly labeled. He would not be one of those exploiting Wynne in that way, even if she had opened herself to exploitation.

He came to a dream whose illustration showed a lady in Renaissance dress—no, a queen, complete with coronet—in attendance at what must be a tournament. Colorful banners fluttered all around, and the lists were visible in the background. Before the queen knelt one of the contestants, armor gleaming.

Arthur selected the dream and quickly completed the purchase. Then he went back and read the instructions more carefully, noting how to increase the chances that the basics of Wynne's dream would control and blend with his own.

Forcing himself not to hurry, Arthur got ready for bed. His old-fashioned pajama shirt had buttons and a pocket. Wynne had sent him a business card when she first started marketing her dreams. He rummaged through his desk drawer to find it. It would do, instead of a handkerchief, as his lady's favor.

With luck, when he dreamed, he would be her knight.

The dream had been all that Arthur could have hoped; and predictably enough, it left him more forlorn than before.

With a wry grimace, he hit "play" on the soundtrack of *Man of La Mancha*, and then began his letter.

Dear Wynne—

I have wondered for years whether, if I had been bolder, I might have had a chance. If I had shown my feelings before you met Harold, would they have found a response? Was there never more than friendship possible between us, or did you simply give up and move on?

Of course, it makes no difference, now. But I wished to declare this once, and once only, that you are my ideal of womanhood; and that you deserve, beyond any possible question, the best of any man's passionate devotion. It is my sole remaining hope that you will value yourself enough to settle for nothing less.

Arthur

He read the letter over, silently, aloud, and silently again. Then he switched off the music, took one last look, and deleted the file.

Arthur had maintained a careful distance from Wynne and her husband. He followed her on social media to the extent he could do so without disclosing the fact. He sent the couple the same Christmas cards he distributed to professional acquaintances. On the rare occasions when he encountered Wynne in public, he made casual conversation and asked no questions. After the explosion, he had come by the hospital several times, but not after she regained consciousness.

Now, with unwelcome time on his hands, it was harder to refrain. He needed to know how her recovery was coming. He wanted to see whether she was happy.

Did he really hope that she was happy with Hal?

How happy could she be if, despite her essential honesty, she had been driven to cheat?

And if Hal had left her so emotionally starved, why had she not turned to Arthur? Had his efforts to hide his feelings been too successful?

Arthur's thoughts screeched to a halt. What was he thinking? Why would he assume, why would he believe, that Wynne had been unfaithful? They had spoken so seldom. Had he picked up some clue, one of those times, and only now seen it surface?

Perhaps, if he saw her again, he could remember that clue—or obtain another.

***

Wynne was not sure what to make of Arthur's visit. He had called ahead—he was unfailingly polite—but he had not really explained why he wished to see her. She would have been happy to remain friends, but he had made clear that this was, for him, either undesirable or impossible.

Of course, she had more visitors and calls since the accident. It took such reminders, sometimes, for friends to realize how long it had been since they had been in touch. Those renewed contacts had been one of the few side benefits of what had happened to her.

In any event, she would make Arthur welcome. It was, in fact, good to have the distraction of a visitor—though she could have wished that her visitor was someone in whom she could actually confide. Hal's "Benedict Black" submission had made the first cut—which had, of course, made it necessary for Hal to reveal his identity. To Wynne's unspeakable relief, the Park Commission still wanted to meet with him. He had left for the meeting hours ago....

Arthur sat perched on the edge of a chair that would have provided more comfort if he had allowed it. Bitsy sat a couple of feet away, observing him intently. She did not appear suspicious, as she sometimes did around strangers, but neither was she attempting to lure him into playing with her.

Every time he sipped his cup of tea, he put it back on the coffee table as quickly as possible. The second time, the saucer trembled and the cup rattled slightly before he could set them down. Something was obviously troubling him. And how had he arranged to visit her in the middle of the afternoon?

"How have you been, Arthur? Is everything—going well?"

Arthur stared at her. "You ask *me* that? Of course everything's all right. How are *you* holding up?"

It took only a little effort to smile. "I'm doing really well, considering. The new hand is well on its way." She thought of showing him the growing bandaged area, but reconsidered: many people found it unsettling. "And I've been getting back to work! Hal's helped me so much."

She was sorry to see him tighten his lips. It didn't look as if he had managed to move on. He was such a decent man—what a shame he hadn't found someone, someone better for him than she would ever have been. Maybe she could do a little match-making.

He seemed to search for words, then looked her straight in the eye. "So you and Hal—you're happy."

She did not want to take offense at his prying. Their shared history might give him some right to inquire. "Yes, Arthur. We're quite happy."

He looked frustrated at her answer, as if finding it somehow insufficient. A troubling thought struck her. Arthur was an investigator: he spent his days poking into people's lives. Had he somehow stumbled on the fact of her affair? And if he had, did he imagine that it provided him with some kind of opening?

Wynne stood and leaned down to pick up Arthur's teacup, taking care not to look him in the eye. "I know how busy you must be. It was kind of you to come. But I'd better let you get back to work—and I'm a little tired."

Arthur stood up, staring at her again, and blurted: "Then you haven't heard?"

She wrinkled her forehead. Was he in some sort of trouble? And here she was being cold to him, when he needed a friend. She swallowed the lump in her throat. "What is it?"

He made no answer. She stepped closer and held out her right hand. "Arthur, is there something I could help you with?"

He jerked out his hand to clasp hers, squeezing it tight. Then he released it, stepped back, and walked to the door. He let himself out without another word.

Wynne leaned against the kitchen counter, waiting for more water to boil. She had made tea for herself as well as Arthur, but had let it grow cold—and she needed the soothing aroma of a fresh cup, the gentle heat trickling down her throat and into her chest, to help her sort through just what Arthur's visit had been about.

The kettle's shrill whistle must have masked the sound of Hal's key in the lock, but as she poured the water, she heard his footsteps, firmer and quicker than she had heard them in weeks, and then his glad call. "Wynne! I got it! I'm *back*!"

Wynne turned off the flame under the kettle, looked longingly at the teapot, and hurried to greet her jubilant husband. As soon as she entered the living room, he caught her under the arms, twirled her around, set her back down, then seized her again in a hug that almost squeezed the air from her lungs. For a moment, she feared for the bud of her left hand—but even in his seeming abandon, he steered clear of that vulnerable spot.

Back on her feet again, she reached for Hal's right hand, held it, and looked in his eyes, feeling her own smile stretching to match his. Then, almost at the same moment, they both laughed for sheer relief and joy.

She tugged him toward the kitchen. "I was about to have some tea, but we probably have champagne somewhere—"

He used his free hand to pat her bottom, then kissed her shoulder. "Why not both? You have your tea while I find the champagne."

The water would still be hot. Wynne fixed her tea, picked up the cup, and took a long breath of the steam rising from it. Her neck and shoulders loosened as if from an instantaneous massage. She took a sip, then looked up at her husband, or rather the lower half of him: he was rummaging deep within the cupboard that served as both miscellaneous dry goods storage and liquor cabinet. She chuckled and waited, savoring her tea, until he had extricated himself with bottle in hand. "Thank you, darling. Now tell me all about it!"

Hal launched into the tale of his meeting with the Park Commission—his presentation, their questions, his answers— gesturing enthusiastically with both hands and sloshing the champagne around until she laughed again and rescued it. He stopped in mid-syllable, seeming to hold his breath until she set the bottle down on the counter. She raised an eyebrow at him. "Really, Hal, I can manage."

He looked down sheepishly. "Sorry. I know you can. I just—"

"You just don't quite believe it. It's all right, Hal. I can deal with you treating me as fragile for a little while longer."

She would have liked to open the champagne herself, after that, but that task was indeed beyond her present powers. She handed Hal the corkscrew and made up for it by grabbing two glasses at once, twining her fingers around their stems and pulling them from the cabinet. Hal extracted them, gently, one at a time, and poured the champagne, managing to keep the glasses from foaming over. He handed her one glass and raised the other in a toast. "To our lives— beginning again."

As she clinked her glass against his, she remembered what Hal's return home had made her forget: Arthur's unexplained visit and his perplexing manner. It was an untimely thought, and she tried to thrust it out of her mind; but Hal paused with his glass to his lips. "What is it?"

"It's nothing, sweetheart."

She half expected him to retreat with relief from hearing whatever might be troubling her. But he moved closer and ran his forefinger down her cheek. "It's all right, love. Please tell me."

She took another sip of her champagne, then put the glass back down. "It's just that something odd happened today. Arthur Kellic called—"

Wynne gasped at Hal's look of sudden horror. She had forgotten—how could she forget?—the uncertainty that still hung over him. But nothing in Arthur's manner had suggested such a threat. "Oh, no, darling, nothing like that! He just—well, actually, I'm not really sure what it was he wanted. Except to come by. To visit."

Hal still stood rigid, his jaw clenched. "So he came here?"

Reluctantly, she nodded. "Darling, please don't look like that! He didn't act as if he was—investigating." Or at least, as if he'd been investigating Hal... "Actually, he seemed rather sad. I thought he might be in some sort of trouble. Maybe he wanted to tell me about it. But he didn't, in the end. He just stayed a little while and then left."

Hal stared at her for another long moment. Then he jerked his glass to his lips and took a gulp, champagne spilling around his mouth and dripping down his chin.

Wynne managed to conceal her sorrow and frustration until Hal had finally fallen asleep. Then she slid carefully out of bed and tiptoed to the living room, curling up on the sofa, clutching her knees with her right arm and clenching her fist.

How long would Hal have to live with this horrible threat hanging over him? How dare they go on hurting him, after everything they had already done to him!

Whoever "they" were.... Of course, she knew one of "them." Arthur had been part of it, almost from the beginning. And she could not help but be angry with him—but the feeling was so mixed in with understanding, and sympathy, and some shame for how she must somehow have led him on or failed to explain things....

But those others! Those officials and bureaucrats who had condemned her husband to horrors—to torture—based on so little evidence, and then lacked even the decency to crawl on their bellies in apology—daring, instead, to hint at more torment to come!

How would they like it? How would they face it, if they knew they could be taken at any moment and thrust into a foretaste of hell itself?

She could imagine it, if she let herself: their smug, placid faces going pale and taut, their eyes bulging, their mouths hanging open, sweat beading their brows, as the fear filled their bellies and they imagined the approaching fire....

She could even dream it, if she liked. She could conjure every detail, to the moans they would utter and the smell of their fear.

Wynne jumped off the sofa, shuddering. Had her dreams not contained enough cruelty since the accident, without her inviting more ugliness in?

She hurried into the kitchen and heated some hot milk. Hot milk always gave her a childlike sense of peace and safety. The taste and feel and scent of it would help her shape some sweeter dream.

Chapter 18

Hal leafed through the sketches, comparing, tweaking, discarding, refining. He could hardly wait to be working in the clay, but he was not quite ready.

He had more or less finished the core of the design. The materials that had become available in recent years allowed for an airier structure, reaching more exuberantly upward. But how to incorporate the human figure?

Should Wynne represent water, somehow? He could see her figure floating, holding hands with the fountain and reaching upward, heaven-bound. Water and spirit, mixed.... He might want several figures, large and small in balanced asymmetry, but all ascending.

How would Wynne feel about it? Would she balk at representing the souls of the victims? Would she consider it presumptuous, or inconsiderate?

He waited for the surge of irritation at the thought of her failing to understand.

It did not come.

He cared how she felt. How she felt mattered.

He took a break, heading toward the kitchen to scrounge for a snack. They should have some good bread and leftover bacon for a sandwich. Bitsy, stationed at the living room window and keeping a watchful eye on the neighborhood, barked a commentary as he passed through, then jumped up and followed him into the kitchen.

As he assembled his sandwich, Hal held up a bit of bacon in Bitsy's direction, dangling it for a moment before popping it in his mouth. Bitsy whined. He really shouldn't tease her: Wynne didn't like it. He tore off a larger piece as an apology and tossed it to the dog, who caught it in midair and gulped it down. He looked at the plate, hesitated, then added a few herb-infused crackers and headed for the kitchen table.

As he had expected, Wynne soon appeared. "Look at this!" As he looked up, she leaned over and stole a cracker, grinning at him impishly, and kissed his cheek as she straightened up again.

Hal patted her hip. "Did you really have something to show me, or were you just distracting me so you could swipe my food?"

Wynne held out the necklace she was wearing. "I wanted to show you my present! One of my fans sent it. See the engraved text? It says, 'Throw your dreams into space like a kite.' I've always loved that quote. And this scarf came yesterday. I guess it's no surprise that it's such a good color for me—they can see my picture on my website—but it's still heartwarming that someone cared enough to get it right."

"It's a good thing I'm not the jealous type. No one sends me presents when I get a sculpture installed."

Wynne looked self-conscious for a moment, then donned an expression of exaggerated sympathy. "Poor Hal. No necklace, no scarf." Then her face shifted toward more genuine concern. "Do you ever feel neglected, really? It's true, hardly any of the people who enjoy your art know as much as your name. It isn't fair."

Hal laughed. "It doesn't bother me. In a way, it makes me feel powerful, especially with the public installations— affecting people, changing where they choose to walk or eat lunch, without their even knowing who's done it."

"Well, I'm glad my fans are so good to me. It makes me feel, oh, reinforced somehow—almost as if I had more family than I knew I had." She paused, musing. "Of course I've gotten more presents and messages since—since I got hurt. But it's funny how many of them say that they'd wanted to get in touch even before, except they were too shy or they thought it might annoy me. And then, when they heard, somehow they knew I would need their support."

Hal held out another cracker. Wynne accepted it and blew him a kiss.

Wynne nibbled away at the cracker until it was gone. Then she looked up at him, with a familiar "should I say it?" expression.

"What is it, baby?"

"Oh… I was just wondering…" Now she looked positively nervous.

"I wanted to do a special dream—a thank-you for my fans. It would be different from anything I've done before—no story, just me doing my best to communicate to each one of them. I could give it away to anyone who's bought one of my dreams in the past."

For some reason, Hal found the idea almost unbearably touching. He fought back tears. "I think it's a terrific idea." He batted away the unwelcome afterthought that it would also be terrific publicity, and might well become a collector's item.

But why would she hesitate to share that idea? There must be more.

"…But it's a little, I don't know, scary to do something so simple. I'll be very—exposed. And I'm still a little shaky. So I was wondering if you'd mind… again…."

Hal pulled her into an embrace. "Of course. I'd be glad to help. It wasn't bad before, and it'll be easier this time." And if fate were kind, any nightmares the helmet gave him would be silent ones, and Wynne would not have to know.

Chapter 19

Tertius had noticed an anomaly.

Several times, over the last few days, he had thought about the boy. Of course he had relived, analyzed, and relished the boy's recorded death, but now and then he had found himself pondering such pointless questions as whether the boy had already chosen a career path and whether he left any family behind. Curiosity was Tertius' most consistent driving force, but these were not the sorts of matters about which he was usually curious. Nor was this the effect his special expertise would have led him to expect from any recording. He had anticipated acquiring miscellaneous details about the boy's life, but not the thirst to acquire even more.

Could the cause be some event unrelated to the recording? Two nights ago, he had attended the performance of a newly prominent composer. Music could have an unpredictable impact. In obtaining the recording of the boy's death, Tertius had risked exposure somewhat more than usual: that flirtation with danger might have some lingering effect even though he had not, at the time, been conscious of special excitement.

But the greatest deviation from his usual habits and pleasures had beyond question been the recording itself.

Well, he could hardly embark on a new set of experiments without encountering some surprises. He would proceed, albeit cautiously; he would observe, and note his observations. Caution was justified; timidity would be beneath him.

***

Arthur had not expected to hear from the office so soon. He fought back the impulse to hope. He could hardly expect absolution after so short a penance. But why had the Deputy Director called on a secured line?

"Art, we've had something come up, and we could use your help. It's a little ticklish, though. You're not exactly the fair-haired boy right now—to put it mildly. Most people here would think I'm crazy to trust you."

Arthur waited. If the Deputy Director needed him enough to risk contact, she would explain without prompting.

"We've had a wealthy society widow disappear from her house. We got lucky—we thought—when a witness identified one of two men who were skulking around the area after dark. A familiar bad guy for hire, out of the pen for a year. We picked him up. He had nothing to say—seemed scared to talk. So we let him stew overnight, and lo and behold, he had a heart attack in his cell."

He had better speak now, or she would think he had sunk into passivity. "Sounds like someone with resources was behind it."

"Naturally, that left us having to work from the victim end. It didn't take long before we found something. The lady had two children, a son and a daughter—until the son died. Want to guess how?"

A chill ran down Arthur's spine. "The explosion."

"Too right. Any more speculations?"

What would be tied to the explosion, and also politically sensitive? There had been the mess about Harold Wakeman's conviction and punishment—but Arthur was the last one to whom the Department would turn if that were involved. What else?

"A son. How old?"

"A youngster. Nineteen years old."

Arthur closed his eyes. "The death recording. The boy who was recorded—it's his mother who's missing."

"Yes, it is. And that just might mean—"

"Christ!" The recording that some insider might have stolen; a kidnapping, linked to the recording, which of course was just one aspect of the bombing; the death of a suspect while in custody....

"I believe I see why you'd like to have someone investigate who isn't officially on duty. Okay. I can play it that way. Except how am I supposed to investigate without apparent authority?"

"We're working on that. You can start doing behind-the-scenes research. You've got access to the databases."

"Which gets recorded. If there's an insider involved, he or she could get to those records."

The Deputy Director pursed her lips, then took a deep breath. "I'll talk to the Director. We should be able to get you some sort of visiting law enforcement credential. In the meantime, with what I've told you, you might be able to make some headway through public sources."

"Don't count on it. But I'll give it a try." A pragmatic question occurred to him, a little late. He was on unpaid leave. Did his new value to the Department change that status?

He almost asked. But he did not want to discuss his humiliation, and quite likely have it reinforced. And he would do this job, regardless.

Did he have to do it entirely alone?

"If you can manage it, I'd like to have Hannah's assistance. You can trust her discretion."

The woman frowned. "I doubt I can swing it, at least not yet. But I'll work on it—if you're on board."

"At least send me the file on the boy. By secure transmission."

"I will. And Arthur—thank you."

"I hope I can do something worth the thanks."

"Stay in touch, Arthur. I have a very bad feeling about this."

That made two of them.

***

Tertius lay in bed, watching the sunlight creep across his bedroom, and reviewed his schedule.

He anticipated with relish his leisurely exploitation of the opportunities his new guest presented. He would play her like an instrument, fine-tuning her moods, her moments of hope, the waning and waxing of her fears, her level of pain; and of course, he would record each variation.

His favorite session so far had been their conversation about the boy. He had led her, deftly, from apprehension at her circumstances into fond recollection of his childhood; then back to remembrance of his death and the return of grief, momentarily overwhelming her concern for herself.

Tertius would decide in due course how fully to experience the recordings. The researchers who developed the process had included ways to modulate the playback, the better to monitor and assess their progress. The general public, of course, assumed that the only alternative was to experience at full blast (so to speak)—the way prisoners were made to do. Tertius, with access to the full operator suite of controls, could choose not only the intensity but to some extent the emotion he would share. And he would dabble in the pain, for its own sake and for the pleasure of cutting it short.

A pity he had only the one recording of the boy. He would not be able to compare the different stages of these related subjects—except, of course, the last.

But there were plenty of other relatives available for the taking.

In the meantime, the woman could tell him more about the boy.

He was interested in the boy.

***

Arthur studied the images and analyses of the ruined fountain. It had not been destroyed as thoroughly as he had imagined. Almost half of the original structure still stood, more or less, with pieces missing but the shape still recognizable.

Had the design of the sculpture, its hollow and solid portions, dictated where the bomb could be concealed? Was there some other explanation for the amount of destruction? Did it, perhaps, suggest that whoever had planted the explosives was *not* a demolitions expert?

The person most likely to have the answers to such questions was unfortunately Hal himself. But Hal would have every reason to latch onto the idea of an inexpert bomber. Perhaps Arthur could, with more study, understand the structural aspects well enough to ask detailed questions, rather than telegraphing a possible conclusion.

And even if he were forced to state plainly what he needed to learn, he could always factor in the possibly unreliable nature of Hal's answers. Arthur would be no worse off with any pittance of information.

* * *

Tertius sampled one and then another of his recordings of the woman, the better to decide what additional experiences to create and record before the final scene. Naturally he varied the amplitude depending on the woman's reactions. Her memories of playing with her baby, nursing him, rocking him to sleep, he did not bother to experience at full volume; other segments, such as her response to his detailed descriptions of the injuries her son had suffered, he allowed full impact.

The additional details about the boy had been gratifying, given his still-unexplained interest in that youngster. But now, he found himself wondering about the woman herself.

How had she come to bear the boy in the first place? What had become of his father?

Unless he had suffered some generalized and coincidental shift in mental functioning, this too must have something to do with the recordings. The effects he had kept secret from his research team, the effects he had been so proud of detecting, must stretch considerably further than he had imagined, creating curiosity about the subject recorded. Only his new and prolonged exposure to the technology had enabled him to reach these new frontiers. Or possibly it took someone with Tertius Shaw's probing intellect to reach those hidden layers. In any event, his current project had borne unintended yet valuable scientific fruit.

He would explore this effect with his usual methodical attention to detail. He would note, immediately, all his thoughts about the woman, and attempt to assess the likelihood that those thoughts originated in the recording rather than in his first-hand encounters with her. With each new encounter and each playback of the same, he would enter comparable data.

How delightful to serve the cause of science and his own proclivities with the same course of conduct!

Interlude

THE LAWYER CHECKED his calendar and saw that the response to his complaint in the substituted recording case—what he liked to call, in Sir Arthur Conan Doyle fashion, The Case of the Plaintive Playback, or the Jilt's Revenge—was overdue. He opened the file to confirm the date. The rejected lover had not, it seemed, hired counsel, or at least not counsel that filed things on time.

He glanced over the notes of his conversation with the federal prosecutor. The prosecutor was willing, if not especially eager, to pursue the matter if the complaining witness would set up a meeting. Had she done so? He sent both the prosecutor and the client a message, inquiring.

Come to think of it, he had heard nothing from his client in weeks. When she first retained him, she had been persistent to the point of annoyance, demanding not just updates but immediate action on a thoroughly unrealistic timetable. But her messages and calls had tapered off and then ceased.

Had she lost interest? Perhaps—but until she got in touch and told him to abandon the case, he was duty bound to pursue it. And there was most of the initial retainer yet to be consumed.

He began putting together a motion for a default judgment. His client would get her victory, and the prankster his comeuppance, whether the injured party still gave a damn or not.

Chapter 20

Wynne's doctor had finally allowed her to return to the farmers' market, just before it closed until the spring. Her hand, while not complete, was no longer dangerously vulnerable to bumps and jostles. She had not been outdoors in a place like this—a place so full of people—since the accident. Sara carried the bags and cheerfully encouraged Wynne to load her down with more and more: apples and spinach and zucchini, brussels sprouts and carrots, onions and cheese. Wynne picked up a bouquet of chrysanthemum and New England asters just before they left.

Back at the house, Wynne found a vase; Sara plopped the bags on the kitchen counter, then glanced at Wynne with mischief in her eyes. Wynne suppressed a groan, knowing what must be coming.

"Now that you're doing so well, are you going to call—*him*?"

Wynne threw a scrubber at Sara. "Make yourself useful, and don't try to make trouble."

Sara caught the scrubber and looked over the produce. "Carrots or zucchini?"

"Carrots. No, I'm not going to call him. Ever."

"You should have seen yourself after you'd spent time with him. You were so lively, so—energized! You shouldn't give that up."

Wynne kept her face turned away from her sister's keen gaze, ferrying items from counter to refrigerator with her one hand. "I can find other ways to be lively. Ways that don't risk my marriage, or lead anyone on."

Sara made a short "hmph" noise that probably accompanied a shrug. "Lover Boy can take care of himself. And right now, Hal isn't going to be looking for trouble."

Wynne closed the refrigerator door, a little harder than necessary, and turned toward her sister. "Right now, Hal is being sweeter and more considerate than he ever was before, even when we were courting! And right now, everything that's happened has made it easy to put an end to what I shouldn't have started. All right?"

Sara brushed dirt off her hands and came over to give Wynne a hug. "I'm sorry I teased you. I just—it was nice seeing you have fun again. You hadn't been, very often, from what I could see."

Wynne looked out the kitchen window at the pinwheel on the bird feeder spinning in the breeze, then drifted over to the vase of flowers and leaned to smell their earthy scent. "There's fun, or pleasure, or joy, easy enough to come by. I just have to notice. I didn't get the easiest reminder of that—but I have been reminded."

She retrieved the scrubber and handed Sara a peeler. "Let's get ready for lunch."

* * *

Hal watched Wynne trotting down the street to the subway with almost the old bounce in her step. She had been working to overcome an irrational fear of the subway, the innocuous and convenient courier that had carried her, on that one day, to such terrible trauma. Hal hoped he had managed to hide from Wynne that he shared that fear. Now, without her there to witness his pretense at indifference, he could not quite suppress the memories: the subway exit, the mayhem he had witnessed, his fear for Wynne.... Her pain, her terror....

He shook himself, almost like Bitsy coming in out of the rain, to cast off the clinging recollections. He would think about Wynne and what she might be doing. Had she managed to produce a salable dream? He would look at her website to check for details concerning any new release.

Calling it up, he admired the photo on the home screen: Wynne in a subtly sensual pose, her outfit alluring though not revealing. The site listed recordings in several categories. He had too little information to guess where the latest might be advertised. Some impulse led him to begin with the selections for adults only.

He smiled at the tone of some of the descriptions. Wynne had complained before about the site team's tendency to sound like hawkers at a strip joint. She was almost, but not quite, dissatisfied enough to take on the extra work of designing and maintaining her own site.

The most recent listing caught his eye. It had become available only a couple of weeks after the explosion. She must have dropped it off at her agent's that very morning, before hurrying off to meet him for lunch.... The guilt and sorrow smote him once again, and he moved to leave the page. But then he did a double-take.

"*Forbidden Journey, or the Pain of Passion*: an illicit encounter brings its own sensual punishment."

What would an "illicit encounter" be, in a dream of Wynne's? Did the phrase mean infidelity? He could not, offhand, remember any of Wynne's published dreams involving such a plot.

He should not be surprised. Probably most married women fantasized about other men from time to time. He had certainly had the matching fantasy himself. But he had never done anything to draw Wynne's attention to those fantasies. And here was Wynne, showing the world—and her husband, should he bother to notice—that she had dreamed along those lines.

Hal had never spent much time looking for hidden meanings in Wynne's words or actions. But now, he found himself wondering. Was this dream a hint of any kind? A confession? Even a way of taunting a husband oblivious to the secrets in his woman's life?

A thought long suppressed fought its way to the surface. Was she, instead, taking advantage of her gift to conjure up a more skilled and satisfying lover?

There was one way to find out more. Though it would mean doing something he had never thought to do again.

The idea made him physically ill. But now that it had come to him, he could not banish it and live with his ignorance.

He took a deep breath, clenched his teeth, and added the dream to his cart.

That night, Hal waited to be sure that Wynne was fast asleep, then carefully climbed out of bed and crept from the bedroom. Earlier, while Wynne was out, he had managed to locate the helmet she had bought him years before, and on which he had sampled a few of her dreams—before she stopped suggesting that he do so. There it sat, in a drawer filled with rarely used tools and various obsolete gadgets. He reached for it and found his hand refusing to obey him. Would it be easier if he delayed actually touching the damn thing? He fetched a washcloth and used it to pull the helmet from the drawer.

Downloading the dream to the helmet would require finer movements. Hal studied the controls, took a deep breath, and punched the necessary buttons. When the display showed the download complete, he used the washcloth to pick the helmet up again and carry it to the living room, tossing it on the sofa as soon as he came within reach.

He retreated to the hallway and pulled a spare blanket from the linen closet. Carrying it back to the living room, he clutched the blanket and stood staring at the sofa. It would be worse actually wearing the helmet. How, with his stomach roiling and every muscle tight with nervous strain, could he possibly fall asleep?

He dumped the blanket next to the helmet on the sofa and headed for the liquor cabinet.

Hal awoke with the throbbing glow of orgasm just beginning to subside, and his own ecstatic groan still vibrating in his chest. A sticky wet patch on the front of his pajamas was fading from warm to room temperature.

No wonder Wynne's dreams were so popular! He pictured his wife slumbering in the next room, no doubt looking as angelic as when he had crept away, and had to laugh. The movement drew his attention to the helmet he still wore; revulsion struck him again, and he hastened to unstrap it and get it off, off, away.... Apparently, it would take more than one jolt of pleasure to reprogram the associations the helmet held.

But the dream! What had it been? The details were already fading. He reached for the vanishing fragments, trying to pull them together.

The dream had been jumbled enough, even while he dreamt it. That might have due to the alcohol or the mismatch of gender. But there had been shivery anticipation, deliciously prolonged; and then pain, controlled by someone else, pain he had somehow accepted and even craved, delivered and withheld and delivered again in measured proportions; and then, warm and soothing pressure obliterating the pain; and then, passionate, abandoned joining....

What, after all that, had he learned?

There was nothing he could say he really knew. It was all guesswork, extrapolation. But the sinking in his stomach told him what he had come to believe.

Whatever imagination Wynne had brought to her creation, no matter what she had added or taken away, he had felt—he had recognized—the presence of another human being.

The lover was real.

Hal's phone had good identification software. A caller did not have to be familiar for his name to pop up in the ID field. But a caller could have security features in place that would keep that name concealed. Whoever was calling had taken that precaution. And the number that appeared did not match any local prefix.

Hal let the machine pick up. Whether or not the caller identified himself, the voice could reveal gender, some rough idea of age, perhaps race or social status.

But he needed no such clues.

"This is Arthur Kellic. I hope Wynne is recovering well—but I'm calling to speak to Harold, on an important and confidential matter." A pause, not quite long enough to cause the machine to shut off. "I'll understand if Harold has no interest in talking to me—but it really is important. I'm not the only one who needs his help."

Another pause.

"I've programmed your number into the secure line. If you call the number your phone is showing, the call will be forwarded where it needs to go. That's if Harold decides to return my call. If—If Wynne wanted to call for any reason, she should use my public number.

"That's all."

Hal stood staring at the phone. He could hardly accuse Arthur of any lack of gumption. As bland and almost sexless as Arthur's manner could be, it took cojones to call the man you'd railroaded and subjected to torture, the man whose woman you wanted, and ask a favor.

The man who had wanted his woman. The woman who might, just might, have....

Was there yet another reason for Arthur's hesitation, his apologetic manner? Arthur might well still believe that Hal was guilty. In which case he would not consider himself to have done him any wrong—in the matter of the explosion.

But if Wynne had actually been unfaithful, who more likely than her old friend and confidant?

Arthur did have the cop thing going for him. Some women found the implicit threat posed by police somehow titillating. Was there a dream about handcuffs somewhere in that directory?...

His suspicions—of Arthur, of Wynne—might be groundless. If he failed to return Arthur's call, the man would have an excuse to call again. And next time, Wynne might be home.

Hal sat in Arthur's kitchen, bolt upright, and analyzed the surrounding odors without success. If he could tour the rest of the apartment, he would have a better chance of discerning any lingering trace of Wynne's personal scent: the smell of her skin, blended with the sachets she put in her dresser drawers and a light touch of floral perfume. But all he could smell here was kitchen, bachelor kitchen, a mixture of ground meat and pizza and unemptied trash.

Arthur had left the room to fetch whatever it was he wanted Hal to see. He returned carrying some large photographic prints and scrolls of what looked like blueprints.

Arthur laid it all on the table, placing the photos face up. The sight hit Hal like a punch to the gut: these were photos of the fountain, Hal's fountain, as it had stood in all its proud grace, and then in charred ruins after the explosion.

But not quite as ruined as he had imagined. He felt a small stirring of pride: his structure had not been entirely defeated by the unknown vandal.

Arthur pointed to the "after" photo. "As you can see, the bomb left much of the fountain standing. Our profilers haven't come up with any plausible reason why the bomber would do that on purpose. What I wondered—" I, not we, Hal noted—"is whether there was an area on or in the sculpture"— Arthur pointed now to the "before" photo—"where a bomb could have caused more complete destruction or a broader debris field. And whether that area was accessible once the sculpture was installed." Now Arthur unrolled and separated the scrolls, revealing x-rays and section drawings of the fountain. "I was hoping you could show me on these."

"This will somehow help you catch the bastard?"

"It might."

Hal studied the photograph and drawings of the dismembered sculpture. If he had been hired years ago to destroy such a structure, to obliterate it, where would he have planted what sort of charges?

"Here." He pointed to one of the taller inner columns. "There's a portal for plumbers to get access, right near one of the principal weight-bearing junctures. And you can see how many branches come off it. That's where I'd have put the charge if I wanted to bring it down completely."

Arthur stroked his chin, pondering the papers. "But would that have spread the fragments as widely as possible?"

"Ah. Sorry, I forgot that aspect." He looked again, then shook his head and swallowed, a sour taste in his mouth. "I don't have experience at that kind of destruction. I'll have to use my imagination more."

***

Arthur watched Hal bend over the papers once again and could not help but believe him. Arthur had spent too many years listening to every kind of liar, as well as the occasional innocent. Hal's response had not been clever misdirection: he had gone first, as people do, to their area of expertise, reinterpreting the problem into one he could more readily solve. And that first answer made sense, on its own terms.

Arthur's professional instincts now told him that Hal was not the bomber.

In which case, what he had done to this man he had never liked or respected—and thus, indirectly, to Wynne—did not bear thinking of. But he could not allow himself to hide from it.

Lost in self-recrimination, Arthur was startled to hear Hal grunt in satisfaction and tap emphatically on the drawing. "There! I could be wrong, but I really think that's where the charge should have been. See how the upper portions, here, would have fallen directly into the path of the blast? And the weight of the collapse, here, would have thrown these branches horizontally." Hal shook his head and actually shuddered. "It's a damn good thing this psycho wasn't an engineer." Then he did a double-take. "That's what you wanted to know, isn't it? And now you actually know something, even if it's negative."

Arthur nodded, pulling the drawing toward him and rolling it up again. "Yes. Now we know something."

Hal's mouth twitched in acknowledgment of the change in pronoun. "Well, I'm glad to've been of service. If you think of anything else I can do to help you catch this unspeakable son of a bitch, just let me know."

Then he stopped short, as if remembering something, and his face went stiff. Of course: the camaraderie of joint effort could not banish for long the man's justified sense of injury.

"I'll be going."

Arthur nodded, and silently ushered Hal toward the door. As soon as Hal's footsteps faded away down the hall, he returned to the kitchen table and sat there for a long time, his head in his hands.

* * *

Wynne pondered the potential necessity of refining her brand. She had only managed to produce two BDSM dreams since the accident, and while her agent had refrained from criticizing, she herself found them distinctly lacking in intensity. She had not yet recovered to the point where she could dream of pain, or more than a little pain, without the dream taking over and heading in the wrong direction. She had no such problem with dreams of binding: she could study up on Japanese Kinbaku techniques.

She checked the agency website for any competition in that specialty and was relieved to find none. While she was on the site, she took a moment to review her past oeuvre, snorting at some of the less subtle cover art.

She read, frowning, the description of the dream she had delivered just before the accident. What would Hal think, should he happen to come to her site for a change and see that entry?

She had to tell him herself, before he found out some other way. If she had any chance to preserve—to deserve—his trust in her, she had to come clean.

And Hal had seemed different lately, more caring, more open. She could not remember the last time he had hurt her feelings.

Which made it harder, in a way, to do what would surely hurt his, and profoundly. But she had to take the chance. It might be her last good chance to forestall marital disaster.

* * *

Wynne sat down across the table from where Hal was reading the morning news.

"Hal—honey—there's something we need to talk about."

Hal looked at Wynne, her face a little pale, her eyes wide, and knew what was coming. His stomach felt cold, and his chest tight. He swallowed and faced her, trying to keep the tension from his face.

She was waiting for something. Waiting for him to help her continue. He forced a small smile. "It's all right, sweetheart. Whatever it is, you can tell me."

She nodded, and took a deep breath.

"Hal... last year... there was—I did something—"

He would not say it for her. What if he were wrong, after all? And besides, he would not abort this act of contrition.

Wynne started to cry. "I had an affair. Oh, Hal, I'm so sorry."

Hal watched his wife crying. Was it remorse? Or fear of what he would say, or even what he might do to her?

Not the last. She trusted him, at some level, more than he trusted himself. She had no fear of physical violence. No, she was afraid he would be angry, afraid he might say something cruel, and above all afraid that she might lose him.

He waited a moment to make sure his tone would be calm and even. "Was it—" No, he would not ask leading questions, not now. "Who was it, Wynne?"

Wynne was sobbing now. It hurt too much to witness and do nothing: Hal got up, put his hands on Wynne's shoulders, guided her out of the chair, and put his arms around her. He held her as she shook against his chest, her tears soaking his shirt. Then he led her to the couch and sat down, placing her beside him. He almost pulled her onto his lap, but that far he could not go. Not until he heard the rest.

"Wynne. You have to take the next step, love. You have to tell me who it was."

At first, when she spoke, he had trouble understanding her. He was so certain he would hear Arthur's name that when she said something else, he could not absorb it. "What?"

In spite of the circumstances, a frown of indignation flitted across her face. She hated it when he failed to listen to her. "I said, I don't think you know him. He does advertising for the agency."

Hal stared at Wynne. Was she telling the truth? He could swear she was. He saw distress, shame, apprehension, suspense, but no hint of calculation nor the uneasy tension of the liar.

His own relief broke from him in a short bark of laughter. Wynne stiffened, her mouth dropping open in shock. He threw his arm around her and pulled her close. "I'm sorry, hon. It's just—" But he could hardly admit what he had guessed.

And the ultimate fact remained: she had cheated on him, and then waited months to tell him. His arm dropped to his side and he moved away. She flinched at his withdrawal, his inappropriate laughter apparently forgotten.

She would expect him to ask why she had strayed. And he needed to know; but he was not yet ready to hear it. He could not really listen while he was angry and hurt. He turned toward her, taking her hand. How much longer before he could hold both her hands again? The thought helped him speak gently.

"I'm glad you told me. I'd like us to wait a while before we talk about it any more. I need some—some processing time."

She shrank back in dismay. "But—"

He allowed himself a note of sternness. "You've told me something that's hard to hear. Something I shouldn't have to hear. I believe I'm entitled to ask you to let me handle it in my own way, at least for a while."

She was crying again, silently, nothing moving but the tears sliding down her cheeks. He could not help but feel for her. He stroked her hand, once. "I won't make you wait too long. And—you're not waiting for a decision, or any judgment. I love you. I'm not leaving. And I won't push you away." He swallowed hard. "God knows, I've done enough of that."

In her sudden slump against the couch, he saw the tension that had gripped her and how afraid she had been. She twitched her hand for him to release it, and stroked his cheek gently. "Thank you, darling. We'll talk when you're ready. I'll wait."

Hal got up from the couch and brushed her hair with his lips. Should he go into his studio and try to work, to take solace in his creations? Or head to his study and return to his investigation?

That brought Arthur to mind. Poor Arthur: no successful rival, after all, but poorer than Hal, so much further from the prize.

What had Arthur made of Hal's demeanor when they met? Well, Hal had plenty of excuse for hostility, and he had no intention of explaining. Arthur was the last person Hal would want knowing that Hal's victory was, after all, incomplete.

CHAPTER 21

IT HAD BEEN beneath him to panic. Tertius felt something resembling shame.

Over the weeks he had kept the woman, he had found himself wondering more and more about her past, and looking forward—with a nervous eagerness quite different than his usual ebullient pleasure in experiment—to learning more about her feelings. He had no mechanism for coping with internal transformation: recoiling from the experience, he had tried to push it away from him, killing the woman simply to remove her presence, with no finesse, no pacing, no artistry at all. He had almost forgotten to put a helmet on her first.

What a waste of opportunity! He would have to start over. Well, not completely over. He could collect another from the same clan. That course, at least, would allow him to use the data he had gathered, and make the comparisons he had planned. And he would plan this time—carefully, exquisitely. He would take pride in his craftsmanship. No more shame for him!

Each capture, to be sure, increased his chance of exposure. It would be prudent to wait a while. But the wasted time made it hard to be patient.

He had, of course, played back the woman's final recording. This time, the subject had appeared to recognize several individuals inhabiting the lighted area. He was almost sure that one was her son—but his own acquaintance with the boy, via the initial death recording, might be biasing his observations. Next time, he might inquire beforehand which departed family members the victim expected to encounter, and attempt to compare that prediction with the eventual result.

***

The Deputy Director's voice was pitched a little higher than usual, and she spoke at a quicker tempo. "Arthur, have you found any leads?"

"That would be overstating the case. I've eliminated one individual suspect and tentatively eliminated a class of suspects. But that leaves quite a wide field."

"Not so wide, given the circumstances we discussed."

That was a matter of definition. With all the people with various degrees of access to departmental locations and files...

"There's been another."

Shit.

"Remember I told you the last one had a daughter? She's been taken."

Arthur closed his eyes in pain. A girl, innocent, unprepared for the cruelty of the world, taken by a monster! Was there any chance that he could learn enough, soon enough, to rescue her?

He was not used to working solo. He had colleagues to consult, and his superiors at times actually helped point him in productive directions. As for Hannah, he had always valued her assistance, but not, he now realized, half as much as she deserved. If only he had it now! He would have to find a way to insist.

So far the only collaborator he had had in this nasty business was Hal. There was irony enough to choke on! But Hal might have something more to contribute, if only a separate opinion, a different viewpoint off which to bounce ideas. He could not shrink from the extreme awkwardness of asking his help again, not with so much at stake.

***

Tertius Shaw congratulated himself on the results of his foresight, which another might have mistaken for luck. He had recorded the newest one, the girl, as soon as possible, the moment he took possession of her, and played back the recording before transporting her. He chose the minimum emotional volume: there was nothing especially piquant about her initial, crude anger and apprehension. But whatever mysterious connection the playbacks might be creating, there was no point in delaying its inception.

The dividends had not been long in appearing! As he drove her home from his employee's rat-hole of a dwelling place, he had had a flash of intuition, a hunch that she would attempt escape from the moving car. She had probably gotten the idea from some second-rate film, without realizing how likely she was to be injured or worse. Which would hardly have suited his plans, even if, as was likely, he could have retrieved her at once.

Now, after an appropriate punishment—recorded, of course—for her uncooperative intentions, she was safely tucked away and available. He could follow his full program. This time, he would not let any new developments deter him. He was still tweaking the sequence of events: he had not, for example, decided whether to reveal to the girl the body of her mother, which he had kept at a convenient temperature for temporizing.

He clapped his hand to his forehead. Why had he not thought of recording himself as well? He must do so henceforth. He would be able to relive his own experience, and compare his unaided, contemporary perception of the subject's emotions to what the recording of the subject later revealed.

A surge of pleasure blossomed in his groin and radiated outward to his very fingertips. How invigorating was the acquisition of knowledge!

*   *   *

"I'm still not sure what you want from me."

Arthur suppressed the impulse to say that made two of them. Not that he wanted to give Hal a more responsive answer. He had reluctantly told Hal about the death recording's existence and disappearance, but he'd be damned if he'd spell out that someone in the department might be involved. "There are—logistical reasons I can't work from the office or use office personnel. I need someone to talk at, to bounce ideas off of. And you already know a bit about the case."

Hal laughed harshly. "You could say that! I suppose you mean our first meeting, talking about the fountain and the explosion. But I know a hell of a lot more than that. I know, too damn well, what the victims suffered. I know about Wynne, lying there in agony, hearing the screams, feeling the flames come closer, smelling the smoke.... *What* did you say?"

Too late, Arthur realized that he had not only been nodding as Hal spoke but had actually muttered the last few words along with him, anticipating them almost flawlessly. He grasped for some explanation that would not be entirely false. "I read the reports, of course. I know what she went through."

Hal's stare made Arthur feel as transparent and vulnerable as glass. "You read the reports, sure. But that's not what just happened—you remembering some report written in bureaucratic jargon. Something else is going on."

Even while writhing inside, Arthur could not help but note that Hal had the makings of a detective. If their collaboration survived, it might be more comprehensively useful than Arthur had anticipated.

Hal's mouth dropped open. Then his teeth slammed shut, and his glare almost pinned Arthur to his chair. "You sick, creepy—you got hold of Wynne's recording. You played it.

That's how you know." Hal clenched and raised his fist. "I ought to beat you into jelly, you freaking stalker!"

Arthur could only return Hal's stare, and shrug helplessly. "I didn't mean any—"

"You didn't mean to invade her privacy? You didn't mean to strip her barer than naked? You didn't mean to wallow in emotions no one should ever share?"

Arthur sat, slowly turning red, and waited to see what Hal would do.

***

Hal dimly realized that the muscles of his hands were cramping, so tight had he clenched them into fists. He ignored the stabbing pains. What could he do? How could he avenge this outrageous intrusion? This man, this rival, had dared to....

"Why would you do something like that? If you wanted to crawl around in her mind, you could have bought a dream like anyone else! Or did you want a piece of her that none of the others could have?"

"No!" Arthur jumped to his feet, righteous indignation taking the place of shame. "I wanted to help! I had to know—" He stopped abruptly and fell back into his chair. "I thought I could learn something. Something that I had to know before I could help her."

Hal looked at Arthur, who now seemed lost in some harrowing thought or memory. Arthur must have known, or had some idea, how terrible an ordeal that playback would be. Hal had had no choice but to endure it, however he tried to find some redeeming value in what was done to him. But Arthur had had every choice. He had risked his career, even his freedom, to take upon himself that unendurable pain. And of course, he had done it for Wynne. No thrill of the chase, no professional obsession, sufficiently explained it.

Hal's hands relaxed and dropped to his sides. He shook his head, slowly, still staring at Arthur. "Damn. You poor damn bastard."

Chapter 22

Wynne was healing. Her hand was almost a hand again. Her dreams almost never betrayed her now. She was almost herself, almost whole.

She would celebrate with a burst of productivity—gratify her customers as never before. What could she give them? What could she add to their experience?

It was remarkable how one could overlook the obvious until one tripped on it. All it took was passing a bakery and letting it lure her in. The warm, moist richness of the chocolate croissant.... All this time, she had never focused sufficiently on taste! Taste and smell, really—she remembered that wonderful Bakery Window room at the spa—but taste especially.

She could, to some extent, turn up the volume on particular aspects of the dream experience. She wouldn't know until she tried how much she could convey particular tastes, but it was worth experimenting. All she had to do was accumulate some vivid experiences: her excellent memory would store the sensations for later use. And the research would be a treat! She giggled. Literally!

But it would not be much fun, after all, to go eating and drinking alone. This was a project to share with friends. How long had it been since she'd had a girls' night out, or for that matter, a girls' weekend getaway? Too long, that was certain, and for no good reason. Had she somehow feared that Hal would resent her girl time? How silly! Or so it seemed now, with Hal being so sweet.

She got out her phone and started calling.

Fate smiled upon her plan. The farmers' market was holding an apple tasting. The four of them descended on the tables. Her friends bounced around erratically, but Wynne would be systematic. She made her inquiries and started with the tart, her mouth wide awake, the flavor zinging and twanging. The sweeter, mealier fruit was sleepy by comparison, but lingered seductively on the tongue.

Another booth offered milk, creamy milk, silky with fat, coating her palate. From there, it was a short step to cheeses: fresh goat cheese, crumbly in texture, unchallenging; Swiss, the shape of the wedge echoing the flavor; and finally, her friends egging her on, the drippy, smelly assault of Limberger.

From cheese to bread, of course. Soft white rolls, softer than dough; hunks of challah, torn from a braided loaf and still hot; then the sour tang of good, stout rye, and its assertive cousin, pumpernickel.

Her friends were groaning and staggering, beginning to rebel. It was time to regroup. She led them toward the path that wound through the market and on toward the river, snuffing up the clean fresh air, stretching her legs with every stride.

And if she happened to know a very special pastry shop along the path, one mile along....

They agreed, easily, to skip dinner, ending the day instead at a bar they had frequented more often in their college days. It, like the women, had matured in the interim: there were flowers and little candle-holders on the tables, now, and generations-old movie posters on the walls. And if dessert wines had been available back then, none of them had known or cared.

Sipping her tawny port, watching the candle flicker in its little round bowl, Wynne sat back in luxurious exhaustion and listened to the friendly banter around her. Oh, she had missed this! She would like to bring this home with her, some evening—to host these companions at her own hearth, relaxing on her own sofa and chairs.

Could Hal, the reformed Hal, be an easy, friendly host to that many people? She was too pleasantly tired to think about it much. But perhaps.

***

Hal uncovered the clay model of the sculpture and stood back to view it afresh. He usually began his sessions in this way: it let him brush away any inaccurate memories or assumptions about how the piece had progressed, and bring to the work any ideas that had occurred to him since he had last seen it.

Today, after that astounding encounter with Arthur, ideas were buzzing around him like over-caffeinated hornets, darting toward him and zooming past before he could do more than glimpse them.

He had thought of the figures of Wynne as largely supplemental, a sort of adornment for the essential element of the fountain reborn. Now that conception seemed almost barren. This work should celebrate Wynne and her survival, and the refusal of her inner light to be extinguished or to dim.

But Wynne loved the sculpture as he had conceived it. She took delight in the idea of the multiple Wynne-derived figures in flight. How could he maintain that concept, and simultaneously make her more central?

His mind drifted to the picture on the home page of Wynne's website, a misty pool complete with water lilies. He could add the lilies around the main structure. And other flowers, flowering vines, climbing the arches and limbs, strengthening them. It would be tricky—such a design could so easily be busy or banal. But he could make it work.

And at the top, he might add one more Wynne, somehow. Or—not Wynne, but her hand, her hand that the bomber had not, after all, been able to steal and destroy. Not a literal hand, no, but something that hinted at a hand, graceful, reaching, opening as if tossing blessings up and outward....

He thought again of Arthur: dogged, devoted, excluded. Was there some place for Arthur in this creation? What symbol could he use, and what would he want it to convey?

* * *

The fans had loved Wynne's thank-you dream. But she might be pushing the limits if she produced a dream with a more ambitious agenda.

Wynne opened the file with her current contract and tried to make her way through it. She had no great head for legalese, but she needed to know what limitations she had accepted as far as dream content. In particular, could she offer a dream that had any promotional elements?

Well, she couldn't promote her own products in any explicit way—no previews of coming attractions, and no insidious dreams about buyers playing the dream and ending up richer, thinner, or the like. Nor could she include a product's name (even if the information was unlikely to reach the customers) in any but the most innocuous, incidental way.

She couldn't tell, for sure, whether what she planned would be acceptable. But she might as well give it a try.

The fountain crumbled, and flames—far less frightening than the actual flames, with a gentler heat, and a crumbly, cement-dust odor in place of the cordite and charred flesh—

She awoke, annoyed with herself. She must not allow comparisons to distract her and sully the narrative. She forced herself to banish negative emotion, to grow calm, to relax and slip back into sleep....

The fountain crumbled, and soft, shimmery flames, in pale yellow and gold, arose to shroud it. An odor as of funeral flowers filled the air. A sad, sweet melody, a single flute, played softly in the distance.

Then the shimmer of the flames became a translucent shimmering of the air. The flute became a trumpet, the sound clearer, still soft but somehow triumphant. The haze began to lift, revealing a glorious new sculpture, the sculpture even now taking shape in Hal's studio. Where the multiple figures of Wynne would float and fly, she saw only tantalizing glimpses, still shrouded in the haze, with here and there a bit of the graceful human shape just barely visible.

And now came people, many people, men, women, children, approaching the sculpture, and the music swelled louder, coming to a blissful resolution and then fading away, as the dream faded through various pastel shades into nothingness.

Wynne's doctor looked in her eyes, his own eyes twinkling. "It's time, my dear! Are you ready?"

Yes, she was ready. She had made a point of rehearsing the moment in a dream three times this week: the unwrapping of the bandages, her restoration to wholeness. Though the dream's musical accompaniment would be lacking.

Of course, she might not have got the details right.

"What will it look like?"

"Just like the old one, naturally! There won't be any scars, even the faint ones you never really noticed. And the skin will look rather like what you see after a sunburn has peeled away—if you've ever seen that."

She had. Her family fretted less than most about exposure to the elements. She should do a dream about the seashore, the luxuriously warm sun, the too-hot sand, the waves....

Back to the moment at hand! She did an internal double-take, almost giggling at the involuntary pun.

"What about using it? What shape will the muscles be in?"

"Well, they're likely to be a bit weak. We've been stimulating them during your visits, of course, and the bandage has been programmed to do a bit more while you were sleeping—"

So that explained how many of her spontaneous dreams had featured piano playing, or sign language, or other intensive hand movements! She had thought it was simply an emotional preoccupation with what she had lost. She chuckled, to her doctor's apparent puzzlement. So much for psychology!

Wynne took a deep breath and sat up straight. "Let's do it."

Wynne tiptoed up to the doorway of the living room. How lucky that Hal was not in the midst of a creative trance, and she was free to interrupt him.

"Darling—would you come here, please?" She waited for him to look up, then beckoned with her unwrapped, revealed, pretty left hand.

It took him a moment, as she had known it would. She laughed aloud as his face progressed from mild curiosity, through shock, to amazement, and finally to joy.

She had yearned for more than careful embraces, during these weeks—craved more—but she had understood. He did not want to hurt her. He knew just how much she had been hurt already. Her poor, poor, Hal—how she hated that he had had to endure it as well.

But now she felt as randy as a pirate, wild with pent-up lust. She ripped off her clothes, then his, and threw them aside. She did not mind a bit that it amused him. She tugged him to the bed, thrust him back toward it, and threw herself on him, kissing all over his wide, grinning mouth.

They had not been immediately compatible, years ago, when they first reached the point of making love. His natural tempo was quicker than hers, and he seemed unable to sense when she needed him to continue what he was doing and when she would welcome variation. It never worked to say anything: discussion of anything sexual, let alone a request, had inevitably killed the mood. She had learned to focus on what she loved about his lovemaking, the urgency of it, his sheer, elemental physicality.

But now, without losing that intensity, he had become newly responsive. She could barely form a wish before he would satisfy it. Satisfy her.

No dream, consciously directed or rising from unconscious depths, had ever surpassed it.

She was hoarse from shouting by sunrise. They slept until noon.

Chapter 23

T ERTIUS S HAW SMOOTHED the large sheets of the morning paper—he preferred his news presented in tangible, old-fashioned newsprint, however expensive such anachronisms had become—and pursed his lips thoughtfully. The disappearance of not one, but two relatives of "Death Boy" (as the media had dubbed the subject of that first recording) had received rather less attention that he expected. Someone must be working very hard to keep the lid on, to avoid panicking the populace. Tertius might want to stir the pot again, to remind them all that he was still among them.

Of course, the police had made no appreciable progress. His deputy had naturally asked him to approve the clandestine assignment of Arthur Kellic as investigator. Among Tertius' subordinates, she at least was not entirely clueless: she realized that the various aspects of this project might be connected, and that their author might be "connected" in a different sense. Choosing a purportedly banished and disgraced policeman as their bloodhound showed some minimal good sense.

Though it would be a shame to allow the man to work without throwing a few complications in his path. It would be easy to arrange.

But now, back to the present. Back to work! His young lady guest had a wide range of experiences to pass through before he was through with her.

* * *

Arthur had mixed feeling about the Deputy Director's call. He would have liked to have more progress to report. But he could use the contact with his old life, even someone with whom he had seldom crossed paths in a typical day. Now that he had finally managed to add Hannah to his team, their calls were a good deal better than nothing, but he could not compromise her by any unnecessary communications.

"Heads up, Arthur." The Deputy Director looked and sounded grim. "The Director brought in a new investigator on the bombing. She might—well, if you don't come back, she might just take over your job. But for now, her brief is the bombing."

The bad news seemed rather speculative and indefinite, compared to the Deputy Director's tone. "I guess I'll have to wait and see whether they bring me in from the cold before it's too late. If I manage to get anywhere on this investigation—"

"You aren't getting it."

Arthur breathed slowly through his nose to keep his patience. "Please explain, then."

A harsh laugh, and then: "Arthur, you're such an innocent. Hasn't it occurred to you who this investigator will start with? Don't you realize who the obvious suspect is, at this point?"

Ridiculous! "If I *knew* the obvious suspect, don't you think I'd have—" Arthur stopped short.

Of course. He should have seen it.

"She'll think it was me."

The Deputy Director rolled her eyes. "The penny drops! Yes, she'll think it was you. And she'll have plenty of company." She hesitated, then plowed mercilessly on. "Spurned would-be lover gets revenge on the woman and pins it on his rival. Outwardly upright model citizen turns out to be all twisty inside. Which confirms many people's jaundiced view of humanity."

Arthur nodded, seeing the narrative unfold. "I could have been having someone follow her, on some excuse or other. That way I'd know she visited the fountain sometimes, and could find out when she was headed there. And if I was seen doing anything suspicious near the site, in person or on tape, I could explain it away or destroy the evidence."

"But then you went too far, blew it, by stealing the recording so you could gloat."

Arthur stared at the screen. "That is a truly sickening picture." Was it really a convincing one?

There was no evidence to support it. But then, what hard, direct evidence had been needed to convict Harold Wakeman? If Arthur was caught in the same trap into which he had thrown Hal, he could only acknowledge the karmic justice involved.

But if he, in his turn, were to be condemned . . . . The memory of Wynne's agony tried to resurface, and he fought to suppress it. He could not afford to lose himself in panic. He would need what wits he had, to save himself and to continue the search for the true murderer.

Somehow, the Deputy Director had not jumped to the supposedly obvious conclusion. Arthur turned back toward her; she was peering at him, perhaps trying to decipher his reactions. "You don't believe it. Why don't you?"

A snort. "I hired you, remember? I trust my judgment. And I've kept track of you over the years, to confirm that judgment."

An exchange in a previous call came back in a flash. "That's what you meant when you said people thought you were crazy to trust me. My God! How did you talk the Director into putting me back on the case?"

She shrugged. "If you can figure out why the Director does anything, let alone predict what he'll do next, you should definitely have my job. At the time, I assumed he knew better than to suspect you. But now he brings in this new bloodhound, and he's got to know what she'll do."

"Unless he told her about what I'm actually doing."

"Not unless she's throwing up one hell of a smoke screen. You can keep up your hopes if you want to, Arthur. But watch your ass."

* * *

Tertius closed the report from the new investigator and chuckled. By now, Kellic must know of the woman's appointment; and soon enough, he would realize his status as target. If only there was some way to observe—or better yet, to record—his shock and dismay!

If the man could continue his own investigation under such circumstances, he was made of rare mettle indeed. And if not, that would be, all things considered, satisfactory.

* * *

That old Chinese curse could be updated: "May you find yourself in interesting workplace situations."

The new hire must regard Hannah as a leftover assistant trying to justify her continued existence, tainted by association with her disgraced and suspended former boss. Hannah's new job title could just as well be "repository of annoying scut work." All the while, she had to continue assisting Arthur without anyone noticing. She could only hope that no one besides Arthur knew how good she was at both hacking computer systems and defending against the same. (The Director might know—and then again, he might not. Omniscient as he sometimes seemed, he had come to the Department years after Hannah's arrival, and by then Hannah had had time to create the appropriate camouflage and shields.)

Her assignment did not include trying to deflect or sabotage the pursuit of Arthur as a bombing suspect. But if the opportunity arose, she would take care not to waste it.

In order to spot the opportunity should it appear, she would need to keep abreast of the investigation—and would very much need to avoid being caught doing so. Her work station now included an unobtrusive modification that could detect the vibrations of footprints or the increased temperature that meant an approaching or hovering human being. In either case, it would substitute a random innocuous document for whatever the screen had previously shown.

And there went her private copy of Arthur's perp file, replaced (Hannah suppressed a grimace) with the week's morale-boosting departmental memo, in need of proofreading. Hannah looked up to find Arthur's new nemesis herself, flash drive in hand. "I need this analyzed by lunchtime."

Hannah smiled as blandly as she knew how, took the flash drive, and put it close to her keyboard, as if to show she would give it the most urgent priority.

The woman lingered. "Excuse me, Ms. Lowe—but I'm trying to figure out just why you're still here."

The attack direct! "Excuse me?"

"You worked for Mr. Kellec. Your loyalties, if any, would most likely be to him. Your file doesn't indicate that you possess any irreplaceable skills."

Well, that was a relief. Though the Director might have knowledge he did not care to include in generally available files.

Hannah turned her chair to face her inquisitor head-on. "You must know it's not so easy to boot out longterm employees with unblemished records. Though there's a more intriguing possibility as well."

The investigator lifted an eyebrow and waited for her to continue.

"The Director's a particularly good judge of character. I'm betting he knows—" Hannah suppressed the colorful adverb that came to mind. "He must know quite well that Arthur would never, under any circumstances, kill or hurt innocent people to pursue a private vendetta. Or, for that matter, hide behind a bomb as a weapon." A lance, borne proudly on horseback, would be more like it. "So while the politics of the thing required him to give you a shot at Arthur, he may be keeping me around in case you'll eventually lend an ear to what I might say about my boss."

"Your former boss."

"My suspended and currently inactive boss. My once and future boss, I hope."

The woman glowered at her a moment longer, then tossed her head. "Get that analysis done. I'll be waiting."

Chapter 24

Hal looked at the diagrams Arthur had drawn up, impressed in spite of himself. Arthur had made separate charts of all the personnel and outsiders (contractors, political sponsors, and the like) who might have access, first, to the death recording, and second, to the cell where the kidnapping suspect had died. Then he had cross-referenced them and made a third chart of those who appeared on both.

"It's too bad," he said to Arthur, "that we can't come up with some neat list of everyone who could have gotten to the fountain unobserved."

"Indeed. We could find out who had reason to know the police patrol schedule in the area, but anyone could have scouted for a while and figured that out. Still, you're forgetting something. Or don't you know about the security cameras?"

Of course. Any public spot, these days, was likely to have at least one electronic eye aimed its way at all times. "Do you have some blurry infrared image of someone skulking about?"

"No, we don't—because the cameras were on the blink and weren't due for service until two days after the blast."

Hal whistled. "Ain't that a coincidence? C'mon, let's see the next chart."

Arthur grinned, which Hal could not remember ever seeing before, and produced it. "This is anyone who might have an excuse to touch the cameras—of course, we can't include members of the general public who might have got to them from areas they don't cover—but also, anyone who could have set or tinkered with the repair schedule."

"Not including hackers for hire."

Arthur shrugged. "I know. We do what we can." He called up yet another document. "Anyway, *this* has everyone who appears on more than one of the other lists."

"No one's on all of them?"

Arthur grimaced. "That'd be too easy. Shall we take a break? I made coffee."

"I could use some. Wynne had another nightmare last night. She'd hoped—we'd both hoped—that they were over with. That she'd regained full control."

Arthur bit his lip. "I'm sorry to hear that."

Hal stood up and stretched his aching back. "It's tough from all sorts of angles. The dreams themselves—well, you and I both know what they're about, and how bad they are."

Arthur flinched, his face trying somehow to show both pain for Wynne and embarrassment for himself.

"And it's harder for Wynne because she's had so few bad dreams of any kind until all this happened. And she wonders whether she's been damaged in this special part of herself, in some permanent way... So all in all, we were up for a while afterward."

Arthur hesitated, then spoke with an obviously forced calm. "I hope you were able to help her." Then, with a burst of sincerity: "I wish to God I could."

That wouldn't be all Arthur wished. Hal remembered, with a vividness that made his skin tingle, the feel of Wynne pressed up against him under the covers, trembling at first, her tears soaking his T-shirt, and then her slow relaxation. She had fallen asleep, for once, there in his arms, and he had waited some time before carefully extricating himself and moving over in the bed.

He could give Arthur nothing of that, even if it had been his to give, and he had not the slightest urge toward any such quixotic generosity.

He found himself blurting out, "For a while, I thought you and Wynne were having an affair."

Arthur's chair scraped harshly against the floor as he thrust backward from the table, his face white, his eyes wide with shock.

What ailed the man? Was he afraid of some attack? But Hal had already implied that he knew better than to suspect him any longer. And Arthur's reaction was not defensive: "flabbergasted" would describe it better.

"Arthur, what's going on?"

"Hal." Arthur spoke slowly, in hushed tones, almost whispering. "What made you think that Wynne was having an affair? With anyone?"

Hal tried to remember. "Well… I was looking at her website. And one of the dreams said something that sort of hinted at it."

"Are Wynne's dreams always autobiographical?"

Hal laughed a little. "Hardly. She's never visited another planet, last I heard. Or been a fairy, living in a tulip. Or—"

"So why did you think this dream was likely to be true? Or based on truth?"

Hal sat back down heavily in his chair. "I don't know. I must have picked up some sort of clue without realizing it. It must have been intuition."

Arthur's mouth twisted in a quick, humorless smile. "I think you picked something up. But not where you'd expect." He hesitated, then went on. "And so did I."

"You what??"

Arthur brought his chair forward again and leaned his elbows on the table, looking steadily at Hal. "I had a notion that seemed to come out of nowhere. I was thinking about Wynne, and wondering—wondering if you and she were happy. And then I was asking myself how you could be happy, if she'd cheated. And I had absolutely no reason to think that that had happened."

Hal got up again and started pacing back and forth across the room. Hal could explain his own suspicions easily enough. He'd had plenty of chances to notice that something was wrong. Wynne's behavior must have offered some clues. He simply hadn't realized what he knew. He had probably suppressed the knowledge, rather than confronting it.

But even if all that were true, what about Arthur? What clues could he have seen? Unless Wynne were deceiving him again, seeing Arthur far more often than Hal knew, or confiding her secrets to him....

But no. He might have been blind to her affair, but he knew Wynne better than that. She was hiding nothing now. The relief she felt at giving up her secrets was clear beyond cavil.

The only other possibility had implications he could barely grasp.

"Arthur, you think it's the recording. That it somehow told you, told us both, something beyond what Wynne was sensing and feeling at the time. Something deeper, below consciousness—far beneath."

Arthur nodded, wordless, his face still pale.

"Okay. Okay. Let me think." Hal tried to find some focus in his whirling thoughts. "Obviously, this is big and hairy, and way beyond us. I can't begin to figure out all the implications. Christ—all those criminals! What have they picked up about their victims? What secrets have they learned? God, what happens when they get out?"

Arthur closed his eyes. "I've got to report this." He opened them again and sagged back in his chair. "But right now, let's get back to our problem. What does this tell us about the bomb, or about the kidnapping?"

Hal's lack of sleep bore him down, stupefying him. "I can't think. Wait a minute—didn't you say something about coffee?"

"Oh. I did. I'll get it. We sure as hell could use it."

Two cups apiece revived them both, but shed no further light. No longer sluggish, Hal's thoughts now raced in circles, getting nowhere.

The only recording that might be pertinent to their investigation was the death recording. But how could that recording shed any light? Unless the boy knew something, something that might betray the perpetrator, and the perp knew it, *and* knew about the hidden reach of the recordings....

Hal offered up this hypothesis without believing it. Arthur cocked his head. "It doesn't make much sense. Doesn't feel right." He sighed. "But I've got nothing better. Which means we've got squat."

Hal got up once again and took his coffee mug to the sink. "I think I'll head on home. We both need time to process this. Maybe we'll understand it more, get some ideas, after we've let it all sink in."

And he needed, as never before, to go home to his wife and hold her warm against him, feel the comfort of her.

Poor Arthur, with no such prospect. He avoided eye contact with his host as he prepared to depart. Arthur would find pity offensive, and Hal could not help but feel it.

Hal jerked upright, gasping, his arms flailing, his right hand knocking the tissue box off the nightstand.

Another goddamn nightmare. Or rather, the same goddamn nightmare, for maybe the hundredth time. Had he made enough noise to wake Wynne?

He turned toward her side of the bed. At least this time he had not disturbed her: she lay sleeping peacefully, sprawled on her back, taking up fully half the mattress as usual.

If he and Arthur could track down the bomber, if this mind-blowing discovery actually proved useful.... Maybe he could get the memory removed, carved or burned away like a cancer, and his nights would be his own again.

But—if they were right about the recordings, then the memories that tortured him had brought with them a new insight into Wynne's nature and needs. Would he lose that as well?

Would it be worth it?

After all, Wynne had loved him before. She had married him, and stayed with him, even if he had sometimes been clueless.

Thoughtless.

And yes, she had stayed, but not without straying.

Would it happen again, some day, if he gave up this chance to know her better—gave it up for a few nights' sleep?

For a mess of pottage.

*   *   *

Arthur stood at the kitchen counter and waited for his tea to steep. Coffee might stimulate, but perhaps tea would help him ponder things more calmly and systematically.

When the liquid had darkened to a rich red-brown, he removed the tea bag, putting it aside for a possible second use, and stirred in a single drop of honey before settling down at the table. He breathed in the steam before taking a first leisurely sip.

He had barely swallowed it when the door buzzer sounded. Arthur looked through the peephole, as always. Yes, it was Hal. The man was early—less than courteous, but suggesting that Hal was just as consumed with the quest as Arthur himself. He blew on his tea and took another swallow before opening the door. "Come on in. Care for a cup of tea?"

Hal's eyebrow twitched upward, but he nodded more or less graciously. "Thanks."

Once they had resumed their now customary seats in the living room, Hal leaned forward and said, "What's bothering me about this idea is why no one else knows about it. Why wouldn't the team that developed the helmets understand them better than a couple of newcomers like us?"

Arthur put his mug down on the end table and stroked his chin. "I can think of reasons. Remember what they were trying to do: reproduce an experience in real time. That's what they'd be looking for and trying to measure. The active test subject skis down the mountain, and the passive test subject does or doesn't report the details of the course or the types of trees along the way. The researchers aren't going to be asking whether the active subject resented his stepfather! And besides—it might take some time for the subject to become even subliminally aware of the background material. By then, it might have been days or weeks since the experiment, and the odds are he'd just shrug it off as random thoughts, or something from a dream."

Hal nodded and gulped down some tea. "I guess that's plausible enough." He paused as if struck by some idea. "But maybe someone, at least *some*one on the team did know something. They could have kept it a secret for some reason—to use later, for their own purposes."

Arthur tilted his head, dubious. "I suppose, though we've got no basis for assuming so." He stopped, disciplining himself to consider the notion. There was no point taking on a collaborator if he refused to examine the collaborator's ideas.

And in fact, an idea soon occurred to him, or at least the beginning of an idea. "Would knowledge of this effect provide any sort of motive for stealing the death recording?"

"Hmmmm. Offhand, I don't see how. The dead boy's emotional history doesn't seem obviously more interesting than the fact of his death. But maybe we should look into that initial research team, just in case. Wynne's sister worked there at the time: she could help."

Arthur suppressed a frown. Once they started investigating members of the team, Wynne's sister could become not only a source but a target. "It's a long shot. Maybe we'll look that way at some point. But it's hardly a priority."

* * *

Before the latest revelation, Hal would have distrusted the impulse to confront Wynne. As it was, he had hesitated for days. Why rock the boat? Why dredge up old grievances, when he had been trying so hard—with at least some success—to reform?

But for better or worse—an appropriate phrase—he had reason to know, now, that if he thought there was something Wynne needed, he was probably right.

So he covered the clay, washed the grit off his hands, hung up his smock, and went looking for her.

* * *

Wynne had not expected to see her husband for hours yet. She had even thought of peeking in to watch him work: she loved to see the clay dust coating his hair, the strong arms lifting the tools and turning the model, his profile tense with concentration or relaxed as he waited for the next whisper of the muse.

But there he came, bearing gifts!—at least, a small stemmed glass with a dark gold liquid sloshing slightly.

"Is that sherry?" She could smell its sweetness.

He nodded and brought it to where she sat, placing it on the end table and sitting down in the opposite chair. "It's a prelude to something. A suggestion."

She lifted an eyebrow. "How mysterious! Well, I'll bite. Or sip, rather." She picked up the glass and wet her lips, then licked them appreciatively and drank several swallows. "That's lovely. Where did you find it?"

"I bought it last week. I thought you'd like it."

She took another swallow, watching him fidget in the chair. "Hal, what is it? I think I'd better hear this suggestion of yours."

He leaned forward. "Hon, could I steal a bit of that?"

She got up and brought it to him, stroking his hair—there was still a bit of clay dust in it—as she put the glass in his hand. Then she sat down again, waiting.

He took a single sip and stretched out his arm to hand the glass back to her. Then he sat back, with a sort of deliberate relaxation. "I think you need to get mad. At me."

She stared at him. He smiled for an instant, then grew serious again. "You've been patient, Wynne. You've put up with, and forgiven, and explained away, and forgiven some more. You've never really let loose. Just a little snark, now and then, a remark with an edge—and even then, you always do something to smooth it over. And you were right. I wasn't ready. If you'd aimed outright anger my way, I'd have sent it right back at you. I'd have roared, and then sulked—and done anything but listen."

She sat, her hands—the familiar and the new—clasped together, gazing at Hal in wonder as he went on.

"But I've been a lousy husband, Wynne. I've been careless and dismissive and self-centered. And God knows how many times and how many ways I've hurt you. I don't think we can move on until you've let yourself feel it and show it—at least once." He laughed suddenly, and looked surprised to have done it. "Once, if I'm lucky." Then he shook his head. "I'm sorry. I've got no business trying to derail this. Wynne, my love—let it out, at last."

***

Hal waited, holding his breath, as Wynne's gaze went unfocused. Finally, just as he had to inhale, she sat up very straight, then stood and started to pace. He stood up straight in turn, just as she whirled around to face him.

"You're right. I put up with a lot. And yes, I got sick of it, your attitude, and your—your disrespect! You were the only artist in the family, the only one who had something *important* to do, the only one fighting any battles that counted. Where did I fit in? When did *I* get to matter?"

He would not tear up, not yet. He could not let her soften before she was done.

"And my time never mattered. If we were supposed to go to a movie or take a walk or meet my friends, I could just sit around and be forgotten, and like it or lump it! And any time we were supposed to... to...."

He stood and faced her. "Any time we were supposed to meet somewhere. What would happen?"

He saw her decide to spare him. "No, Wynne! Say it!"

She was shaking now, glaring at him. "You'd be *late*, Hal! You kept me waiting, almost always. You kept me waiting, that day. *You were late!*" She broke into sobs. He ached to hold her; but he could not touch her yet. He waited for her to grow quiet, and then knelt at her feet.

"Darling, I'm not asking you to forgive me. Not yet. I'm only asking, or hoping, that you've already started to."

With a grace he could only envy, she sank down to her knees, facing him. She did not yet move to touch him. "I have. And I will." Then she reached out her new left hand and smiled at him. "Come on, help me off the floor."

He put his hands under her elbows and gently lifted her up, then stood holding her arms for a moment before letting go. He had turned to walk away, to leave her some space to absorb what had happened, when her voice stopped him. "Hal—thank you. Somehow you knew what I needed. I didn't—know, that is. I must have needed that for quite a long time."

He came back toward her and moved slowly to put an arm around her, watching for any stiffness or pulling back, finding none. "Lover, I hope to give you what you need, from now on. Until death us do part."

She shuddered in his arms, and he cursed himself for a clumsy fool. He stroked her cheek with his finger, the way she had always loved, hoping to make her forget. And whether she forgot or no, her muscles relaxed, and she turned to kiss him.

So maybe it would be all right.

Chapter 25

The joke was on Hal.

He had now and then accused Wynne of being excessively sensitive. He listened to her as much as most husbands, probably more. If she had something important to tell him—important to him or important to her—then sooner or later, she would make certain he heard her.

But this one time, he had insisted she tell him something, and then failed to hear it. And he could hardly insist that she tell him again—not that painfully confessed secret.

But what the devil had been the fellow's name? He could not recall even a syllable.

It had probably never occurred to her, once she decided to admit adultery, to withhold the details. That wasn't how her mind worked. She would not have leapt ahead and imagined him searching for the man, obsessing about him, torturing himself with comparisons.

And he should do nothing of the sort, he supposed. His moment of inattention could save him from himself.

To hell with that!

After the name—if she had even uttered it—she had said that the man worked for the agency. Or had she? No, she had said that he "did advertising" for them. He might work anywhere, any company that had the agency for a client.

Would he have to hire a private detective to find the fucker?

Of course, Hal knew a detective, if not a private eye. Arthur could doubtless track the fellow down in a matter of hours. But this was none of Arthur's business. And besides, who could say what Arthur would do to a man who had defiled his lady love?

So how could he find the man? He had to find him. How else would he ever know just how he had failed, what he had lacked?

...He might have another choice. The knowledge could be lurking inside him, entangled with the rest of the helmet's legacy, if he opened himself to seeing it.

Hal shuddered away from the thought. Sizing up the interloper was one thing. Absorbing Wynne's own assessment of both men, her comparison between the two — that he found himself unready to face.

He would have to find some other way.

Hal wove his way through the throng of holiday shoppers at the outdoor mall, checking directories whenever he could find them. The chocolate shop had to be here somewhere. He rarely ventured into such places any time in December, but Wynne would like one of the shop's Christmas boxes, with their intricate packaging and whimsical combinations of flavors.

The crowd parted and gave him a glimpse of the storefront before a surge of shoppers blocked his view again. Another shift in the masses of people, and he saw it again, the door opening and a man walking away.

Inside, behind the counter, a middle-aged woman with carefully styled gray hair was putting away samples and muttering to herself in some unfamiliar European-sounding tongue. Sensing Hal's presence, she looked up and smiled. "Welcome! Come and see what we delights we have to offer!"

Hal looked at the array of candies — round and square, glossy and soft, dark brown and lighter brown and brightly colored and multicolored — and almost backed away from the counter. "It all looks delicious, but I wouldn't know where to begin. Could you put together a selection — a dozen of...." How could he describe Wynne to this woman, to guide her in choosing? "Whatever you think an artist would enjoy."

The shopkeeper beamed at him. "But of course! It would be a pleasure. And how nice to have such an appreciative customer, after—well, I shouldn't complain. But some people just go out of their way to criticize and be unkind, don't you think?"

Hal arranged his face in sympathetic agreement, while recalling an episode or two when his own conduct might have deserved such a description. His response appeared to encourage the woman: she continued her tale of woe as she deftly selected, arranged, and packed the chocolates. "That man! One look at him and I knew he would leave without buying. He tells me he needs just the right chocolates, for— what did he say?—'for a *very special* guest.' And then he leans over the counter so close that I had to wipe his breath off the glass afterward, and walks back and forth, and makes such faces! And then he wrinkles up his nose and says, right out loud where anyone walking in could hear him, that he should have *known* he wouldn't find anything *sufficient*. Bah! I pity that guest, whoever she is."

She paused in her work and looked at Hal as if expecting him to chime in. He had better say something, if he wanted his chocolates. "Sounds like a very unpleasant character."

The woman nodded vigorously, three times in succession, and then finished tying an iridescent ribbon around the box. "Here you go, sir. And my best to your artist friend."

Hal paid the bill, which was higher than he enjoyed but less than he had feared, and made his escape with relief.

Hal and Wynne sat companionably on the living room sofa, ignoring the dishes from Sunday breakfast. Each leaned against one end of the sofa, their legs intertwined. Christmas lights twinkled on the artificial tree, a benign accompaniment to the wind whistling outside the window.

Both were reading, but neither read what they might have chosen a few months before. Hal had disdained police procedurals, and abhorred them even more after his Kafkaesque passage through the grotesquely misnamed "justice system"; but now, as he became ever more involved in Arthur's detecting, he had begun to skim through them, acquiring some sense of the world that he seemed to be entering. Wynne, now that she was posing for his sculpture—now that he was soliciting her opinions and ideas, from time to time—had begun scooping up his past issues of art magazines.

Wynne's phone trilled its ring tone for general callers. She fished it out and glanced at it. Her legs, lying against Hal's, stiffened convulsively; she jabbed hard at the phone and then threw it on the rug by the sofa.

Hal stared at the phone, and then at his wife. Wynne never threw her phone. Indeed, she treated it with a respect that had always amused him, a sort of incongruous courtesy. "Who or what was that?"

Wynne had gone pale, as pale as the day of her confession, and tears stood in her eyes. "Someone who needs to stop calling me."

Her lover. It had to be. The man must be hoping that Hal's arrest and conviction had given the interloper a new opportunity. But here was Hal's opportunity: he could get hold of the phone, find the man's number, and track him down.

But to what end? It was Wynne's heart, after all, that he needed to read. And here she was: no longer stretched languorously beside him, but huddled against the end of the sofa, clutching her legs with her arms, trembling.

It was time to ask.

"My love . . . please tell me why."

***

Wynne hugged her knees and gazed at Hal. Ready or not, she would have to try to answer him. Any evasion would be a blow against the foundations of their marriage, one it might not survive.

But he was starting to answer his own question, sitting on the sofa and facing away from her, elbows on knees, staring at the rug.

"I know I've been—aloof. And impatient. It's just as you said the other day: I took you for granted, and I didn't bother to listen to you. I was full of myself and my all-important work. I pushed you away."

Wynne scooted over to him, sitting beside him, thigh against thigh. "That was part of it. It was. But—sweetheart, I knew that about you, all along. I knew I would sometimes find it hard to—to get through. I knew you would spend a lot of time in your own little world. I knew I would sometimes get lonely. I could live with that."

Hal ran his fingers through his hair and made a little moaning sound that pierced her heart. She put her arm around his broad back and leaned into his side. "No, love, listen! I'm trying to get to the part that matters. All that, it may have upset me more than I expected—but there was something else, something that wasn't your fault.

"Maybe the best way to explain it is—you know how you moved a lot, as a child?"

Hal nodded. "My father's commissions took him all over. Sometimes he went alone, but for the bigger jobs, we trailed along after him."

Wynne nodded at the familiar explanation. "You told me once that the good part, the silver lining, was that you could try to start over—shed the mistakes and embarrassing stories, and reinvent yourself. I know it never worked as well as you hoped—because we always take ourselves along, don't we?—but here and there, it worked a little. Right?"

The phone's ring tone sounded again. Hal started, then kicked the phone across the rug. She shivered at the sudden violent motion. Neither she nor Hal might know, entirely, how much anger lurked within him, waiting to somehow escape. But she must go on.

"Well, what came over me, last year, was the other side of that. You knew me so well—at least, the me I had been, all these years since we've known each other—so well that I couldn't be anything else. Even if I wanted to change, it seemed impossible—because you knew I was the same."

Hal had turned; finally, he was looking at her. "Why did you want to change?"

"I was tired of myself! I looked at my life, and it seemed so—so tame. With a stranger, I could try being someone different. Wilder." She blushed. "Kinkier, even."

She could see him stop himself from rolling his eyes. "That would be something to see."

She could not entirely suppress a flare of indignation. "There, you see? To you, it's silly, because you know I'm not like that." A pause. "He didn't."

She saw this reminder of just what they were discussing hit Hal like a new blow. She gave him a moment to recover, then went on. "It's little things, sometimes, but they couldn't be that little, could they? For example: you know I don't sleep well if you're holding me?"

Hal nodded again, his mouth twisting a little. It had been a sore subject when they first became involved, the way she got restless and twitchy if she tried to sleep in the circle of his arms.

"You know that about me. And because you know it, you long since stopped offering, or trying, to hold me when we came to bed, unless we were making love."

Hal wrinkled up his forehead. "But—has *that* changed?"

Wynne sighed. "No, not really. But it feels so lovely, lying beside you, your arm around me...."

"Wait—are you telling me that when you slept with this lover of yours—" (she winced, but he had every right) "—that you could sleep beside him, up against him? That he got to hold you—all night?"

Now she was the one to look away, but she kept hold of him, even as he sat up straight and stiff. "I—I used a sleep inducer, with a delay. It was obvious, of course, but I never told him why. He thought I needed it just to sleep. He—he thought it was funny, a professional dreamer who couldn't get to sleep without help, but he didn't know any better. That was the Wynne he knew. And so, when I stayed the night with him—not so many times, of course—"

Because it was so hard for her to lie to Hal, or to skirt the lie, deceiving him all the same, and she could rarely bring herself to do it....

She must force herself to say it all, and then Hal could do what he had to do, to her or to them both.

"I could lie there, with someone's arms around me, and it wasn't as good—it could never be as good as your arms would have been. But at least, I didn't have to suggest, and overcome doubts, and explain. I could just be someone who fell asleep—and woke up—in her lover's arms."

She shuddered, remembering. "But almost as soon as I woke, I would feel him, see him—and I felt horrible. What was I doing there? That was how I felt, every time. And after a couple of months, I realized. I had tried being someone different, but I never wanted to be that other Wynne, the cheating one, the one with the wrong man's arm around her shoulders, ever, ever again. Oh, Hal, I'm so terribly, horribly sorry."

Finally, now, she could allow herself to cry.

She sobbed all the harder when Hal took her in his arms.

* * *

Wynne did not cry often enough to treat the matter casually, and crying herself out tended to exhaust her. She accepted, gratefully, Hal's suggestion that she take a nap. He led her to their bedroom, kissed her forehead, and swallowed hard at her loving, sleepy smile. Then he tucked her in and headed back to the living room—where Wynne had left her phone.

Had she had done so purely by accident, or had she subconsciously given him a way to identify her lover? She had already made clear that she wanted nothing further to do with the man. She might be enlisting Hal's help. His protection.

Hal picked up the phone, resisting the impulse to handle it only with the edges of his fingers. Dropping and breaking the thing would be an unfortunate complication.

Hal reached out to access Wynne's contacts—and jumped, dropping the phone after all, as the ring tone trilled again. The phone fell on the sofa cushion, and he heaved a sigh of relief. Should he let it go to voice mail? Could it be anything urgent? He glanced at the screen.

The caller's face had not appeared, although Wynne usually set her phone to show the caller. But the screen bore a name. "Max."

Hal barked a short laugh, then looked guiltily toward the closed bedroom door, hoping the sound had not disturbed his sleeping wife. He looked back at the phone. He was irrationally certain of the caller's identity. "Max." Was that the real name of Wynne's lover, or had he chosen the nickname to hint at possession of a big—

The trilling stopped. Carefully, as if the phone were radioactive, Hal picked it up and checked the Recent Calls listing. "Max" had called twenty and twenty-five minutes ago as well.

The corner of the case was jutting into his palm. Hal made himself relax his hand and put the phone back on the sofa.

At once, as if in protest, the phone sounded again.

Slowly, Hal reached for the phone, grasped it, and brought it to his ear. "This is Wynne's husband. And Wynne doesn't want to talk to you."

There was silence for a few seconds before the caller spoke. "May I speak to Wynne Cantrell, please?"

Well, that was one way for the fellow to play it. He had to give him credit for keeping his cool.

"She's sleeping. And as we both know, she hasn't been taking your calls, awake or asleep. So leave her alone."

Another silence, a little longer.

"Harold, isn't it?"

He did not want this man calling him by the same name Wynne did. "Close enough."

"This may sound strange, but I'd like to talk to you. Face to face. And you must have questions—questions you don't want to ask Wynne. Let me buy you a drink."

"No."

A barely audible sigh.

"Okay, you don't want to drink with me. Understood. Just meet me somewhere for a few minutes."

Hal fought back the urge to drop the phone and kick it across the room, as he had done a few minutes earlier. Knowledge was power. The more he knew about Max and what he wanted from Wynne, the better. He could stand it.

He would choose a place that he knew inside out, with his own creation standing sentinel. "Meet me in the central plaza of Riverside Park, under the arch, in fifteen minutes." The arch had been Hal's second commission. He and Wynne had had their engagement photos taken beneath it. Too late, he recoiled at the thought of this man standing near where Wynne had stood, her smile almost blinding....

"I'll be there." And the caller was gone.

The cold breeze sent last autumn's leftover leaves skittering past as Hal reached the plaza. A man stood beneath the arch, shifting from foot to foot and looking around. Max, in person, was tall and husky; in jeans, hiking boots, and quilted jacket, he lacked only an ax to make him a lumberjack. Hal waved to attract his attention, then pointed to a bench. The bench had been installed only a few months ago: it had not been part of the photo session. The arch loomed overhead, commanding the scene.

Max nodded and walked over to the bench, his gait unexpectedly graceful. Reaching it, he hesitated and then sat, looking up at Hal. Hal remained standing. "Why did you want to talk to me?"

Max cleared his throat. "I wanted to apologize."

That, Hal had not expected.

"I didn't mean to cause problems, or hurt anyone, or interfere in anyone's marriage."

Hal looked down his nose at Max, glad he had remained standing. "Let me guess. You didn't know she was married. Did you ask?"

"I didn't think I had to. Where we met—not in person, but the chat room where we first encountered each other— well, it wasn't a place you'd expect to find anyone who had… obligations. Or maybe I should say, restrictions."

Hal sat down heavily on the other end of the bench. He stared up at the arch, its component strands intertwining as it soared to its peak. Max seemed to be waiting for some response. "A meeting place for people ready to play."

"Pretty much. To play, to explore, to push a few boundaries."

Max didn't look much like the reckless, boundary-pushing type. But then, neither did Wynne.

And Hal was not the only one Wynne had misled. Had cheated.

He turned toward Max. "If that's true, then you don't owe me an apology." And Wynne had already made hers. Though he might need to hear it again. More than once. "How did it end?"

Max leaned back against the bench and blew his breath out through his lips as though smoking a cigarette. "We were supposed to go to this club. I went; she didn't show. It's in a pretty rough neighborhood, so at first I was afraid she'd had some trouble on the way. I called and left messages, asking if she was okay. The next morning, she texted back, just saying she was sorry I'd been worried. And then, three days later, I got another message saying she wouldn't be seeing me again."

Max was sitting forward now, hunched over, his large hands hanging between his knees. Hal had a momentary urge toward some expression of sympathy.

Max looked over at him. "I wasn't quite straight with you just now. When Wynne and I first met, I didn't know she was married. But I found out after a while. I looked her up. I wanted to know more than she'd told me. I saw her website—the dreams—and I saw she was married. But no kids, right?"

Hal shook his head. "No kids. Not yet."

"It would've worried me, if the two of you were living together and had kids."

"So she called it quits. Why have you been calling her?"

Max heaved a heavy sigh. "I didn't know what to think. I was concerned. And I missed her. She's—life was different with her around. Super-charged. More intense. I miss that, too."

It was hard to believe they were talking about the same woman. But maybe that's what Wynne could do, when a man gave her all his attention.

Time to put an end to this.

"What you've said, about how you two met, fits what Wynne's told me. She was restless, trying to find out how it felt to be somebody else. And—she didn't like it. She's done."

Hal saw Max's eyes flutter, his mouth twitch, at the words "didn't like it." He could practically see the memories playing in the man's mind like a dirty movie. Hal looked away and clenched his fists, and then his teeth. He counted silently to himself as he fought to fend off the thoughts of

Wynne, Wynne moaning and crying out, writhing ecstatically beneath the man's powerful body....

The worst thing was that the thought triggered not only anger and sorrow, but arousal. By coming here, by existing, Max had turned Hal into a voyeur, peeping and leering at his own wife.

He started to stand up, then stopped as Max spoke again. "I guess, in a way, I'm lucky she's a dream artist. I can still have some trace of her in my life—just like her other customers. And she won't even have to know.

"Or do you object even to that?"

Well might he ask. Hal had frozen in place, his mind racing. The man was already making a nuisance of himself. But if Max started playing her dreams, absorbing God knows which of Wynne's secrets, things could get so much worse.

He could try persuasion. He could even try intimidation, dubious as that prospect seemed. There was only one tactic that might work. And it would make Hal look like a complete heel, and a lousy husband to boot.

There was a certain justice in that.

"Yes, I object. You're damn right I object! How do I know the two of you haven't set all this up? She'll stop running off to hop in your bed, but she'll make sure her dreams are just what you're missing—both of you. Well, I'm onto you. And you can bet I'll be watching. Let her sell you one dream, and I'll make her sorry!"

Max turned toward Hal, his eyes wide in disbelief. Then he was breathing hard, his large fists half raised. Hal concentrated on looking unafraid, belligerent, and vindictive.

Max stood up and spat in Hal's direction.

"I'm going to write to her, telling her that I'll always be there if she needs me to help her in any way at all. And then I'm going to leave her alone, and hope like hell that she leaves you. And when she does, then God help you if you ever come near her again."

He strode off, through the arch, without looking back. Hal sat on the bench long enough for Max to get out of sight, then hurried home. Wynne could be done napping any minute.

***

Wynne, half asleep, heard Hal leave the house and relaxed into the nest of pillows and blankets. She found it hard not to censor her dreams when Hal was near. With his departure, she could give herself the comfort of physical intimacy and sexual release. What she really wanted was Hal, in the waking flesh. But she could not bring herself to suggest it, mere moments after he had heard her confession.

Putting Hal through his paces in a dream, puppet-like, seemed dishonest, an evasion of her own responsibility for the reluctance he might be feeling. She would know, no matter how she scripted the encounter; it would be hollow, and the hollowness would mock her.

Except for that one commercially motivated dream, she had refrained from dreaming about Max even during their affair. And to create that one dream, she had lingered in a hotel room after Max had left. She had been ashamed to bring the thought of Max into their home, let alone their bed. But now that she had forever closed the door on that relationship, she could allow herself one short dream, just one, as a farewell.

She sent herself to sleep.

Ocean waves, breaking on the beach. (Even with her quest to push old boundaries, she had never seriously considered making love on the beach: how could anyone want sand finding its way into all those tender places? But in her dream, the sand could retain just enough of its texture to be novel and stimulating, and stay where it was wanted.)

And there stood Max, naked, all those lovely muscles on display, watching her approach in her own nakedness. He reached one strong arm out to pull her close....

She couldn't.

Wynne turned toward Max and raised her folded hands toward him, in wordless prayer for his forgiveness. Then she turned and ran toward the surf, splashing through the breakers, diving in. And the waves, warmer than waves would be, obedient to her will, held her and tossed her and caressed her, again and again, so that her pleasure built and crested like the waves, and then crashed down on her in glorious tumult.

* * *

Hal took off his coat and hung it on the coat tree, then looked around for any sign that Wynne had awakened. The bedroom door was still closed, and he heard nothing.

He still felt shaken, and faintly sick, after the scene with Max. He could use a drink, a good stiff drink, a double.

He tiptoed across the living room and slowly, carefully, opened the bedroom door. Wynne was curled up in bed, facing the door. He had made no sound, but her eyes opened. She gazed at him in what seemed like longing, and reached out her hand.

He kicked off his shoes, stumbled to the bed, and lay down, wrapping himself around her, burying his nose in her hair.

Interlude

The lawyer, unlike many in his profession, prided himself on keeping his clients informed. His clients usually appreciated his efforts. Not today! The woman's outraged visage filled the phone screen, obscured by little drops of spittle as she sputtered.

"What do you mean, you'll be getting a default judgment? And for 'intentional infliction of emotional distress'—that sounds like what you're doing to *him*! And what's all this nonsense about federal prosecution and mail fraud? What are you *doing* to the poor man?"

"But madam, you gave me very clear instructions, which I confirmed in the written exchange after our meeting. I did just as you asked, and now you're on the verge of obtaining substantial redress for the emotional trauma you suffered from that deceptively packaged recording. And—"

"You must stop it. All of it! Leave him alone."

The lawyer tried to think. "If we moved to dismiss the lawsuit after this much time, you could have costs and fees assessed against you. The judge could even order sanctions." And the judge's displeasure at such an abrupt reversal might carry over onto other cases. He had not come this far in his profession by antagonizing judges.

But of course, if the case had been settled, dismissal would be a matter of course. "If you are truly intent on this, it might be necessary to offer the defendant—"

"Don't *call* him that!"

"—some compensation. The court would be considerably more tolerant if it appears that the parties have agreed to resolve their differences without further judicial action."

He expected her to balk; but she replied at once, "That's fine. That's only fair. After all, I did hurt him—dreadfully.

He trusted me with his dreams and made me part of his future. And I simply *kicked* him away."

"But the recording, the way he tricked you—"

The woman actually chuckled. "Yes, that was naughty of him. But he knew I wouldn't listen any other way. He wanted me to understand.

"And I do. I really, really do."

Chapter 26

Dream Daemon leaned back against the wall at the head of his bed, closed his eyes, and visualized a giant roulette wheel, spinning round and round, painted in improbably fluorescent green and purple and orange, the ball rolling and clattering around and then sliding downward. Just as it settled into place, he opened his eyes and jabbed at his screen, making the connection.

He had no idea what recording he had hacked into—that was the fun of it, the whole point of his latest game. Already he'd found himself juggling torches, flying over canyons as a giant bird, and rolling in the sack with a truly hot little number. Good thing he always, always locked his door: his mom had heard the noises he made and hammered on his door, all upset. He'd startled so hard it made the helmet reset. And with the random selection setup, he couldn't even go back and finish....

Enough of that! Time to find out what fish he'd caught this time around.

It was a girl's point of view. And she was scared. Not thrill-scared like someone skydiving or bungee jumping, but really scared, enough to feel sick with it. Why would someone pay money for a recording that made them feel like that?

And what was that? Something in his, her, mouth. Mmmm! Chocolate, really good melty chocolate, expensive-tasting. She was still scared, but confused. And there came more chocolate.

And more. Piece after piece, shoved into her mouth. More and more, until she was choking on it.

She tried to spit it out, but someone put a hand across her mouth, pressing tight....

Just as he broke the connection, he thought he sensed relief, a gasp of air. So the girl hadn't really choked or suffocated to death—he didn't think.

He pushed the tablet away and lay down, curled up in a ball, clutching his pillow until his heart stopped pounding and he could breathe without panting.

He didn't know who sold that kind of horrible stuff, and he didn't want to know. No more roulette! He'd go back to the regular vendors, the ones he'd started with. There were lots of dreams he hadn't sampled yet, and lots of clever switches he could make.

* * *

Wynne saw her agent's number on the phone and winced. Her output had still not reached its former level, and the agency might well be ready to hint at some impatience. Indeed, with the New Year imminent, they might be going through their list of suppliers, pruning the less productive.

"Wynne?" The agent's voice was grave, and her heart sank: she had been right about his errand.

"Wynne, I wanted to tell you not to send us anything for a few days, at least."

At first, before he finished the sentence, she thought he was firing her, and tried to decide whether to protest. Then her ears caught up with what he was actually saying. "What's going on?"

"We've been hacked."

"*What?*"

"Hacked. Someone's been following our downloaded dreams, playing them for free and even messing with them."

Wynne almost dropped the phone. "I had no idea that was possible!"

"We knew it might be. We hoped it wasn't, or that no one would manage it. Someone has."

"What have they been doing?" Had they altered her own dreams, sabotaging her clients' experiences? What damage might her clients have suffered?

"Just minor mischief so far. We're looking for common threads, for any relationship between the customers affected. I suspect we're dealing with some young punk who isn't as clever as he thinks he is. We'll get him sooner or later. But in the meantime, we're stepping up site security. There's no point in delivering anything new until then."

She was about to say goodbye when her agent spoke again, hurrying to add a final word. "Oh, and Wynne? Please don't mention this to anyone. Well, to Hal, if you must. But no one else. We'd rather it not get around."

Naturally not. It could ruin their business—the agency's, and the dreamers' as well—if word got out that people might be subjected without warning to malicious dreams. She shuddered. If the hacker was not found and stopped before long, she might consider herself obligated to disobey the injunction of secrecy. But she would wait a little while and see what happened.

Wynne hung up the phone and sighed in frustration. It was never easy to thank Hal's father for anything. He always dismissed his actions as nothing, not worth fussing over, what anyone would have done. Well, no one else had, this time, except Hal's lawyer, Mr. Medved, who was paid to do it. Hal's father had saved Hal—or almost saved him, saved him from so much worse than even what he had been made to suffer. And she was darned well going to find a way to show her gratitude. Harold Senior's birthday was coming up, so he would, for once, accept a gift from her.

She thought of the photograph, the old-fashioned fabric-style print in an old-fashioned frame, in the living room of what had been the family home. Now the old man lived there by himself, with that looming reminder: the family, Hal and his parents and the sister who lived so far away, perched on all sides of a picnic table, in a meadow with hills all around.

Wynne could give him that picnic, that day. She knew all the people involved: Hal's mother had been herself, still, when Wynne and Hal met, and for a few years thereafter. If she needed to, she could pump Hal for more information. Thank goodness the recording could actually transmit such details as facial features when it involved people Harold Senior knew so well.

Maybe, instead of the family in earlier days, she should imagine the family as it could have been, up to date: Hal, his parents, his sister, and Wynne herself, all picnicking together. It might be as well to get Hal's consent to that approach, but surely he would give it.

Now there was a way to make herself useful, while the agency tracked down whoever was attacking it!

Waking from such a dream might make the old man sadder. But Wynne thought she could see just well enough into his heart. He would bear that sadness and be grateful for it, to see his wife's eyes sparkle once again, and hear her sing the family anthem just a little flat; and for her to know, again, who was her husband, and who her son.

Wynne saw Hal's father's number on the incoming call and wondered whether Hal could be interrupted. He was in creative ferment, more or less inaccessible. She picked up the phone and prepared to assess the call's urgency.

"Dad, it's so nice to hear from you! I'm not sure if Hal can come to the phone right now—"

Harold Senior smiled warmly; his deep voice sounded firmer and stronger than she had heard it in years. "Wynne, my dear, I didn't call to talk to Hal, this morning. I called to talk to you."

"Oh! Oh, how nice. How are you?"

"I am well. I had a wonderful night's sleep—and much, much more."

She would have trouble speaking if she tried. But Hal's father clearly had more to say.

"You're so young, Wynne. I doubt you can grasp, at your age, how much the old can long to remember the past. And for most of us, we can only—" (he chuckled) "—we can only dream of the good fortune of truly recalling the past in dreams, without distortions and absurdities. You come like an angel, Wynne, blessing me with a dream of my family."

She did not know whether he had actually experienced the dream as she had crafted it, with her and Hal included, but it did not matter. She had succeeded in giving him joy, and that made her joyful. "I'm so glad! I was happy to do it."

"I was wondering...." Now his voice was less certain. "What would happen, do you think, if I gave the dream to Evelyn? Could she understand it? Would it disturb her, or frighten her? Could it do for her anything like what it did for me?"

Wynne had never considered such an idea. She knew nothing about the dreams dementia sufferers experienced, let alone of what assisted dreams they were capable.

"I have done a bit of research. Those who suffer from my wife's condition tend to dream less, or at least, they have less REM sleep. Would that prevent your dreams from functioning?"

"I don't think so. The helmet picks up the entrance into REM sleep. As long as she has some, that's enough. And the benefits of REM sleep aren't reduced by assisted dreaming."

"Excellent!" She had never heard him sound so buoyant. "Would the dream you gave me work for her?"

Wynne considered. "I think it might be best for me to tinker with it." She could emphasize all the identities involved. And she knew how to provide a more general sort of heightened reality. In the past, she had used it to give her customers a sense of intoxication, similar to certain drugs but without the side effects. This would be, if successful, a far more important use of the technique.

She had almost forgotten that Harold Senior remained on the line when he spoke again. "I do not wish to impose. When would it be convenient for you to make these adjustments, and give me a dream for my wife?"

Wynne smiled. "It's really quite an imposition. I doubt I could manage before this afternoon."

He laughed, the deep rolling laugh she had not heard in quite some time. "I believe I can adjust to this delay. Thank you, dear lady. Thank you so very, very much."

***

Harold Wakeman, Sr., knocked on the door of his wife's little room and waited for her to invite him in. Sometimes it was an aide who responded, but he preferred, even then, to hear Evelyn's voice as well. There was little he could do to add a touch of dignity to the life she was living.

Evelyn seemed to know him today. She winked at him as he approached, an old signal from lover to lover, not entirely appropriate to the circumstances but still to be cherished. He leaned down to kiss her cheek, and then, as she turned, her lips. Kneeling beside her, he held out the gift-wrapped box. "I brought you a present, darling."

Her face lit up, childish again, and she bounced in her chair, laughing shrilly. He tried not to wince, and managed to smile along with her. "Yes, presents are lovely, aren't they? Shall I help you open it?"

"*No!* Mine!" She pushed his hand away and tugged at the bright pink ribbon. He had taken care to tie it so loosely that she could not accidentally tighten it. The ribbon slid off onto her lap, and she opened the lid. Inside was a helmet, sized from the hats tucked away in a usually undisturbed closet.

She picked it up and turned it this way and that, confusion on her face.

"May I tell you what it is?"

She nodded, her lip starting to tremble. Harold moved his hand, slowly and gently, to take hers. "It's for dreams, my love. To make you pretty dreams. See how nice and padded it is, inside, and how the outside goes flat when you press it? You can wear it when you sleep. For pretty dreams."

He examined her face for signs of comprehension.

"Dreams? Nice dreams?"

"Yes, sweetheart! That's right. And—do you remember Wynne?"

She wrinkled her forehead. "My friend?"

"Your friend, and our son Hal's friend. Wynne sent you a present, too. It's in here—in the—" The word "helmet" might alarm her, with dim associations of battle. "It's in this special hat. It's a dream she made, just for you."

Suddenly her look was one of rational, adult skepticism. "Wynne can make a dream? For me?"

He grinned, nodding. "She's very special, our Wynne! She can do just that. And she made one for you. I think you'll like it."

She turned the hand he was holding, to take his and squeeze it. "Will you be there? In my dream?"

Harold's eyes filled with tears. He raised her hand and kissed it. "Yes, my dear. I will."

Chapter 27

THE INDOOR EXERCISE room at Holdark Correctional Facility had televisions at all four corners, playing nonstop. To prevent conflicts over programming, their settings were constant: one news, one sports, one soap operas, one game shows. To be sure, fights still broke out constantly—over political contests, football wagers, whether the doctor had been correct in accusing his patient's sister of seducing the doctor's wife—but at least there were none about whether to change the channels.

The jaded prison guards rarely found much to surprise them, but those on duty this morning were a bit bemused when a weathered old convict who had been playing Solitaire near the news broadcast let out a sudden cry of anguish, sweeping his cards aside and breaking into violent sobs.

The con's roommate, alerted by some prisoner, hurried over from the game show corner. "What the hell, buddy?"

The con gestured wordlessly toward the television, where the broadcaster was obligingly repeating the story that had been responsible. "To recap: industrialist and billionaire Sheldon Packer, founder of Shell-Pack Industries, has been found dead in his office at the age of eighty-one."

"Packer. Isn't that the…" The roommate stopped abruptly, appearing to consider his comment indelicate.

The shorter guard pointed to the television. "Sheldon Packer. That's the one whose daughter got snatched a few years back. Had a rough time, I hear, before they rescued her." He did a double-take. "Wait a minute—that old bastard crying on the table—he's the one that snatched her, isn't he?"

The taller guard peered at the prisoner. "I think you're right. What the hell is he crying about? Is he thinking he should have waited until the old codger died and the girl was rich herself?"

"Naah, that can't be right. If she was the rich one in the family, who'd be able to pay the ransom if she got snatched?"

Apparently they had been talking loud enough for the prisoner to hear. He raised his tear-drenched face and glared at them. "Don't you have a heart? Her father's dead! She loved him! They were so close...." His sobs broke out anew.

The two guards looked at each other, shaking their heads in bewildered unison.

The shorter guard's shift was over. He made his way to the locker room to shed his uniform and don his street clothes. As he buttoned his shirt, the unwelcome tickle of duty kept disturbing him. He really should report the incident in the exercise room. It might mean something to someone. It might even be important.

He hesitated, then left the room and turned not toward the outer doors and the bus home, but down the corridor to the Chief of Security's office.

* * *

Years ago, Arthur had provided Hannah with her first training in the fine art of preemptive protection, or what he had called, in a rare hint of vulgarity, CYA (for "cover your ass"). But Arthur had demonstrated recently that his grasp of the subject was incomplete at best. Hannah could only hope that she had deployed adequate tripwires and backup plans to protect both Arthur and herself, in case this business of Arthur's clandestine assignment blew up on him.

Her current task was quite sufficiently ticklish: find out what reports might be lurking in anyone's files, anywhere in the sprawling bureaucracy, concerning unusual effects or events involving playback helmets. She had been openly skeptical, attributing the request to Arthur's unfortunate obsession with Wynne Cantrell; but she had in fact found a fair number of anomalous incidents, and had duly summarized them. The greatest number had come from various prisons—not surprising, given that most other uses of the helmets had no direct government connection.

As she was about to send Arthur her report, Hannah's searchbot pinged again with one more find from the Holdark facility. At first it seemed to add little to the previous reports, but as she scanned it she realized that it did, in fact, include a different element. None of the other incidents had involved such intense emotion.

She copied the key language, pasted it into her report, and sent it to Arthur by the established secure channel. It had better be secure, or it would be her—insufficiently covered—ass.

* * *

Arthur reviewed Hannah's latest compilation while Hal made coffee in Arthur's kitchen. Hal was pouring hot water into the filter when a sudden shout from Arthur made him spill some on the counter. He swore, jumped back, and looked around for a towel.

"Hal! Come here and tell me whether I'm crazy!"

"Just a minute!" He found the roll of paper towels, wiped up the water on the floor, and was about to wipe the counter when Arthur hollered again. "Forget about the coffee and get in here!—please."

Hal defiantly finished his cleanup and checked to make sure enough water had made it into the filter before sauntering to the breakfast nook where Arthur had set up shop. "What's the latest?"

Arthur thrust his tablet in Hal's direction. "Read this. Just read this."

Hal took the tablet and scanned the report. "Holdark again. But I see what you mean. It's different. It's not just about unexplained information, not this time. This sounds like—I'm not sure what to call it."

"I have a word for it, I think." Arthur pushed his chair back, stood up, and headed for the kitchen. "And I need that coffee, after all."

Hal put the tablet down and trotted after him. "Thought you would.... But what word, already?"

Arthur turned toward him, his eyes wide. "Empathy."

"Let's examine this notion of yours." Hal took a gulp of coffee. "You're saying playback doesn't just reveal information—that it actually induces empathy for the recorded subject. Well, you and I...." He trailed off. He did not like where this train of thought was heading.

Arthur and Hal had both experienced Wynne's recording. Could that playback explain the greater understanding Hal had seemed to have, lately, of Wynne's emotional needs? Where Wynne had been giving him credit for a new level of caring, for emotional maturity, had he simply been feeding off an artificial effect?

And Arthur—that was worse. Arthur had not, after all, been the one who (his shoulders went tense at the thought) slept with Wynne. But all unwitting—yet still as a result of his voluntary action—Arthur had apparently connected with Wynne on a deeper level, penetrating not her body but her psyche. Her soul.

The coffee was bitter in Hal's mouth. He took the mug to the kitchen, poured its contents down the drain, and spat the mouthful into the sink.

"God knows when we'd have figured it out if Hannah hadn't tracked this down." Arthur sat shaking his head, staring at the tablet. "You and I—neither of us would have wondered why we cared about Wynne and felt empathy for her. We'd have stayed clueless."

Hal was more than ready to change the subject. "It's a pity the goddamned kidnapper didn't record and play back his victims. He'd be a lot less dangerous to them if he had."

But wait…. If their hypothesis was correct, the death recording was somehow mixed up in all this. The mastermind behind all these linked events was particularly interested in, and informed about, helmet recordings. Was it really so unlikely that he would record his victims and play those recordings?

And if he had done so, and had still not repented, had not turned himself in or at least turned the women loose… what sort of monster were they hunting?

INTERLUDE

THE SENIOR INTELLIGENCE official reviewed the agenda for his meeting with the President and felt the familiar pang of guilt at what it omitted. The increase—an uptick, really, but still an undeniable increase—in operatives betraying a dangerous degree of sympathy for terrorists and other targets would come to light sooner or later, and by failing to inform the President, they were putting him at risk of public embarrassment or worse. But until they had some explanation, the report would discredit the Agency without actually addressing the problem.

What had changed in the last few years that could possibly explain it? What procedures had been abandoned or put in place? What defect in their recruitment process had led to the harvest of so many bad apples?

The official knew nothing of how playback figured in the ritual hazing of new recruits. A political appointee, he had not come up from the ranks, and the field operatives did not hold such appointees in particularly high regard. Many were the secrets he had never been told.

Chapter 28

Hal lingered over his breakfast, reluctant to start the labors of the day. He would not be able to work this morning, even if he could concentrate on the sculpture: he had promised Arthur he would come by and go over the charts again. There must be something they were missing, something too obvious to have occurred to them.

Wynne had gone off to visit Hal's mother. Her absence made it easier for Hal to face the problem that had been lurking just below conscious awareness. What did his and Arthur's new hypothesis mean for Wynne, and for Wynne's work?

Before the explosion and everything that followed, he had been somewhat dismissive of what he saw as Wynne's pretensions to creative stature. He could not recall, now, just why he had considered her crafting of dreams, her calibration of how to include architecture on which her clients could build, as somehow more trivial than his own work. In a way, he was sorry to have left behind that point of view, however indefensible. It would be comforting to be able to dismiss as unimportant any impact (aside from economic) that would flow from the possible disruption of the lucid dream market.

He had stalled on bringing Wynne up to date. How could he tell her that her "clients" had been learning, to an unknown and probably unknowable extent, about secrets to which even Wynne might not have conscious access? How could he look in her eyes and explain that when she thought she was selling her visions, she had been selling her heart?

And would it move her or frighten her to know that in earning her clients' custom, she had also been winning their love?

***

Wynne hoped the call from her agent meant an end to the hiatus. They could use the advances for her latest dreams—to put it mildly. And she had news. The dream for Hal's mother had been a success. Evelyn had awakened the next morning and told an aide all about it, speaking clearly, though it most often took her hours to achieve coherence. And when Harold Senior visited—Wynne still got choked up, remembering what he had told her. "She remembered the dream. And she was happy, all morning. And all morning, she knew me." ... Since then, Wynne had been bubbling over with ideas. She was determined to explore the possibilities of using dreams to help other victims of dementia. And had anyone teamed with a psychiatrist to create therapeutic dreams?

As she had hoped, her agent sounded a triumphant note. "We got the bugger. Some young punk, just like I thought, playing games to get back at people. But he left a wide enough trail!"

"So I can bring in my latest?"

"Sure, sure! Your fans are hammering down our doors— virtually speaking, of course. I hope you've got a few spicy ones for us."

Well, she had done her best. The combination of the Japanese rope fetish offerings and some straightforward hot action might satisfy the agent, if not all of her usual customers. And she was increasing her sweet-and-light inventory to compensate for the sparse offerings in the kinkier department.

Her thoughts returned to the culprit. "Did you have the hacker arrested?" She hoped he would not get into too much trouble, not enough to spoil his future prospects permanently.

"Uh—no. We didn't think that was entirely prudent. The publicity, you know. So far, we don't think the news has spread. You didn't tell anyone?"

"No one but Hal." And he had been at least as perturbed as she, but had reluctantly agreed to hold his tongue for a little while. It would be a distinct relief to tell him the matter had been settled.

"So what are you going to do about the hacker?"

"He'll be signing the nastiest, scariest cease-and-desist plus nondisclosure agreement our lawyers can cook up, in exchange for our forbearance. He tries it again, or brags to anyone, and he's toast."

Some idea was stirring in the back of Wynne's mind. She needed to get off the phone and give it some room to emerge. "Thanks for the good news! I need to do something, just now, but I'll let you know later when I'm coming in."

She hung up and turned her chair toward the window into the garden. Just a bit of distraction should give the idea a chance to emerge and blossom.

Wynne opened the door to Hal's studio as quietly as possible and peeked in. He was working, but in a relaxed sort of way, cleaning up edges, smoothing surfaces. He could be interrupted. "Honey?"

Hal looked up and smiled. "Hey, there, sweetheart! Did you want to tell me something?"

"To ask you something, actually. Do you and Arthur still think that helmet recordings are an important piece of your puzzle?"

He nodded, his expression more somber. "It's getting tangled, or even twisted. But yes, we do."

"Well, I just found out something, and I was wondering… do you think it might turn out to be useful if you had someone who could hack those recordings? Or at least, hack into dreams?"

Hal wrinkled his forehead and put his chin in his hand, in his almost comical "deep in thought" posture. "Hmmmm.

I don't know. It's too soon to say. But if you could set up the possibility, we might end up taking you up on it."

Wynne called her agent back as soon as she had kissed Hal and left his studio.

"Before you get that mischief-maker's signature on an agreement, can I talk to you about something to put in it? If it's any trouble, I could compensate the agency—waive one of my advances, or something. If you're free this afternoon, I'll head straight in."

Chapter 29

Tertius removed the helmet, the playback confirming his initial impressions, and fought to overcome his disappointment. He should not allow himself to be disappointed, when only his failure to recall and extrapolate from available evidence had led to his unsatisfied expectations.

He could still take pride in the modifications he had made to the helmet, allowing his subject to play a recording while he in turn recorded her experience thereof. But he had looked forward to exquisite unhappiness on the girl's part as she finally relived the death of her mother. It had begun well: the girl's first sight of her mother's frozen body, before Tertius started the playback, had made for a most piquant moment of grief and despair, as the girl realized what she was about to experience and drew the appropriate conclusions about her own probable fate. But then, toward the end of the playback, she had experienced a sense of calm, even comfort, that he had by no means intended.

He had had sufficient data to predict this outcome, yet had failed to do so. After all, he had posited, when first reviewing the mother's recording, that she believed herself to be encountering and recognizing various loved ones. Naturally the girl would recognize many of them as well, from photographs and the like.

Tertius's blunder might well have cascading consequences. The girl's own death would almost certainly be affected by what she would now expect to see. Not only would her terror be reduced, but her experience might be tainted by anticipation of particular images, and Tertius would have no way to isolate that effect.

And he had invested so much time in this subject already!

But no, he must maintain a positive attitude. While the data might lack the rigor he preferred, he would still be the first to record a death experience affected by the subject's own experience with death playback. And more precisely calibrated experiments could follow.

* * *

Wynne had shared with Sara as many updates as she could extract from Hal. After all, Sara's intuition needed the fuel of facts. And Sara, in her turn, had given Wynne access to her dream diary—at least most of it. She had reserved the right to do a little editing. Wynne opened the file chuckling, imagining the sort of secrets her little sister might have decided to excise.

"Since Wynne told me that a death recording was somehow mixed up in the case, my dreams have been wandering around the lab. My old boss keeps popping up, in the oddest ways. Three nights ago, I dreamed he came up to my cubicle wearing a mask—but the mask was his own face. He kept taking it off and putting it on, and every time he took it off, his expression would be different; and then, when he put the mask on again, it would have changed to the new expression. In the dream, it all seemed natural enough. It was only when I woke up that it creeped me out.

Then last night, I dreamt I went into his office to get his approval of something, and he had all sorts of strange stuff on his desk. There was a row of little perfume bottles—sample sized—and a cluster of really delicious-looking chocolate truffles; and then a set of scrimshaw carvings in an arc in front of him. I kept trying to get his attention, but he just kept touching one or another of the objects and muttering, 'Exquisite. Simply exquisite.' A little weird, but not as weird as it sounds. The guy really was like that, kind of—is 'epicure' the word? He'd go out of his way (or send someone else out of their way) to get the best coffee, or some exotic fruit, or whatever. And people who'd been to his home talked about his collections: butterflies, I think, and crystal, and I don't know what."

Butterflies. Wynne remembered the butterfly garden at the spa, and shivered. She found herself imagining a middle-aged man, fastidious in his dress and movements, moving slowly around the garden and plucking the butterflies one by one out of the air, dropping them daintily in a flask of some chilling, deadly liquid....

Did she know the name of Sara's former boss? Wynne had a vague sense that she'd heard something about him, about where he had gone after leaving the laboratory, but she couldn't quite bring it to mind.

*　*　*

Tertius Shaw closed his copy of Arthur Kellic's research notes, took another slurp of his tea (an almost unobtainable Da Hong Pao blend), and sat back to consider.

It had been amusing watching Arthur stumble around, searching for Tertius's trail—but the man was starting to pick up a few too many clues. The obstacles placed in his way had proved insufficient. It might be time to simply cut him off.

*　*　*

Hannah thanked her lucky, or at least vigilant, stars for her habit of mimicking paranoia. She had set up the trace on her reports to Arthur without any expectation that it would prove necessary or fruitful. Yet here it was, notification that a copy had been duplicated and diverted to an unknown computer address.

She sent a message to one of her own contacts, a probationer with a stake in keeping Arthur uninterested in his recent activities. Hannah had several such arrangements. She could not let her boss' sometimes unrealistic probity keep her from protecting him as needed.

Half an hour later, she received a reply. Looking quickly through it, she absorbed the essential information and relaxed. It was only the Director's home computer. It was hardly surprising that someone with such weighty responsibilities, and so many interruptions to his office hours, would catch up on some developments at home.

She had almost forgotten the matter when she next checked her email and found something to dismay her. The Director had sent a message to accounting, cc'd to her attention, cutting off the funding for Arthur's investigation into the theft of the death recording and related matters. And to underline it, he had revoked Arthur's access code to the confidential department files.

Forcing herself to be patient, she worked, or pretended to work, for another hour before feigning the onset of a nasty cold, complete with hacking cough, and leaving the office, allegedly for home. Instead, she walked to the subway, went down the entrance and up an exit, then found a taxi to take her to Arthur's apartment.

***

Arthur looked at the kettle and shook his head. After the latest startling developments, tea might not suffice. He would allow himself the rare indulgence of a vodka tonic.

He measured the vodka carefully, added enough tonic to fill the glass, and took his drink back to the kitchen table where he had left his handwritten notes. Sometimes old ways were the best, after all: there was no hacking pen and paper.

He looked through his summaries of all his discussions with Hal, and frowned at the mention of the helmet research team. He had not yet checked on the members of that team or their relationships with any current police department employees. That loose end must be addressed. He had little reason to fear that Wynne's sister would be implicated in anything sinister; and if the facts turned out to surprise him, he would deal with the matter then.

Turning to his tablet, he logged onto the Department site—but the site rejected his password. Annoying, but this was hardly the first time that one or another government web page had gone buggy. He would start with public sources, and then try again if necessary.

The usual online encyclopedia gave him the necessary dates. It took considerably more digging to find an obsolete staff directory covering that period. The ice in his drink had melted, diluting it further, by the time he had what might be a complete list.

Arthur frowned. Had he known that the Director came to their department from this research project? He vaguely recalled something about a scientific background, but doubted he had ever heard the details.

There was a connection, to be sure! But—how absurd, surely, to suspect the Director of involvement.

And yet, he had been looking for an insider....

His increasingly troubling thoughts were scattered by a loud, repeated rapping at his front door.

Arthur peered through the peephole, then flung the door open wide to greet Hannah. What a pleasant surprise! And so good to see her in person instead of on the phone, after all this time.

Except—she seemed upset.

She hurried in, looking over her shoulder as she entered, and shut his door herself. She looked up at Arthur, her coat still on, her large black eyes wide and frightened. "I need you to tell me if I'm crazy. And I really hope you can."

Chapter 30

Wynne tiptoed out of her mother-in-law's room, leaving the older woman nodding in her chair and drifting toward sleep. They had had a pleasant visit, if not as productive as Wynne had hoped. She wanted to give Evelyn another dream, a dream of her youth, including some of her favorite activities. Harold Senior could provide some information, but it would be better to hear what the dreamer-to-be thought of first and ranked most highly. Unfortunately, the slight improvement in Evelyn's mental state since the last dream had not sufficed to make a detailed, focused conversation possible. At least not today.

Wynne headed toward the office to return her visitor's badge and almost ran into a man who was leaving it. He looked familiar, but she could not immediately place him.

"It's Mrs. Wakeman, isn't it?" The man held out his hand, smiling and genial. Mrs. Wakeman? For a moment she was disoriented; then she realized he must be using the old-fashioned reference to Wynne's marital status. Hal's mother, indeed, called herself Mrs. Wakeman, as she must have done in her youth, but it had never occurred to Wynne to do the same.

The man's smile grew wider (surely not at her discomfiture?). "We met a few years back, at the Policeman's Ball. You came with Mr. Kellic, as I recall."

Of course—it was Mr. Shaw, the Director, Arthur's boss' boss. Wynne had indeed attended as Arthur's guest. But she had not been married to Hal, then.

"How nice to see you again. Are you visiting someone?" Too late, she wondered if the question would be considered impolite. But there was nothing to be ashamed of in having a relative living in this place. Though some people were ashamed, when they were unable to care for a family member at home.

Mr. Shaw, she saw with relief, took no offense. In fact, he seemed somehow pleased with the question. "Actually, no. I'm here in an official capacity. Our fraud unit has been working with nursing homes and other such facilities, throughout the city, to help them put some protocols in place to protect their residents." He shook his head solemnly. "You know how reprehensible people will prey on the elderly."

"What a good idea.... You'll excuse me, won't you? I have to be going." She had no great urgency about departing, but the encounter had an awkwardness about it. She extricated herself with a few more social pleasantries and headed to the parking lot. The subway came nowhere near the nursing home, and the bus ride was long and awkward, so she had taken their carlet. Since she was driving anyway, if Hal had not yet headed to Arthur's, she could pick him up and drop him there.

* * *

Tertius Shaw waved goodbye as Wynne Cantrell trotted off. She seemed almost offensively cheerful. How could she remain so warm and friendly, so blatantly benevolent, after what she had endured? It showed a want of feeling, a sort of poor taste.

He could go after her and bring her home, recording her current frame of mind and then correcting it. But she had already, though unintentionally, shared her psyche with two men, her husband and her would-be paramour. Tertius preferred exploring virgin territory.

He had, in fact, been considering plucking one of the residents from this facility. It could be very interesting to sample the mental state of someone with a deteriorating mind. And for consistency, he could choose a subject who, like the previous and present subjects, had some connection to the victims of the fountain explosion.

To be sure, he had not quite finished with the girl, but he could, with a bit of re-arranging, make room for a second guest. Why not?

***

Hal found it difficult to make light conversation as Wynne drove him to Arthur's apartment. He was still trying to decide what to tell Wynne, and when, about what he thought of as The Effect. If he continued stalling, she might find out in some accidental way and know he had kept the secret from her. But he could hardly spring it on her now, while she was driving!

He let her get out first when they arrived, following her up the musty stairwell. To his surprise, Arthur's door was open, and Arthur himself was standing in the doorway, shifting around restlessly, looking down the hall and stepping back. As soon as he saw Hal and Wynne approaching, he waved them in. "Finally! Hannah's found out something, and we may need to scramble."

Hal followed Wynne into the apartment as Arthur shut the door, almost slamming it in his haste. Arthur led them into his living room, where his assistant Hannah sat on the edge of a sofa, sitting bolt upright, hands clasped together, eyes darting around in nervous excitement.

Hal turned toward Arthur. "All right, what's going on?"

Arthur gestured toward Hannah in an oddly courtly flourish. "Hannah's the one who found out—just when I was starting to suspect, for other reasons. And if she hadn't taken what I assumed were unnecessary precautions, we'd be in even more danger than we are already."

Hal stepped between Wynne and the others, as if the danger somehow emanated from them, before he caught himself. He forced himself to breathe evenly and deeply as he waited to hear Hannah's report.

Hannah bit her lip. "I think—it sounds nuts, but I think our Director may be the one you're looking for."

"The one we're looking for, for what?"

Arthur rolled his eyes, a sign that anxiety had overtaken his habitual courtesy. "The one! The guy! The bomber! The thief! All of it!"

Hal stared at Arthur, then turned back toward Hannah. "Ms.—"

"Oh, call me Hannah. You want me to explain. Of course."

Hal listened closely as Hannah described her surreptitious trace on Arthur's confidential reports, the diversion of a copy to the Director's home, and the abrupt suspension immediately thereafter of all that made Arthur's investigation possible.

Hal turned back to Arthur. "Are you sure you aren't making too much of this? There could be all sorts of bureaucratic reasons for this latest development, and the timing could be coincidence."

"Is it also coincidence that Shaw used to head the helmet research team?"

"He *what?*"

"You were right. I should have checked as soon as you raised the idea." Arthur paced back and forth across the small room. "We have to take precautions. If the man we're hunting knows all about our work, he could go after us, any of us, at any time! And besides... I've been doing this a while, Hal. I have a sense of when I'm—when my team is onto something. The back of my neck says it isn't just coincidence. And remember my charts? We couldn't find anyone connecting all three, and that seemed like disconfirming data for our hypothesis that the bombing and the stolen recording and the kidnapping were all connected. But the Director could have falsified the records I used to make those charts."

"Could anyone else have done the same?"

Arthur stood still for a moment. "I need to look into that. You're right—I can't go off half-cocked here. I could miss something else."

"And we still don't know how, or whether, it matters that he ran that research team."

"I only just found out about that." Arthur turned to Wynne. "I imagine you'll be concerned about your sister—but there's no reason at all to believe she's involved in any way."

Without a word, Wynne dug around in her purse and pulled out her phone. Her hand shaking slightly, she punched the button to call her sister. "Sara? Please say you aren't too busy to talk. I need to know, right away—what was your old boss' name? The one you've been dreaming about?"

She listened, her face growing pale. "I've got to go. I'll call you as soon as I can—and thank you." She hung up and turned toward the men. "Hal, you know about my sister, how good she is at putting two and two together in her dreams. She was wondering who planted the bomb, and I suggested—well, you can guess what I suggested. And she's been dreaming about your Director. Mr. Shaw. Arthur—you really think the Director..." She held up her hand, her new left hand. "He did this? And all the rest?"

Arthur nodded, gazing at her.

Wynne grasped her left hand with her right. "I just—I just saw him. Talked to him."

Hal grabbed her shoulder. "*Where?*"

"At your mother's place. The nursing home." She paused, her forehead wrinkled and her lips parted, obviously trying to recall as much as she could. "I knew I'd met him, but I couldn't place him. And he greeted me. He called me Mrs. Wakeman and said we'd met at the policeman's ball years ago. I came there with Arthur." She turned to Arthur and Hannah. "Hal and I weren't married then. In the back of my mind, that got my attention, but I didn't really think about it. He was connecting me with Hal. That would make sense, if he was thinking about—about the explosion, and Hal's arrest. But he didn't say, oh, I heard what happened, how dreadful, are you all right? He was—jovial, and talking about seeing me with Arthur—and still he called me Mrs. Wakeman. It was—odd."

Hannah stirred uneasily on the sofa. "Arthur, a moment ago you said that if the Director really is the one, that he could turn on us, any time. And Ms. Cantrell—Wynne—you said you met him where Hal's mother lives?"

They all stared dumbly at Hannah. Then Hal grabbed frantically for his phone and started punching numbers, muttering. "Answer, God damn it, answer!"

* * *

Wynne held her breath as she watched Hal's hand, gripping the phone so hard she thought it might fall to pieces.

"Hello! Hello? This is Hal Wakeman. Evelyn Wakeman's son. We're going to be coming to pick up my mother, quite soon. She's—she's going on a trip with us. I know I hadn't mentioned it. I was going to call next week, but we got a chance for a discount if we moved things up. Please have someone pack a bag for her, right away."

He paused, listening. The he breathed in sharply and turned toward the rest of them, saying hoarsely into the phone, "Would you repeat that, please?" He set the phone to speaker and held it toward them.

The voice of the woman on the phone sounded a little confused. "I said, I know about the trip. Your driver is already here, and we're packing your mother's bag."

Hal took the call off speaker again. "My driver." Hal was whispering; Wynne wondered if the woman could even hear him. Then, suddenly, he was speaking slowly, distinctly, into the phone, with an eerie imitation of calm. "Please listen to me. Please listen very carefully. The man—is it a man?... That man is not my driver. That man is not my agent in any way. Do not, repeat, DO NOT release my mother into his custody. Do not let him be alone with her. Do not let him anywhere near her. *Do you understand?"*

Hal's face relaxed just a bit as he listened to the woman's response. Then he went on: "I know you've been talking to him, but get a good, long look at him. Try to memorize his face. If you can come up with an excuse, take a photo of something and get him in it... I know that may not work.... If you can do it without arousing his suspicions, then please try to stall him. Say there's something they're trying to find, something the old woman insists on taking with her. You can laugh about it, about silly old women and their whims. Offer him something to drink. Ask him if he's going on the trip. Keep him talking, and keep him there, for as long as you think it's safe. I'm on my way."

He hung up, already running for the door. Wynne called to him. "Here!" She tossed him the keys to the carlet. He grabbed them without stopping and yanked the door open.

"Hal, God damn it, hold on!" Arthur ran after him.

"No! You stay here! We don't know that my mother is the only target. Why would she be? You stay here with Wynne, Wynne and Hannah." Hal bit his lip, his face drawn. "I'll go pick up my father as soon as my mother is safe. We'll meet back here—no, I'll call you when I have them. We'll decide then where we're going."

"Hal, wait! How are you going to deal with this 'driver,' if he's still there?"

Hal closed his eyes for a moment. "If he's still there, I'll let the staff take care of Mom, while I deal with him. If that happens, I'll call you and ask you to go get Dad. But I don't think he'll be there. I think as soon as they start to stall him, he'll disappear."

And Hal was gone, thundering down the stairs.

Chapter 31

Hal stamped on the carlet's gas pedal and cursed the vehicle's limitations. If they had bought the muscle car that had tempted him, he would be almost there. Unless, of course, some traffic cop, always suspicious of a car with old-fashioned power, pulled him over. It might be just as well he could not yield to temptation.

He ignored the parking lot and pulled up in front, jumping out and racing up the ramp, then pulling up short to avoid crashing into the office administrator standing in the open doorway. Her demeanor, fluctuating between nervous and defiant, told him that his quarry had escaped. He stalked silently past her; she scurried after him, talking to his back. "I told him you were coming yourself, that you'd changed your mind about having anyone else fetch your mother. I thought he was going to hit me for a second! Then he left. I had to think of the safety of the patients. All of them, not just your mother."

He spun on his heel and glared at her, then realized he could not afford the luxury of showing such anger. He took a deep breath and tried to force a smile. "I'm sorry. I'm just—concerned. I shouldn't have put you in such a difficult position."

The woman relaxed a little. "I did try to memorize his face. I could do that without him knowing. And I jotted down some notes." She held out a paper. He grabbed it, folded it and thrust it in his pocket before turning away and walking, as quickly as he could without running, to his mother's room.

She was standing by her bed, leaning a little on the metal frame at its base, looking small and frail and bewildered. He swallowed the lump that came to his throat and went to embrace her. "I'm here, Mom. And I'm taking you with me for a while. You and Dad are going on a little trip with Wynne and me and—and a couple of friends."

He released her and looked for whatever suitcase the staff had packed, just as she pointed toward it. "The aide, that nice young man, said something like that. I wasn't sure I'd heard him right. You're taking me away?"

"For a little while. Then—then, we'll see." He picked up the suitcase, fetched his mother's cane, and handed it to her. He escorted her slowly to the door, then down the hall toward the front of the building. The administrator hung back, evidently not eager for any further confrontation.

They had just stepped out into the open air when his mother stopped short. "Oh, I forgot!"

Hal sighed. Of course. "Is it something you have to have, even for just a few days?" Not that he knew how long they might have to hide.

Her lip trembled, and her eyes filled. "My dream. The dream Wynne gave me. Couldn't we go back for it?"

Hal's nerves screamed at him to say no, to hurry her away. Wynne could make another: she would no doubt take her special recording helmet with her, wherever they went. Then he reconsidered. Their adversary's agent might return, or another might come, searching for clues or for anything else to use against them. He would not leave that dream, full of their family's history and prepared with such love, for the enemy to seize.

As quickly as Hal could manage, he and his mother returned to her room. She hobbled to the bureau, opened it, rummaged around, and pulled out the helmet, a momentary gleam of triumph lighting her face. Hal checked that the recording was in its slot before ushering her back out the door.

***

As soon as Hal's pounding footsteps died away, Arthur turned to Hannah. "I'm going to pack a few things. I'm not sure what we should do for the two of you—whether we should risk going to your homes for any belongings or just stop at a Wal-Mart somewhere."

Wynne tried to think. "My helmet's in the car, and I always keep a few blanks with it. That's all I really need that I couldn't pick up at a store."

Hannah shrugged, with a who-cares twitch of her eyebrows. "Hey, Wal-Mart for me! Who do I need to impress with my fashion sense?"

Wynne thought she saw some brief, faint protest in Arthur's face, but he said nothing more and headed to his bedroom. Hannah laid her hand gently on Wynne's arm and ushered her toward the sofa. "Let's sit down while we wait. There are some things we haven't had a chance to catch you up on—and you need to be fully in the loop."

* * *

Arthur tiptoed to the bend in the hall and peeked around toward the living room. He could hear only the rise and fall of voices, without the actual words. Hannah was holding Wynne's right hand.

He saw Wynne flinch backward and stare at Hannah, eyes wide. He trudged back into his bedroom to close his suitcase, then resumed his station in the hall. He would make sure not to interrupt them too soon.

* * *

Wynne shook her head in wonder. "So when Hal had to share that recording of what happened to me—it helped him understand me better?"

"More than that, we think. Of course, he already cared for you, loved you!—but that caring would have been reinforced as well."

Wynne laughed a little, then sighed. "And I thought he was cherishing me more because he almost lost me... that he was trying harder. But you're saying it wasn't his doing—not really."

Hannah raised an eyebrow. "We can't know that. What you assumed very likely did happen. The playback made it easier, maybe. And there's nothing wrong with that."

Wynne tried to absorb what Hannah had said, to think it through. "My recording..." She gasped. "My dreams! All the dreams out there! My God, are all my clients—"

"We don't know. The data we're piecing together has more to do with the recordings used in the justice system. But it could be. In retrospect, is there anything that's happened, that you know of, to suggest a similar effect from dream recordings?"

Her fans, so devoted, and sometimes so insightful..."I'm not sure. But maybe so."

Wynne gazed off in the direction where Arthur had gone, presumably to his bedroom. "What does Arthur make of all this? It must seem very strange to him."

Hannah looked unaccountably embarrassed. She raised her voice from the soft tones she had been using. "I think Arthur should answer that question."

* * *

Arthur ground his teeth at the way Hannah was forcing his hand, but obediently came into the living room, setting down his suitcase. Hannah patted Wynne's hand and stood up. "I'll go make us a snack—something we can eat on the road. We'll need to get going as soon as we can."

Wynne gestured toward the vacated section of sofa, smiling at Arthur. "Do sit." Then she laughed. "Listen to me, playing the hostess in your own apartment!"

"It's quite all right." He sat as close to her as he dared.

Wynne bit her lip. "Arthur, I'm trying to make sense of all this, and I'm not sure how. I'm a bit worried about Hal. If dream recordings do act like the others… do you think he'll be jealous? Of my clients?"

How to get from this peripheral concern to his own confession? "I think Hal knows there are a lot of other things to think about and worry about first."

She looked at him with sorrowful concern. "I'm so sorry you've got dragged into all this. Just because you did your job so well, you've got to throw in your lot with us and even go into hiding. It's terribly unfair!"

Arthur closed his eyes for a moment and heaved a giant sigh before opening them to see Wynne's bewildered expression. "Actually, I haven't been dragged in. I dragged myself in. And I owe you—and Hal—the most profound apology."

* * *

Wynne stared at Arthur, now sitting against the end of the sofa with his face flushing red and looking down at his clasped hands. She could hardly believe what he had told her, but he could not possibly have lied.

Arthur had endured that hell—and for what? Surely not from mere investigative zeal. He was dedicated, yes, but no fanatic. Had he wanted so badly to prove—to believe—that Hal was guilty? Had it been some unconscious romantic need to share her suffering?

And now, whatever his motivations before, he was trapped. Already, so unfortunately, carrying an unextinguished torch for her in spite of her marriage, now he had unwittingly made himself even more her slave.

She reached out to take his hand, then thought better of it. "Oh, Arthur. You poor, dear, foolish man."

Hannah re-entered the room, carrying a bulging paper sack. "I made every kind of sandwich you had the fixings for, and threw in some fruit and cookies." She threw Arthur a smile. "I'm glad to see you know the first rule of housekeeping: the kitchen must have cookies!"

Wynne caught the flicker of appreciation in Arthur's eyes and stashed it away for future thought. There might, after all, be some better future for Arthur than hopeless and artificially augmented devotion to another knight's lady.

* * *

Hal offered up a silent prayer of thanks that his parents had kept their large and unfashionable car. There was no way the entire party could all have crammed into the carlet. In this behemoth, Hal and Wynne and Arthur could fit in front, with Hal's parents and Hannah in the back.

And in the glove compartment, of course, was Harold Senior's even less fashionable gun. Hal had always regarded it with a mixture of queasiness and contempt. Now, he thanked heaven and his father's intransigence that they were not entirely defenseless.

The car was too conspicuous; they would have to hole up somewhere as soon as possible, to reduce the number of people who noticed it. The witnesses' huffy disapproval would make them all too likely to remember what they had seen.

He would have liked to ask Wynne to drive. He was still feeling shaky from the ebb of adrenalin. Reluctantly he kept the wheel: Wynne had never driven anything this large and heavy.

After consultation with the others, they had chosen a destination to which he knew the way. Arthur's various proposed safe houses all shared the same potentially fatal disadvantage: they were known to one or more members of the department and referenced in various official files. Hal had searched his memory, caucused with his father, and come up with a campground that had enclosed and fairly comfortable cabins, not many hours away and reachable by uncrowded routes. They did not even have to go online to check on its status: Wynne, once they mentioned the place, had seen an ad for it in a throwaway paper at her beauty parlor, only weeks before. They would head there and hope for a vacancy. They were likely to find one: the campground stayed open through the winter, but relatively few people took advantage of the fact.

Hal tried to think of what he might be forgetting. He could tell there was something, something important. Did he have any meetings scheduled? Only tentatively, and if he failed to confirm, the Parks Commissioner would probably grumble and concentrate on more urgent business rather than trying to make contact. Was anyone coming to the house, to check for pests or—

He started and almost swerved onto the shoulder. "Wynne—the dog!"

"Yes, darling. I already called the neighbors and asked them to look after her for a few days. I told them where the key is hidden. Arthur helped me work out what to tell them."

He relaxed against the seat. Of course, he should have known she would remember.

Wynne's phone buzzed for her attention. She fished it out, peering at the number. "It's the neighbors. Could the key be missing?" She answered the call, listened, gasped, and burst into tears.

Hal scanned the road ahead frantically, looking for a turnout. He saw one that might be just big enough, swung into it, and slammed on the brakes. His mother squealed, and his father mumbled some protest; Hal apologized and turned to Wynne, who was listening again, clutching the phone, nodding as she cried.

Finally she spoke. "I'm so sorry you had to see that. Thank you so much for—we'll collect her when we get back into town, and—and lay her to rest. I'll call you."

She hung up, found a tissue and blew her nose. Then she threw herself across the front seat and clung to Hal.

He stroked her hair. "Bitsy?"

"They went over together to play with her and take her for a walk. Th-they found her... Someone..." She burst into sobs. He held her until she quieted enough to continue. "Someone *stomped* her to death."

Hal clenched his left fist so tight the nails cut into his palm, all the while continuing to stroke Wynne's hair with his right hand. "Did they see any sign of who might have broken in?"

She gulped and shook her head. "Not exactly. But—they did see blood. On the floor. And not—where they found it, it didn't look like Bitsy's blood. They think she must have bit whoever it was. I think they're wondering whether it was a burglar she attacked, who killed her in self-defense."

"I suppose it might have been."

She looked up at him. "You think it was somebody the Director sent."

"Yes, I do." If only it had been the man himself, if Bitsy had drawn their enemy's blood as her final act! But it must have been just another hired henchman.

* * *

Tertius Shaw held the cloth saturated with hydrogen peroxide against his ankle, grimly enduring the sting. He deserved the pain. It had been intolerably self-indulgent of him to go to the couple's residence in person. He knew better than to take such risks—even if exposure, rather than a ravaged ankle, was the more likely outcome.

He had felt thwarted, naturally, when his agent had reported failure in obtaining the old woman. Harold Wakeman had somehow anticipated him. Tertius had been concentrating too much on Arthur and his investigation, and had missed something. Any such failure of course irritated him, but irritation was no excuse to make other errors. Targeting Wakeman's wife, after initially rejecting her as tainted goods, was such an error—and attempting the pickup in person certainly had been.

He would need to find ways to focus, to calm his mind. Another session with his current subject might serve. And if not, he could proceed to the final phase of that experiment.

CHAPTER 32

IT TOOK A WHILE to decide who should go into the campground office. They had no way to know which of them the Director might have publicized as a dangerous felon. Arthur's credentials might be useful, if the clerk was not too diligent about confirming them; but Arthur was relieved when Hal's father was eventually selected, as possibly familiar to the staff. Arthur could imagine all too well proving to be the weak link that brought their pursuer down upon them.

Once they had checked in and claimed their cabin, they all felt too restless to sit inside. Hal went out to scout, and came back reporting that the campground was sparsely populated, with no one else appearing to have rented a cabin in their little cluster. The group of cabins had its own fire pit, largely clear of snow, with wood and kindling stacked nearby; they quickly agreed to stare at a bonfire instead of simply each other. Just too late, Arthur was struck with appalled remorse: would fire serve as a trigger for Wynne's memories of torment? He could compartmentalize the secondhand memory, but what of her?

Wynne, however, showed no sign of any feeling but pleasant anticipation. Afraid of his own daring, he tried to clear his mind and let his illicitly gained knowledge of Wynne's feelings provide an explanation, and soon he had a sense of childish delight in a succession of Yule logs, blazing in the same family fireplace. Mercifully, the explosion had not tainted that memory.

Hannah helped Hal's father navigate the short, leaf-strewn path, while Wynne guided Hal's mother and the younger men built the fire. As the flames leapt up, Arthur sat down heavily on the long log bench, watched the fire dance, and began to relax.

Wynne was the first to speak. "I've been thinking about something we could do. It might not work, and there might be some—some objections to part of it. So let me ask, first: does anyone have any plans I don't know about yet about how to find out for sure if the Director is the one you're after, or what to do if he is?"

Arthur looked around the circle and saw the others doing the same. He himself had had no time to think since Hannah's stunning revelations, and he doubted any of the others had gotten any further.

No one responded. Wynne took a deep breath and went on. "Hal, I've already mentioned this to you—the beginning of it. Let me get the others up to where you are. For a couple of weeks, my agency had to stop delivering dreams, because someone...."

As Wynne told her tale of a teenage miscreant invading people's minds, distorting their dreams for his vengeful amusement, Arthur found it harder and harder to sit still. This was the sort of perp he would take great pleasure in bringing to justice. But the injured party, like so many such, had chosen to act outside the system, letting the guilty go unpunished for its own commercial ends.

And now Wynne had some notion of borrowing this hacker's illegal methods, using them against Shaw. She wanted him to try eavesdropping on any recordings Shaw might play. And she seemed to have some second stage in mind, something she didn't want to explain just yet.

Wynne's scheme, amorphous as it was, made him think of the phrase "so crazy it just might work." Arthur was not among those who used that phrase or tended to believe it. "You want to trust this juvenile delinquent with all our lives??"

Wynne bristled at him. "I don't want our lives to be in danger! I don't like any of this one bit! But we have to do *something.*" She calmed down quickly, as always. "And I think we can trust him to grab this chance. We're giving him a way to keep playing his little game. And we're giving him a—a monster to play *against*. He'll be thrilled."

Hannah spoke, for the first time in some minutes. "Or scared to death."

***

Wynne heard Hannah's words and felt them reverberate inside her. Scared to death. Scared. Scared.

Terrified.

She did not think any of the others had followed her train of thought far enough to know what she was facing. And she could leave things that way. She did not have to do what she was planning, even if it turned out to be possible.

But there might be nothing else to do.

***

Dream Daemon had fallen on his feet, for sure.

He'd been busted, but he wasn't in jail. He wasn't stuck in some halfway house with nothing computerized within reach. He wasn't on probation, with snooper software ensuring that his life was too boring to live.

No, he was out in the wilderness, with a bunch of crazy older people who needed him for some important, secret project. He could see why: they didn't seem very tech-savvy. It had been up to him to make sure that no one had planted a bug on him before the cold, silent dude picked him up at the rendezvous point. That guy, Arthur Something, was the only snag (so far): he didn't seem one bit happy to have Dream Daemon around. Some sort of cop, he smelled like. But somehow, he was in on this caper, whatever it was.

And now, the sexy older woman was going to explain his mission. At least the first part of it.

"First, D.D.—" (a reasonable abbreviation, and much better than Bert) "—we need to try to find out whether our suspect is really the culprit. We have his address, and we need you to find whatever helmet is in use there, while it's being used, and then help us do some eavesdropping."

That should be simple, at least for him. And very, very illegal. Was this some sort of elaborate sting operation? If he did what this babe suggested, would the glowering cop type clap the cuffs on him?

"You all want me to do this." He looked around the circle. All of them nodded, with varying degrees of apparent reluctance.

"Then you need to, I dunno, sign something, or let me record you telling me to do it. And I'll stash the record somewhere safe."

The cop and the babe's husband looked at each other. The husband said to the cop: "I know you don't like any of this. But we're up to our eyeballs already. It won't make things any worse."

The cop looked like he'd eaten a lemon in one gulp, but he nodded.

The babe smiled at Dream Daemon. "We'll do it. Whenever you're ready."

With the CYA taken care of, Dream Daemon took the information provided and set to work. First he checked for helmets at the address they gave him. He found one and set up an alarm to let him know when anyone used the helmet to record or play.

In the background, the two men had a pretty heated discussion going. Every once in a while, one of the women would try to interrupt, with "I don't see why I couldn't—" or "I'm perfectly capable of...." Every time, the men ignored or squelched what the women were saying. They were pretty rude about it, too.

Finally, the cop came up to him, his face flushed. "Has anyone used the device since you set your alarms?"

Dream Daemon smiled smugly at him. "Just recorded something a few minutes ago."

The cop went from flushed to pale. "I need to tap in on the next playback. How long will it take to set up?"

Dream Daemon tapped in a few commands and picked up the helmet they had given him. "Once the time is right, you just put it on and hit this button."

The cop took the helmet, his hand actually shaking. The poor sap looked terrified.

* * *

Arthur vividly remembered the last time he had felt this ill—after playing Wynne's recording. He locked his jaw, fighting the nausea. He would try with all his might to wait until afterward, until he could walk off into the woods and privacy, before giving way.

It could be hours, or even days, before the signal—but Arthur thought not. The Director (or so they were assuming) had just made a new recording. Surely he would be eager to experience it.

The others had tried hard, all of them, to claim this duty. They must be relieved at their defeat. He was the officer of the law, charged with hunting down predators like the one they were pursuing. He had chosen, long since, to be exposed to the twisted and evil side of human nature. And alone among their band of conspirators, he had chosen, as well, to break the law and play a recording in pursuit of that calling.

So there was no use wishing that somehow this cup would pass from him.

The excited young voice from the other side of the cabin made him jump. "He's doing it! It's about to start!" The hacker held out the helmet, then pulled it back toward himself, his eyes wide. "But he's doing something weird. He's set his helmet to record and play back at the same time. Like he's recording himself playing the recording? Huh."

There was no time to think, to weigh the consequences if he did as he had promised. At least, whatever the price to be paid, Wynne and Hannah would not have to pay it.

Arthur felt as if someone else were reaching for the helmet, placing it on his head, and pushing the playback button.

There was a moment of transition, a buzzing that went through his teeth and down his spine—and then it began.

He was young, female, and very frightened; immobilized, tied in a spread-eagle position with some sort of bindings, soft but strong. He was looking at a mask. The masked figure held a bottle, a small one, and looked her up and down, his gaze lingering as if in appreciation on her neck, her breasts, her thighs.

And then the masked figure spoke. (In that corner of his mind where Arthur remained Arthur, he knew that he was transforming the vague impression of speech, and the speech's emotional content, into his own words.) The tone was smooth, almost soothing. "You've been a very good guest, my dear." (The submerged Arthur recognized something about the speaker or his voice.) "But your visit will be ending soon, in a few days at most. Before then, we have some more experiences to share."

Mesmerized, she watched as the man, with delicate, almost surgical movements, slowly unscrewed the cap of the bottle, and replaced it with a sort of eyedropper. "Ready?"

He came closer, very close, near her exposed armpit. Then he placed the dropper against her upper arm, above the armpit, and squeezed the acid onto her skin.

Arthur screamed and tried to thrash about, but could not move. She screamed again as the torturer stepped to the other side of her and applied the acid to the same spot on her other side. There was a moment of what would have been respite, if not for the throbbing of the burned places. She opened the eyes she had squeezed shut in her agony and saw the clever fingers at work again, exchanging the dropper for a nozzle. A nozzle for spraying....

Arthur swam back toward consciousness, the smell of vomit in his nostrils. The helmet no longer pressed against his skull. He felt the hard floor beneath his back and legs, and something soft beneath his head and shoulders. Wynne, sweet Wynne, was sitting on the floor and holding his head in her lap, as warm drops of water fell on his face, one by one.

"It's him." Arthur could not stop shaking, not yet, but he could speak, even if his teeth rattled as he spoke. He sat between Hannah and Wynne, drawing comfort from their warmth. "I'd have trouble explaining how I know—but I know. It's him."

Hal cleared his throat. "Is there anything else you remember that you think we need to know? Is... is the latest victim still alive?"

Arthur forced himself to recall what he could. "I think so. I don't know if I made it to the end, but.... Wait a minute. That's odd."

They waited for him to explain.

"I remember now. I didn't pass out until just after it was over. But it wasn't over. The playback—it cut out in... in mid-scream."

CHAPTER 33

THIS WAS GETTING entirely out of hand.

Tertius had not even finished the latest playback. A most unnatural and inconvenient feeling had disturbed him: a sense of discomfort at the sight and sound of the young woman's suffering. He had turned the helmet off and even flung it across the room.

He inspected the device. It showed no sign of damage. That was fortunate: it would not, under present circumstances, be entirely prudent to obtain another. The remaining prototypes he had retained when leaving the development team lacked his most recent refinements.

But would he have needed a replacement? Should he accept that this entertainment came with too many unquantifiable and undesirable side effects?

He could return to his previous habits and abandon this latest permutation, this indulgence that might—if trends continued— threaten his enjoyment of many of his pastimes.

And yet... how bland the old days seemed, in retrospect, without the added immediacy and intensity of playback!

He tucked the helmet back in its usual place, and headed off to grill a veal chop for his lunch. He would ponder the matter with the help of a bottle of Chateauneuf du Pape.

* * *

Arthur sat in the cabin's kitchen nook, wishing he could somehow get warm. From the demeanor of the others, he was the only one who felt cold. He had found extra blankets and wrapped two of them around himself, but they helped only a little.

Hannah took one look at him, handed him a mug of coffee, and told him to sit while she fixed him some breakfast. The campground had its own little store, so they had not had to risk the outside world to buy food.

He sat warming his hands on the coffee mug for a few minutes before he bestirred himself to take a sip. Hannah soon reappeared with a mug and plate, steam rising from both. The plate held scrambled eggs, and—waffles? The cabin kitchen had its luxuries, then.

She put the plate in front of him and stood over him, waiting, then sighed and put the fork in his hand. "Eat, boss. We've got things to do."

He tried to think through the fog in his brain. "Things...?"

"Eat!"

He managed to get a forkful of eggs and lift it to his mouth. Oh, he was hungry. He ate with increasingly sure movements and gulped down the rest of the coffee. Hannah pulled up a chair and sat down next to him. "First, we'll need to get a search warrant."

"A warrant." Of course. And later, backup, and plenty of it. But how? Already a suspect, and now on the run: he could hardly trot into a courthouse and talk to a judge. Whom could he trust?

"I've got the Deputy Director's private number."

Bless the girl! But would even that be safe? Was the deputy still uncorrupted? Had she ever been?

"Boss, we've got to take some chances. This is one."

He swallowed a bite and laughed. "Stop reading my mind."

She leaned over and patted him on the head. "Part of my job, boss. You'd miss it if I quit." He jerked his head toward her in alarm. She chuckled. "Quit reading your mind, I mean. I don't plan on quitting my job. Someone needs to keep you out of trouble." Her face grew grave. "Though I haven't been managing so well, it seems. You've been getting good at finding trouble."

Neither of them spoke further as he finished his breakfast. Arthur carried his plate and fork to the sink and swung by the stove for more coffee. "The search warrant, then. Let's get cracking."

Arthur swallowed his scruples and ordered the hacker to set up a call: untraceable, untrackable, voice only. When the boy had the Deputy Director on the line, innocently waiting to speak to the mayor's appointments secretary, Arthur took over.

"Arthur Kellic here. Things are happening, and I'm going to need your help."

"*Arthur*? Where the devil are you? I've been trying to keep anyone from knowing that you disappeared, but sooner or later someone in the department will figure it out —"

"Where I am is on the trail of our bomber, also our kidnapper. And if you thought things were ticklish and likely to blow up in your face, brace yourself, because they're actually a lot worse...."

Arthur was almost sorry that he had not, after all, made the call with visual included, in spite of the security risks. He would have liked to see the Deputy Director's face as his revelations sank in.

But she moved with admirable speed from astonishment and dismay to grim efficiency.

"So you'll need all the resources and access available to a senior department official on active duty—without anyone at headquarters, no, anyone else on staff, knowing about it ahead of time."

"Can you manage it?"

She answered with an unfamiliar low chuckle. "Just don't ask me how. Maybe I'll tell your assistant later. She'd probably appreciate the details."

They arranged a second phone call for two hours later. By then, she had set up the essentials, starting with a secure number he could use to contact a generally accommodating judge. It was time for the search warrant.

He had had to lie.

If he had not known about the hacker until afterward, he could have taken the information as a gift. A civilian brings him a civilian informant: acceptable. An officer of the law connives with a civilian lawbreaker to perform an illegal search: unacceptable.

Maybe he could have stopped Wynne from explaining the scheme in his presence. He had not been operating at his normal capacity. Ever since the explosion, ever since Wynne was injured, he had let events and his own impulses take control.

Arthur left the cabin and stood on the porch, gazing into the woods. Hannah came out and joined him, standing silently beside him. Finally he spoke, still facing the woods.

"This is my last case."

"I know."

He turned toward her. "Resigning's too easy. I should be fired. Maybe I'll tell the whole story afterward, and let them fire me."

Hannah shook her head. "You can't. Whenever you told it, you'd be letting him loose."

"Maybe not. Things have changed. There are so many exceptions now."

"You can't take that chance. Unless you think your public penance is worth letting that—that creature get out and keep preying on people, you can't say anything."

Arthur blew out his breath through pursed lips, producing a small puff of fog in the chilly air. "We're getting ahead of ourselves, aren't we? He's still out there, preying on people with impunity."

"And you've decided to stop him, the only way you can."

"But—I—"

Hannah took his hand. "I know. And you'll be paying for it. You love your job, and you'll be giving it up." She stood there, holding his hand, as the breeze carried to them the quiet winter scent of the woods. "What will you do? Instead?"

He had no answer. So he said nothing, letting her hold his hand, breathing the breeze, watching dusk fall.

* * *

Wynne looked across the campfire at the teenager hunched over his tablet, busy with who knew what mischief, and decided to make some attempt to get through to him.

"D.D., do you ever have nightmares?"

The boy preened at the sound of his chosen nickname, then registered the substance of her question. He glanced quickly in her direction, then looked back down at his screen. "Sure, sometimes. They're no big deal."

Wynne sighed. Perhaps, some day, when she was years older and more experienced—when she became a mother, a mother of a son, and understood both children and men a good deal better—she would know what to say next in such an exchange.

* * *

D.D. turned his face away from Ms. Cantrell in case he wasn't managing to control it completely. Out here in the woods, surrounded by strangers and on the hunt for a killer, he was jumpy enough already. Thanks a lot! He'd hardly thought about that old nightmare in years, and now he couldn't stop remembering, running it over and over in his mind....

(He's stranded on a rock, a slippery rock almost too small for his feet, and the fog is rising. Fog shouldn't smell, but this fog smells like rotting meat; and eyes keep appearing and disappearing, glowing evil eyes, getting closer and closer.... And his mom and her boyfriend, and even his dad, are standing somewhere nearby—he knows they are, even though the fog hides them—and when he yells for them to help him, the fog parts to show them standing together looking at him with that Oh Not Again expression, and then the fog hides them and he's alone again, alone in the fog, and he knows that any minute it will swallow him all up and he'll disappear forever....)

***

Wynne could only see the side of the boy's face, but she thought he looked pale. Maybe she'd made an impression after all. Maybe it was worth going on.

"We all have enough bad dreams, don't we?" She could not have said that, once. But she had earned the right, since the accident. The attack.

The boy jerked his head up and looked at her, face full of indignant protest. "But I don't give anyone really *bad* dreams! I just...." He sputtered to a stop.

"That's good to hear." She made a point of speaking gently. "But it's hard to know, sometimes, how a dream will seem to someone else. Did you ever have a dream that didn't sound strange or frightening when you told someone else about it, but somehow it just *was?*"

The boy's gaze turned inward with remembering, and he shuddered.

Perhaps she'd said enough.

***

No, he couldn't think of any dreams that were scary without sounding scary. But now he was remembering that other dream, or whatever it was—the one he'd found playing roulette, the one with the chocolate and the choking. If she knew he'd found *that* and had kept it to himself, maybe she'd know he wasn't some sort of sadist.

And he probably should tell someone. If it wasn't a dream, then there really was a girl getting hurt, or there had been. Wynne could tell that police fellow. Maybe they could put a stop to it.

***

Wynne listened to D.D.'s halting description with increasing dread. Hadn't Sara said something about her old boss—Tertius Shaw—and some sort of special chocolate? And hadn't she said he always sought out the best of everything? D.D. might actually have blundered upon a recording that Shaw had made, a recording of one of his victims. It might be the missing girl. Though there was no way to know how recently the recording had been made.

But D.D.'s experience certainly supported their hypothesis that Shaw was using helmet technology. Her plan, far-fetched as it had seemed when she first thought of it, might just provide an avenue of attack.

"Hon, what is it you think we should do next?"

Wynne took a deep breath. This would be the tricky part. She had to persuade them that what she planned was necessary. Both Hal and Arthur would be appalled, and either could prevent her from proceeding. She should have told Hannah first, privately, and tried to secure her support before this confrontation. Well, too late now.

If her plan were even possible.

"D.D., I know you can substitute one dream for another."

The boy sat up straighter, looking wary.

"Can you substitute a dream for a recording of waking experience? Is there any technical obstacle?"

The boy considered for a moment, then shook his head. "Don't see why not. Can't say for sure, but I bet I can."

Wynne slumped against the tattered leather armchair. The boy had no idea of how much, in spite of everything, she had been hoping for another answer.

(And when she explained, he would remember what she had said to him about dreams. He would probably think her a hypocrite and reject what she had said. But she had no choice.)

She turned toward the men. "We don't know exactly how someone like the Director—a deviant, maybe a sociopath—responds to playback, either to the content or to the more general effects you've discovered. But it's still worth trying to—to get to him, the only way we can." She smiled a little. "The way only we can."

Of course she would have to spell it out.

"I'll make a dream especially for him. To try to take him down."

The young woman they sought to save might be almost out of time. But Wynne needed to build up her strength and endurance before she could make the attempt.

They spent that day together, all of them: hiking, and playing in the stream, and talking very little. She tried to soak up all the peace and beauty of her surroundings, that she might have some wholesome and welcoming place to return to from where she would have to go.

Finally, at dusk, she faced the boy and Hannah and Arthur, trying to smile in reassurance. Then she turned toward Hal, his face drawn in anticipatory anguish. She could not wait much longer before starting to cry. Just in time, he opened his arms, and she nestled in his embrace for a few precious moments before taking the helmet into one of the small side bedrooms and closing the door.

She had never attempted anything remotely like this dream. She mapped it out beforehand with special care, even making notes of the sequence and reading them over and over. She had to get it right, as right as in her ignorance she could manage. It would be hours or days before she'd be in any shape to try again—which might be too long. And she must craft the sequence in such a way that it would follow its path no matter how the initial stages affected the dreamer.

She had thought of using pain, agony such as she herself had endured, but discarded the idea. His response to pain might be complex; he might relish receiving as well as inflicting it. But nausea—surely nausea, the worst kind, seasickness that made travelers wish they would drown and end it—such nausea would not arouse even a man like this.

And then must come the terror: terror that disarmed and unmanned, terror to leave any man gibbering and drooling and helpless.

Then, sorrow, the sorrows of the ages, sorrow to drown in.

And then, in a burst of realization that might just pierce the man's protections and overcome his inborn limitations—guilt. Horrified, paralyzing guilt. She would dredge up every trace memory of childhood remorse, every exaggerated penitence for misunderstood offenses and every stroke of justified shame for genuine wrongdoing, and intensify them as much as she was able.

And finally, she would move from emotional paralysis to physical. This, if nothing else, should affect even their quarry: to be trapped, entombed in rock like the ancient fossil of some long-ago cataclysm, utterly beyond any hope of moving until centuries had worn one's prison to dust.

If they planned exactly right, and if all their plans met with the favor of the fates, the man might be paralyzed and helpless for long enough that they could reach him.

***

Arthur hovered in the cabin's common area, knowing there was nothing he could do. Wynne was putting herself through hell, and her husband stood ready to comfort her, and Arthur had no place in this scene.

He could, at least, make sure that no one else in their party needed assistance. He stood outside the room shared by Hal's parents, an awkward intruder, listening to a whispered conversation he was glad he could not quite decipher. Then he moved on down the hall to the room where Hannah kept their hacker company—and under surveillance. All was quiet: Hannah might be reading, and the youngster was probably engrossed in some game or other.

He headed back toward the common area and the cabin's front door. The sounds coming from Wynne and Hal's bedroom were terrible. Hal stood just outside the room, his eyes wide, his face white.

Clenching his jaw, Arthur reached the front door and spoke to Hal's back. "I'm taking a walk. I won't go far—call if I'm needed." Then he stumbled out into the night.

***

Hal made himself wait, clutching the door frame to keep himself from bursting in, until the racking sobs, the pleading, the muffled cries, had finally ceased. When all was quiet within, he opened the door slowly and slipped inside. He stood over the bed where Wynne lay sleeping, the pillow beneath her head drenched with her tears, the sheets a tangle from her tossing.

It took two attempts before he could force himself to touch the helmet on her head and remove it. He dropped the thing on the chest of drawers and returned to his wife, smoothing the twisted strands of her hair and kissing her forehead. He stood by the bed for a few minutes, listening to her soft breathing, and then slipped out the door.

Chapter 34

Hal did not even try to sleep that night. Somewhat incongruously, the cabin came equipped with sleep inducers for those guests unused to the quiet (or the few but unfamiliar noises) of the forest; but even the thought of lying down motionless for hours made him more restless. He checked on Wynne once more, then secured a flashlight and tiptoed outside. He checked as well as he could around the cabin and told himself not to go far. Then he bundled up and strode out on the nearest path, taking deep gulps of the chill night air, savoring the smell of earth and snow and crumbled leaves.

As he walked, the moon appeared between the trees and then hid again, never lighting his path for long before the shadows returned to hinder him. Just when he was reluctantly concluding he would have to turn back, he noticed a large flat rock in a small clearing, and saw also that he was no longer alone. Arthur sat on the edge of the rock, hunched over, his chin in his hands, staring off into the darkness of the trees beyond.

Hal walked forward, then hesitated. Arthur turned at the sound of footsteps, smiled a little, and gestured toward the rock. "Sit down, if you'd care to."

Hal accepted the invitation, seating himself carefully to avoid the rougher parts of the rock surface. He waited a moment before he spoke. "Big, hairy day tomorrow."

Arthur snorted. "You might just be understating the case." He shook his head, then sat up straighter; Hal could feel the sudden tension in him. "There's something I haven't said, and need to say. If you hadn't turned up, I was going to try to get you away from the others before we left." A pause. "Though I suppose I should do it more publicly. But I don't want to wait any longer."

Despite that declaration, Arthur paused again, long enough that Hal was growing irritated and ready to prompt him. Then Arthur inhaled audibly, turned toward Hal, and said, "I don't know how to apologize, how to apologize *enough*, for what I did to you."

Hal looked down at his own suddenly clenched fists. He had managed to forget, most of the time, the role Arthur must have played in Hal's prosecution and conviction. But if he had had any doubts, Arthur had just banished them. Did Arthur have any idea just what—

Not at the time, perhaps. But now he knew full well what Hal had suffered. Though if not for Hal's father and lawyer, that would have been just the beginning. The very thought of that narrowly escaped fate made Hal's gorge rise. He would surely have gone mad....

Arthur cleared his throat and spoke again. "I guess I still haven't done it, have I? I'm genuinely and terribly sorry. I know there's nothing I can do to change what happened. I believe you understand why I jumped to the conclusions I did. But my training and experience should have kept me from doing it."

"They sure as hell should have. I just hope you never did the same to anyone else, based on any other personal agenda."

Arthur flinched. "I don't think so. I really don't. I've never had much—much of anything personal, besides Wynne, that could cloud my judgment."

Hal turned to look at Arthur, still staring into the woods. "I suppose you'd like me to forgive you."

Arthur shrugged. "You'd think so. But I'm not sure what that means. It isn't absolution, even if I believed in absolution. I'd still be as guilty. You'd still be as wronged."

Hal pondered for a moment. "That's all true. But they do say that forgiveness is more for the benefit of the person wronged. If they're right, and I could manage to forgive you, it might make me feel better. Which I imagine you want—or you think you're supposed to want."

"I do want it. God, I'd love to know that you're suffering less, for any reason." Arthur picked up some pebbles at the base of the rock and started tossing them into the wood. He did not seem to be aiming at anything, and they fell haphazardly, some with the quiet "thunk" of impact with a tree trunk, some coming to rest almost silently on a blanket of leaves.

"Well, then, I guess it'd be a kindness—of a sort—to tell you something. And if it hurts you, in another way, then that can be part of your punishment."

Arthur turned toward Hal, eyes wide in the dim light. Hal went on, watching Arthur's face, measuring the impact of his words.

"Something good has come of what happened—what you did to me. And you must already know it, or you have reason to. Getting the helmet, going through that playback— you know what it can do. And it has. I understand Wynne better. I've become less of a selfish bastard, where Wynne is concerned—maybe just in time. And she's very, very glad about it. We're closer than ever. We're solid. We've become what a husband and wife should be."

Arthur bowed his head and turned his face enough that Hal could no longer see his eyes. He might guess that there were tears to be hidden, and he could take some satisfaction from that guess; but he would not act to see if it were so.

Hal stood up. "I'm going back to the cabin. I think I'll make myself sleep. You should do the same." He hesitated, then went on. "We're going to—we're all going to need you tomorrow. You should sleep."

* * *

Wynne still seemed fragile the next morning, pale and shaky, but Arthur reluctantly agreed that they could wait no longer. Every hour lessened their hope of saving the current hostage's life, and they themselves were in constant danger of discovery and the horrors that could follow.

Hal's parents would stay at the campground. Arthur arranged, with some persuasion and expense, for the staff to deliver ready-to-eat food and to check frequently that all was well. The rest of them would have to risk relocating to somewhere very near the Director's house. The dream was as long as Wynne had been able to make it, but they would still have only minutes to reach the house, break in, and — with exceptional good fortune — find the Director sufficiently distracted and disabled that they could overpower and arrest him. Whether Arthur in fact retained the authority to do so was yet another uncertainty.

The Director, naturally, lived in a neighborhood with no abandoned storefronts or obviously vacant houses. Hannah had scanned the real estate listings for the area and found three homes for sale within a few blocks of their target. Once again, Arthur had the hacker set up a secure line with which they could call real estate agents from the road. Hannah made the calls:

"I'm looking for a home for my in-laws, something quiet, not too close to the neighbors. They'd be particularly pleased if the owners had already moved out, so it'd be easier to imagine their own furniture and paintings and so on as they'd look in place...."

And on the final call:

"Wonderful! They'll be arriving next week to see the possibilities. Let's set a tentative date and time.... I'm looking forward to meeting you! Until then!"

She hung up and waggled her eyebrows at Arthur. "Am I good or am I good?"

He could not help but smile. But the scheme had a potentially fatal flaw. "What if they show the house to someone else in the meantime?"

The hacker cleared his throat. "They must have their calendar online. I could—I might be able to, ah, get a look. And if there are appointments, I could send some messages...."

Arthur grimaced. He was long past keeping his hands clean in this business. The stakes were too high for him to try.

They said their goodbyes to Hal's parents: his father solemn, his mother fluttering about in confusion, calling them by an assortment of names. This time, Arthur had no excuse to sit beside Wynne: he climbed into the back with Hannah and the hacker. Hannah, looking at his face, placed herself in the middle, keeping Arthur and the hacker as far apart as feasible.

They located the house easily enough. Arthur consulted his own records and found the patrol schedule for the local police. If he used his special master key, they could open the front door quickly, but it would be just as well to have no official observers.

They had an hour or so to wait. Since leaving the campground, they had not bothered to stop for food; now they used the delay to find the least objectionable drive-through option. As they approached the house again, Arthur tried to quiet his increasingly nervous stomach. He must have spent entirely too long behind a desk if he now found the prospect of action so disconcerting.

Or was something else trying to get through to him?

"Hal—wait. Pull over, please. I have to think for a minute."

Hal's shoulders stiffened, but whatever irritation he might be suppressing, he obeyed.

"Something's wrong."

Wynne turned around to face him, concerned for him in spite of her own condition. "Are you all right?"

Hal studied him with an appraising eye. "That recording you tapped into. Shaw recorded himself while he played it. Was that enough for the effect to kick in? Did you learn something?"

Arthur tried to focus, to follow the elusive thread that was tickling at him. "Maybe. I don't know. It's just...." The feeling crystallized, became a warning. "We can't go there. To that house."

Hannah took his hand in hers. "I know how hard this must be—but can you tell us anything more?"

Arthur gritted his teeth and fought his own reflex to recoil from the tainted knowledge lurking inside him. "I can't get to any details. But he'd notice if anything changed there. Maybe he always walks that way. Maybe he knew the people who used to live there. Maybe he's thinking of buying the house! All I know is there's a risk."

Hal made a hissing noise through his teeth, too impatient to be a sigh. "There's a risk. We're taking risks left and right. We can't avoid taking risks."

Wynne turned toward the hacker. "D.D., could you track our target's helmet and send the substitute dream from the car?"

The youngster smirked. "Sure. Piece o' cake."

"We could go back to the mall where we got our food. It's big enough that we could park in out-of-the-way spots and move every couple of hours. If nothing happens by nightfall, then if we have to, we can come back to the house and take our chances."

Arthur tried to remember what he knew of mall security. "We could try it. If someone notices that we're hanging around, we'll have to have some story—and then make ourselves scarce, as soon as it wouldn't look even more suspicious."

Hal said nothing more, but turned the car around, whistling some tune under his breath. After a moment, Arthur recognized it: a theme from the movie *The Charge of the Light Brigade.*

* * *

Tertius strolled around the neighborhood for his usual evening constitutional and paused outside the house around the corner, clucking at the state of the flowerbeds, which had not been properly prepared for winter. Even before the owners moved out, they had been derelict in their care of the garden. A few months back, noting its bedraggled condition, he had amused himself by returning surreptitiously at night and fertilizing the flowerbeds with some cremated ashes he had handy, mixed with an appropriate soil additive. The flowers consequently thrived; he made a point of congratulating the lady of the house, when next they met, on the beauty of her garden, and she had preened and thanked him with a truly ridiculous smile. He had toyed with the notion of converting her, in her turn, for the benefit of her garden, but had resisted indulging himself with someone so conspicuously close by. The flowers, naturally, soon returned to their previous lamentable condition; he assisted them once more, but the effect wore off even before the advent of winter.

There was a moral to be drawn, or a metaphor, concerning the futility of human endeavor, or at least of attempts to improve one's surroundings. He shook his head and continued on his route. He had, after all, a guest awaiting his attentions.

He had decided, for now, to use the peculiar effect of the playbacks as a positive, a tool, rather than recoiling from them. Surely he had that degree of self-discipline! Now that he seemed especially attuned to the subject's emotional reactions, he would play upon them as upon an instrument.

He might, indeed, be developing a novel art form, the creation of emotional lyric lines, with exquisitely timed rise and fall.

And her death, when it came, would provide a profound and solemn coda.

Chapter 35

Hal, watching the cars zooming in unpredictable directions across the parking lot as he moved their car for the second time, found himself distracted by the fidgeting of the teenaged computer expert in the back seat. The boy had not seemed to care that Arthur kept glowering at him, but now he seemed almost agitated. As soon as Hal pulled into their next spot, he turned around. "What's eating you?"

The boy looked nervously around the car. "I, uh, it's just that I forgot to mention something."

Arthur made a noise remarkably like a growl. "And just *what* didn't you tell us?"

Hannah shushed him. "That's not helping, boss. D.D., what is it we need to know?"

The boy's eyes darted around the car again. "It's the guy's helmet. There's a special setting on it. It lets you, him, the user, it lets him change the volume, you could say. Dial the intensity higher or lower."

Wynne moaned softly. "If the dream isn't completely as I recorded it, it may not work. It probably wouldn't."

Hal glared at the boy. "Well? Can you hack this special setting?"

The boy wriggled again. "I guess so. I mean, I've never done it, but I think I can. But it's going to be hard to do everything at once."

"Then do things one at a time, dammit! Once he starts playing a recording, crank up the volume on it and then swap ours in! Or no, the other way round!"

The boy shrank back against the rear seat. "Yeah. That makes sense. I'll try that."

Arthur leaned toward the hacker, crowding Hannah as she sat between them. Hannah shoved against his shoulder, then patted it. She shook her head and blew out her breath in a long, low whistle. "God of our fathers, look down upon this sorry crew and save our asses. Amen."

***

Wynne forced herself to stay awake. It would be so pleasant, just now, to escape into some playground of her making. She was exhausted from yesterday's labors and cramped from sitting in the car, desperate for movement and fresh air. As tired as she was, she could fall asleep in moments. Then she could bathe in a waterfall, or sing her heart out atop a mountain. Or zoom through a nebula, with no such bother as a need for air. Or indulge in a rollicking, mind-blowing, sweaty interlude of sexual congress with any partner, real or imagined.

But the others had no such respite to retreat to. And none of them could know who might be needed at any moment for some new curve ball or crisis. They had already had what seemed a call of action, when their young consultant had announced excitedly that the Director's helmet had been activated. But as they should have expected, it was set to record, not to play back. She tried not to think about what it might be recording. At least, if he continued making his recordings, he was likely to play one back sooner or later; the abrupt termination of the last playback had not been a permanent abandonment of his pastime.

Some of the others did seem to be trying to nap. The hacker was nodding over his keyboard. Hal leaned his head against the side of the car, his eyes closed, his breathing a bit heavy as it became when he was about to fall asleep. Sensing her eyes on him, he cracked one eye open and smiled faintly. "Hanging in there, sweetheart?"

She took his right hand and held it between hers, savoring the sensation of having two different hands with which to feel the texture of his palm and knuckles. "I'm fine. But I've never liked waiting, any more than you."

He snorted. "You've done a pretty good job of hiding it, more than once. So you're as impatient as I am?" He paused, as if consulting some unseen source. "I guess you are, at that."

She had always seen herself as the more insightful and empathetic of the two. It was strange to think that their positions might now be reversed. And she wanted so much to know him, all through, to know and to cherish....

"Hal? When we're finished with this, when we can go home again and have some time together, would you consider...." She stopped, remembering. How could she ask him to do something that might trigger that memory?

"What?" When she did not answer, she felt him tense, and then deliberately relax again. "Wynne, hon, what did you want me to do?"

Her throat had gone dry; she tried to swallow. "I'm sorry. I forgot, for a moment what it would mean."

He growled a little under his breath. "Didn't we just establish that we're both impatient? You're driving me nuts here. Come on—now you have to tell me."

The utter stillness from the back seat told her that they had acquired an unwanted audience. She beckoned him closer and whispered, "Could we get out of the car, just for a moment?"

Hal turned to the others in the back of the car. "We're going to stand outside, for just a few minutes. Arthur, if you're willing, could you climb up here and be ready to honk the horn if you need us back sooner?" Without waiting for an answer, he got out and came around to open her door.

He led her a little farther away from the mall, then turned to face her and placed his hands on her shoulders. "All right. What is it?"

She put out her hands and rested them on his hips. "Hal, my dear... I want to know you. To know you as well as I can. Better than I have. And we've stumbled on a way for me to do it."

His hands on her shoulders went rigid. "You want to record me?"

She bit her lip. "That's why I didn't want to tell you. I know how you feel—how you have every right to feel—about the thought of letting a helmet touch you. But... if you ever feel that you can somehow let that go, I'd like so much to have that gift—the gift of knowing you as you've come to know me."

He hesitated before answering her. "I hope I wouldn't disappoint you. I'm not sure you'd like me any better for knowing me."

She had no words to give him, but came close to him and fitted herself against him, holding him close. He squeezed her tight for a moment before releasing her and taking her hand, leading her back toward the car.

They had almost reached it when the horn started blaring.

* * *

Arthur gazed out the window of the car at Wynne and her husband. He had a pretty good notion what she had wanted to say to Hal. Would Hal have the courage to take her offer? Could any man who loved her refuse it?

He jumped at the shout from the back seat: the hacker, bouncing up and down in excitement. "It's starting! He's turned the helmet on!"

Arthur pounded the horn, once, twice, then slammed open the car door and cleared the way as Hal ran back to jump in the driver's seat. Arthur scrambled into the back as Wynne hastened to resume her own seat. He buckled his seat belt with some difficulty as Hal burned rubber toward the exit. "Slow down, man! We don't need to get stopped right now!"

Hal let up slightly on the accelerator; Arthur turned to the hacker. "What's happening now?"

"Shhhh! I have to get into the volume control!"

They all held their breaths, while the hacker pecked frantically away. "He's already pushed play... There it is!"

"DON'T turn up the volume yet!" Hal barked at him. "Send the new dream first!"

"Yeah, okay...." More punching at the keyboard. "It's on the way. And UP goes the volume! All the dials maxed. That sucker's gonna have quite a ride."

Hal sped up again. Arthur clung to the seat belt with one hand and extracted his phone from his pocket with the other, hunting for the emergency number that interfaced with the police radio frequency. He struggled to dial it even as the swerving of the car around a corner threw him against Hannah's shoulder.

Instead of the monotonous voice of a dispatcher, there came the shrill whine of a disconnected number. What the hell? He forced himself to breathe steadily, trying to clear his head.

Hannah reached for the phone, took it, and tapped away at it with brisk efficient movements. Of course! The number had changed; he remembered, now, a message from Hannah telling him to update his phone, a message he'd glanced at and forgotten. There was no time to thank her: she had already put the phone back in his hand. As he listened to the ringing, he had time to wonder if the Director had thought to leave some standing order, preventing emergency personnel from being sent to his house without confirmation from him. He could only hope not.

"This is Senior Detective Arthur Kellic! I need backup to this location, stat! I have a search warrant for premises containing possible violent felon and kidnapping victim!"

He held his breath again. Had the Deputy Director managed to clear the way for him?

He exhaled in one emphatic gust as he heard the dispatcher's flat, efficient tones, summoning the cavalry.

Now they just had to lead the charge. But what if their plan, their experiment, had failed? What if their quarry was too inhuman for any nightmare to overcome?

Chapter 36

Tertius Shaw loaded the helmet with his guest's penultimate recording. He had extracted all the variety of which she was capable, at least without an undue investment of his own energies. Indeed, he could not adequately explain just why he had kept her alive this long. Had he suffered so much emotional contamination that he was actually reluctant to kill?

Well, he would not indulge such weakness any longer. Tomorrow he would record her last moments and compare them to those of her brother and mother.

He had not given the girl as much pain as usual in their most recent session. The respite should make her response to tomorrow's encounter even more piquant. Still, he made sure his intensity controls were at twenty percent, high enough to savor but not enough to overwhelm.

It began, as before, with the girl's sense of Tertius' presence and her emotional reaction to his mask. Her—

What was happening?

He could no longer feel the viewpoint of the captive girl. She had melted away, somehow; he was himself, fully himself, more himself than ever, and something was terribly wrong, someone must have poisoned him, because he felt terribly sick. He had never been so nauseated, so appallingly ill. The room was lurching, heaving, spinning, throwing him around, falling away, rippling beneath him.... He had never felt anything so horrible. He would die if he could not vomit, vomit up whatever was killing him, killing him, something was killing him! He was afraid....

Afraid. *Afraid.* He was AFRAID, AFRAID, AFRAIDAFRAIDAFRAID—

He was the center of the universe, true, but such a small, fragile center, so easily crushed, and all around him, closing in on him, there were things, *things*, THINGS WITH TEETH LONG DRIPPING HORRIBLE TEETH AND GIANT SHARP BLOODY CLAWS CLOSERANDCLOSERANDCLOSER AAAAAAHHHHH

***

Wynne craned around and shouted to the hacker, "Where is he? How far into the dream?" The boy held up his screen and showed her the graph.

***

Unfair. Unfair. Things were poisoning him and attacking him, and he could not see them, had no way to fight them, and it was all unfair. He would die and be swallowed, and the universe would end, and all the wonder and beauty and intricacy and cunning that had been Tertius Shaw would be gone, gone, nothing but emptiness…. He grieved, keening, for the tragedy of it, the terrible loss.

***

Hal swerved the car to the curb in front of the house and slammed on the brakes. Arthur snapped open his seatbelt and lurched forward to place a restraining arm on Hal's shoulder. "We can wait a minute for the backup to arrive." He glanced over at the screen. A minute, perhaps; but they could not wait for long.

***

What had he done wrong? He had so many enemies, but he had always been cleverer than they. What had he missed, how had he failed? It was all his fault, this loss, this ruin, the end of everything, all his doing. What was it the Catholics said? *"Mea culpa, mea culpa, mea máxima culpa"*...my fault, my fault, my most grievous fault.... He had spoiled everything, everything....

* * *

"There they come!" Hannah shouted and pointed down the street. One car, only, but it should be enough. If they hurried. . . . The car pulled slowly to a stop. Arthur jumped out and ran toward it, dancing with impatience.

Hal looked at Arthur and the policemen. Arthur was speaking urgently, gesticulating, perhaps arguing; the body language of the police suggested skepticism. By the time Arthur could spur them into action it might be too late.

Hal grabbed his father's pistol from the glove compartment, shouted to the boy and the women to stay behind, and ran into the house.

* * *

If he had fallen short, perhaps he could still make amends. He had always been able to solve any problem. Tertius Shaw would rise to the occasion!

But he could not rise. He could not even move. The world had contracted around him. His legs, his arms, his chest, his head, every part of him was gripped by a cold, hard vise. There was no light. There was no sound. And all he could smell was dust, dust and age, a smell that would linger at the ending of the world.

The world had ended. The story was over. Nothing would ever happen again.

***

Hal stood in Director Shaw's living room, bits of slush from his boots melting on the deep plush carpet, gun hanging heavy at his side, and stared at the figure in the luxurious black leather armchair. The recessed lighting was turned low, as for a seduction, but he could see the contorted figure all too well. He was like a man writhing in agony and then flash-frozen, a sculpture (Hal felt the bile rise in his mouth) of anguish and terror. The light glinted dimly on the smooth polished surface of the helmet.

Arthur and the pair of policemen came running up behind him. The trio passed Hal and skidded to a stop, staring. One of the policemen let out a long, lyrical whistle. The other stepped forward and put a hand on the helmet. "Let's get this off him."

"Wait!" But Arthur's call came too late, or went unheeded; the helmet dangled in the cop's large slab of a hand. Hal stepped back quietly and brought the gun up to his hip.

Shaw's body melted back into normal human shape with astonishing rapidity, and his eyes opened. He snapped the back of the armchair to vertical and put his hands on the arm rests. The policemen put their right hands on their holsters, and the one without the helmet put out his left hand in warning. "Sir, we have a search warrant, issued in connection with the kidnapping of—"

"Oh, my stars." Shaw had summoned an expression of amusement, but his eyes glinted with hatred. "You're here with this disgraced employee, this obsessed paramour who broke laws left and right, and now you've invaded my home on his say-so? This farce has gone as far as it can, and now that he's pulled you into it, your own careers are in jeopardy.

But if you depart and leave me in peace, I'm prepared to forget your faces, and your badge numbers, Mr. 43562 and 71921 —" (what vision the man must have, to see the numbers in this light!) "—and to confine the disciplinary and legal consequences to Mr. Kellic and his friends."

Arthur pulled out the search warrant. Hal felt a certain pride that Arthur's hand did not shake. "Where's the girl, Mr. Shaw?"

"Kindly let me see that paper." The Director held out an imperious hand. Arthur hesitated, then passed the warrant to him, and watched as their quarry ran through a gallery of astonished, incredulous and contemptuous expressions. Then he tossed the paper on the floor at Arthur's feet. "We both know, don't we, that you obtained that warrant through some new act of malfeasance?"

Arthur picked the warrant off the floor and folded it neatly before sliding it into his pocket. "I really don't think he's going to help us." He looked deliberately around the room, then turned back toward Shaw. "I can see you care about your things. This is a lovely home. It'll get a good deal messier if we have to search every inch of it."

Shaw made a tsk-tsk sound. "Threats, now? You may be sure that I'll catalog anything damaged or made to disappear."

Hal gestured to Arthur, then led him out of Shaw's hearing. "What can we do, the women and I? Will they let us help search? Or can I hold him at gunpoint so the police can do it?"

Arthur looked toward the tableau of Shaw and police, and slowly he smiled, a grim, chilling smile. "Wait a moment, and we'll see." He moved back toward the police, and reached out his hand for the helmet. The policeman holding it shrugged and handed it to Arthur.

Arthur held the helmet in his two hands as he approached the Director. "Since we've intruded so unceremoniously, and since you don't care to assist in our search, we'll let you return to the dream we interrupted."

Shaw's face flooded with terror before he caught himself and banished the expression. "No, thank you. I prefer to remain awake and aware while my home is ransacked."

"As you wish, of course." Arthur turned toward the police. "Mr. Wakeman and I will stay here with the suspect while you conduct the search. If he decides to provide any information, I'll ask one of the civilians to find you."

Shaw looked at the police, already moving away from him; at Hal, standing behind the police, pistol at his side; and back at Arthur, dangling the helmet in his hand.

Without directions, it might have taken them hours to find the girl, if they ever did. But with Shaw choosing to cooperate, it was easy. And she was still alive.

* * *

After an ambulance took the girl away, Arthur huddled briefly with the police before they left with their prisoner.

"She's got a creepy damn story to tell." The policeman shuddered. "Ya know, he told her he was going to take her ashes, mix them with her mother's, and use them to fertilize some garden down the street. Sick. I wonder if he's done it before. Those must be some strange damn flowers."

Arthur staggered toward the wall and leaned heavily against it, closing his eyes.

CHAPTER 37

She had had to do it. How else could they have stopped him? And he had to be stopped.

But....

Wynne vaguely recalled some comic or cartoon, vintage even in her childhood, where the superhero was enjoined to use his powers only for good. Or was it a fairy tale, where some god or fairy gave a gift of special magic, only to withdraw it after it was used for selfish ends?

It hadn't been selfish! To stop a madman?

But if he had not blown a hole in their lives, and wounded them both, and threatened them again, and threatened their loved ones—would she have made it her mission and used her gift to bring him down?

She had brought down a torturer by torturing him with dreams.

Did she deserve, any more, to be protected from the power of nightmares?

She went to sleep that night without planning any dreams. And when she woke, hours before dawn, she was not sure whether she had crafted the dream, or whether it had come to her as dreams came to others.

She had found herself in a Catholic church, one she had seen long ago when spending a weekend with a friend. It was old, small, with rough blocks of stone in the walls, and small bright panes in the stained-glass windows. The real church had had two or three confessionals, but in her dream, there was only one. Darkness loomed beyond the folded accordion door.

She knew she had to enter.

Inside, the area for the penitent was tiny, so that she had to press up close against the wrought-iron screen. The darkness was complete. She could see no cracks of light from the nave of the church. But even though the space was so small and confined, there seemed a vast, echoing silence around her. The priest must be there, only inches away, but she heard no breathing, no movement.

"Bless me, Father, for I have sinned."

The silence waited.

"I made a dream of terrible suffering, knowing I would use it on another human being. And I was proud of it. Proud of what I would be putting him through."

A chill wind blew through the screen, carrying a smell from some ancient crypt.

"Will you absolve me, Father?"

This time, the wind brought a memory: herself, enduring the dream as she made it. A wave of sickness swept over her, and she clung to the screen with cramping fingers.

"Was that my penance, Father? But what I did to him came afterward...."

She felt the faint warmth of another person, someone beyond the screen. And there was light, first faint and then growing, gentle light filling the little space, letting her see her hands and her arms.

Now that she could see herself, she thought she knew the rest.

"I have to go and do good, from now on. To use my gift to help and to heal. That is my penance, isn't it, Father?"

And now, finally, came words from the other side of the screen. "*Deinde, ego te absolvo....*"

The words echoed in her memory as she looked around the darkened bedroom. There, beside her, was Hal, fast asleep. And there, on the nightstand, was her helmet, which she would use again. Here was her home, and some portion of peace.

She lay down close to Hal and let herself sleep.

***

"You could do it now. We both could. The erasure."

Hal looked up from his work to see Wynne standing in the doorway. He studied her face. She did not look as if she were asking a question, or making a proposal. She bore that expression of curiosity with which she tested some hypothesis she had formed, usually one concerning his likely behavior.

"What's going on in that profoundly interesting head of yours?"

Wynne chuckled, then went back to scrutinizing him. "Do you still want to? You could forget all that pain, all the fear. None of those memories would ever sneak up on you again. Or—" She shook her head a little, perhaps unconsciously. "Or find their way into your dreams."

"What about you? You may be able to defend your dreams, but I'm sure the memories have their ways of ambushing you. Do you want them—removed?"

Wynne stuck her lip out in a gentle parody of stubbornness. "I asked you first."

"Then—no."

She lifted her brows. "So quickly? You're that sure?"

"Love, it didn't take you asking to make me consider it. I've been thinking about it ever since they locked up that psycho. I have new paperwork: a blanket pre-authorization, any time I choose. I would even get the government discount."

He had not told her when the paperwork came. He had not wanted to mention it until he decided what to do; and then, once he had decided, it had ceased to matter. Arthur's choice had led him to revisit the question, but only briefly: his own circumstances were very different.

Wynne did not look surprised, exactly, but he knew that she wanted him to explain.

"I've got a couple of reasons. First, I don't know what the memories might take with them."

Wynne nodded. "The empathy effect."

"Yes. That's—it's very precious to me. I think you might have given up on me, in the end, otherwise. I didn't deserve your patience or your loyalty. In a way, I still don't—it wasn't any noble decision or intention that changed me." He felt his mouth twitch in something like a smile. "But even if I don't deserve my second chance, I damn well paid for it.... Anyway, I couldn't take the chance of losing what I've gained."

Wynne gazed at him, her eyes huge. "I don't want you to lose it."

"And even if I could somehow keep that connection without the memories that came with it—I feel like I'd be, I don't know, hollowing myself out." He shook his head in frustration, searching for the right words. "It'd be like plastic surgery. Making me less of who I've become."

Wynne had been leaning against the door frame. Now she straightened up and moved inside, and he saw that she had been holding a worn cloth-bound book in her right hand, her forefinger marking a page. "May I read you something? Because I think I know what you mean."

She held up the book and showed him the cover. It had a title embossed on the front in flowing gold script, much faded: *Adam Bede*. In smaller straighter letters below the title, he could just make out the author's name: George Eliot.

"It's an old book, from 19th century England. This bit comes near the end."

She opened the book and read:

For Adam... had not outlived his sorrow—had not felt it slip from him as a temporary burthen, and leave him the same man again. Do any of us? God forbid. It would be a poor result of all our anguish and our wrestling, if we won nothing but our old selves at the end of it—if we could return to the same blind loves, the same self-confident blame, the same light thoughts of human suffering, the same frivolous gossip over blighted human lives.... Let us rather be thankful that our sorrow lives in us as an indestructible force, only changing its form, as forces do, and passing from pain into sympathy—the one poor word which includes all our best insight and our best love.

He came to her, bent down, and kissed her forehead. "That's it. That's exactly it."

She gave a short nod of satisfaction. "I thought so. And that's how I feel, too. I'm not saying other people shouldn't be able to—to escape! But if I can manage, as I am, with the memories I have, that's what I want. And I know you'll help me. We'll help each other."

She moved away as if expecting him to return to his work; but he put a hand on her shoulder to detain her, and drew her into his arms.

***

Wynne brought up the recording of her meeting with the latest family of clients. She angled her screen so Hal's mother could see it, set the speaker to maximum volume, and pressed "play."

They both watched intently as the family brought out photographs and mementos, and as they took turns telling their favorite anecdotes about their afflicted relative. From time to time, Evelyn would tap Wynne on the arm and point to the screen, giving her opinion on what items or stories would be most effective at reviving the patient's memory or triggering his emotions in a positively stimulating way.

Both women then jotted down their thoughts on what the story of the dream should be, who should be in it and where it should take place. When they were done, they traded drafts, although only Wynne would make immediate use of either.

Evelyn's notes were not always legible, but today the handwriting posed no obstacles. Wynne read rapidly through her mother-in-law's ideas. "Hmmm... I'm not sure we know enough for that one.... But oh, that's lovely! I hadn't paid that much attention to the quilt, but you're perfectly right!"

Hal's mother beamed proudly. Wynne got up and went to kiss the older woman's cheek. "The team does it again! Now let's have some hot chocolate and scones."

Evelyn's face lit up with glee. "Chocolate! Chocolate!"

Harold Senior stuck his head into the kitchen. "Did I hear the magic word? I could use a snack myself."

Wynne cocked her head. "What do you think? Should we let the men have any?"

Evelyn smiled slyly and shook her head. Harold Senior pouted dramatically. "What sort of way is that to treat your husband? Don't I remember something about love, honor, and cherish? And about sharing all our worldly goods? Since when is hot chocolate not included?"

Evelyn's face fell, and she looked as if she might burst into tears. Her husband moved quickly to embrace her. "I'm only teasing, dearest. Would you like me to stay with you while you have your snack?"

Evelyn relaxed and nodded. "Have some. You too."

Wynne, watching, had to blink away tears. He was so sweet to his wife. People always said you could tell what sort of husband a man would be by watching his father and mother together. Her future was in good hands.

* * *

Tertius Shaw retained little that he had ever valued or enjoyed in life. But he did have his privacy. The other prisoners had rioted at the possibility of his being housed among them. And he had so many nightmares, and screamed so often, that no roommate would have let him live for long.

In fact, because of the nightmares and the noise, they had put him in a soundproof cell.

The irony did not escape him.

He had great variety of torment to fill his nights. They had forced upon him the helmet he had used for such exquisite enjoyments, and filled it with crude, unfiltered physical agony, admirable only in its intensity. And then there was *the* dream, Wynne Cantrell's creation, recurring, returning, refusing to be forgotten.

When he was awake, he was subject to a different torture, his unending and unsatisfied curiosity. They would tell him nothing of the lives or fortunes of his victims. He yearned to know about them, and could know nothing. And Wynne, winsome Wynne! How he longed to know what filled her days. Had she remained with the sculptor, now that the man's exoneration was complete? Was she still dreaming? Was she happy?

And no one, no one would tell him.

Chapter 38

Once again, Hal confronted the nauseating associations of a helmet; but this time Wynne was there to help him.

He started by simply touching it, and then taking it in his hand. Within a few days, he could sit in an armchair, reading an absorbing novel, with the helmet on his lap. Then, once more, he placed the helmet on his head. The first time, he snatched it off again and hurled it away, barely managing to aim at the sofa rather than the wall. But once he had worn the helmet for half an hour without much discomfort, he could consider just what he would allow it to record.

Wynne caressed his cheek, tracing along the edge of the helmet. "Are you ready, lover?"

He snared her fingers and kissed them, then let go, smiling up at her. "I do believe I am."

He could not help tensing at the click of the switch; but of course this time nothing happened, or nothing that he could feel. Recording had no sensation associated with it. He relaxed and let his memory float back over years, to a foggy day and a path by a river.

He had been up late the night before and early that morning, studying for a test in Civil Engineering, and felt as foggy as the weather. The fog was so thick that he could hear people and bicycles approaching before he could see them. Even so, he was late in dodging one bicycle, only barely getting out of the way, and still got clipped on the elbow by the rider's backpack.

From behind him he heard a woman's voice, or a girl's. "Are you all right?"

He turned to see the girl, glowing against the fog, a fuzzy orange hat like a winter halo on her head, chestnut curls peeking out beneath it. She came up to him, her eyes almost on a level with his, and made nothing of placing a soft gloved hand on his arm. "Did you get hurt?"

He could not remember what he had answered. He did not know whether he had managed to answer at all, or simply stared, gaping, at the sweetest expression he had ever seen on man or woman....

Hal came back to the present and looked up at Wynne standing beside him, older, still radiant, gazing down at him. He lifted his hands to the helmet, feeling for the switch and pressing it to end the recording. He removed the helmet slowly, ceremoniously, and handed it to her: his gift, his tribute.

* * *

Wynne had picked up lunch at one of her favorite bistros so that she could enjoy the unseasonably warm weather and eat outside in the plaza under Hal's arch. Approaching it, reveling once again in its soaring, graceful lines, it took her a moment to notice the man standing a few feet away from the arch's base, and then to recognize him.

"Max!" She started to ask what he was doing there, and then caught herself. He had every right to be wherever he chose—and no doubt he would explain himself, if she gave him the chance.

Max looked toward her to-go box and held out a somewhat crumpled paper sack. "Join me?"

Wynne bit her lip, then put her box down on the bench. "All right. Just give me a minute." She fished for her phone and sent Hal a quick message: *Ran into Max, will need to talk to him. Wish me luck.—love, Wynne.*

She put away her phone and looked up to see Max standing by the bench, bitterness and concern at war in his expression.

"Whatever you say to him, it won't be enough. Jealous men don't get over it."

Wynne suppressed a sigh. Hal had told her about his encounter with Max. He had apparently been too skilled an actor. Or perhaps he had simply allowed certain feelings free rein for the occasion....

"How can you stay with a man like that? Do you need any help? I may not be a famous sculptor, but I can deal with a bully well enough."

"No! Max, I'm sorry, but nothing is quite as you think it is. And I can't tell you all the reasons why. But I'm fine. I'm not in danger, and I'm not afraid of my husband. Whom I love."

At that last word, she saw a look in his eye that she had never seen—or had failed to see, because she had wanted him to be merely an an adventure, an outlet.

"Even if you love him, there's something he didn't give you—something I could still give you. It could be excitement, pushing boundaries he won't push. Or if you don't want the kink any more, that's fine — I don't care. I still want you, any way I can."

What had she done to this man?

What *had* she done? "Max—have you been buying my dreams?" She held her breath, afraid of the answer.

Max shook his head, frowning. "No. Not yet. But not because your—your *husband* warned me off." He stood up straighter. "It's none of his damned business." He slumped again. "And if I've got no chance of getting you back, at least I could have that much."

Oh, no.

He must have seen her flinch. "If it'd feel wrong to you, having me dream of the two of us being intimate, I could steer clear of that kind. I remember you telling me about some of the other dreams." He blinked hard. "They sounded lovely. I would be happy to share any of them—anything you imagined."

She needed time to think. She gestured toward the bench and opened her lunch. "Please, Max, sit down and eat."

He hesitated, then sat, neither next to her nor at the other end, and opened the paper sack, bringing out a mammoth sandwich. She looked away to hide her smile, which faded almost immediately.

For a moment, she consider explaining it all. But the playback effect was still a secret, it seemed: no one was talking about it anywhere, and her agent hadn't called in a panic.... And what if Max *wanted* that to happen?...

Was there any of the truth she could tell him?

Extracting her four-cheese wrap, she took a bite and then another, hardly tasting it, arranging and re-arranging words in her mind.

"About my dreams: I don't think it'd be a good idea for you to play them. You see—my dreams are meant to... to draw the customer in. To seduce the customer, really. And not just the erotic ones—all of them. After all, I don't want them wandering off to some other dreamer, when I could keep them coming back to me."

That was as close to the truth as she could come. And it was more truth than she had admitted to herself, before everything else had happened.

"My dreams are meant to seduce people. And I don't think that would help you move on."

Max finished chewing a bite of his sandwich, swallowed, and looked her in the eye. "That's the actual reason? You're not trying to protect me from your husband?"

"No, my dear." The word slipped out, and while she had not meant to say it, she did not wish it unsaid. "I'm trying to protect you from me. Please."

He sat silent for a moment, holding the sandwich, and then wrapped it up and dropped it back in the sack. "All right." His mouth twitched in a small, sad smile. "But I don't promise not to dream of you anyway."

He stood up, still gazing at her, then turned and walked away.

Wynne fumbled for her napkin and held it in front of her face for a moment, allowing herself just a little time to cry. Then she wiped her cheeks and her nose and finished her wrap, chewing slowly, pausing between bites.

When she was done, she found a wastebasket, sat back down, and called her agent.

Chapter 39

Dream Daemon stared at his equipment and hissed with frustration. After all that excitement, after he'd helped take down the baddest of bad guys, they were still treating him like a kid! Why else would they have forbidden him, on pain of prosecution for his past pranks, to access any more recordings—not just to hack them, but even to buy?

Well, he might just show them. He could get hold of one, any time, without their ever knowing.

Though he might be kind of busy. They had arranged for that scholarship. Hadn't his mother been surprised—and hadn't Sleazy Boyfriend been *really* surprised!—that he had the chance, all of a sudden, to go to the National Combined Institute of Scientitech, without even having to sit through the rest of his senior year of high school!

Maybe the profs and the other students wouldn't have that much to teach him. But they just might. And then, and *then*, he could really have some fun.

* * *

"So they're hushing it up!"

Arthur closed the refrigerator door and brought the beers to the kitchen table. "Are you surprised? I thought I was supposed to be the naive one in this cabal."

Hal twisted off the top of his beer and took a hearty swig. "I just can't believe they're going on as if nothing had happened. What about the prisoners? And all those dream customers out there?"

Arthur took a more restrained swallow. "Well, so far, the effect on the prisoners seems to be benign. The recidivism rate for helmeted criminals is distinctly lower than average—

unless you count misdemeanor stalking offenses. The authorities have at least put an end to jailhouse weddings where playback may be a factor. They didn't need to reveal any information to do that—just let the red tape multiply, the way it wants to do anyway."

"Wynne's pretty ticked off about the secrecy. She'd like to see helmets used in marriage counseling and the like. We could be the poster couple for that idea."

Arthur's face went carefully blank. Hal pretended not to notice.

"She's cut back on the dreams, you know. She says that until she's allowed to tell people all the possible consequences, she won't let anyone new—except the special clients, the old folks—be exposed to her dreams. I haven't raised the question of what repeated exposure might do. Do you have any data on whether it strengthens the effect?"

Arthur snorted. "None that they're telling me. Our escapade hasn't exactly made the authorities trust me any better."

Hal licked foam off his lips. "At least they got rid of that woman they hired to nail your ass."

Arthur shrugged. "It wasn't her fault. I hope she's doing all right."

They drank a while in silence. Hal was the first to break it. "Any news on our sociopathic friend?"

Arthur shuddered. "He keeps asking about Wynne. And trying to send her messages."

Hal glowered. "If he ever gets loose—"

"I've made sure I'll know at once. And it's hardly likely. He's not the mastermind he was. And he's got nothing to bribe or threaten with. He's staying put."

Hal raised his beer in a toast. "I'll drink to that."

Watching Arthur take a particularly large gulp of his own beer, Hal struggled briefly with his curiosity and then gave in. "Have you noticed any more effects from your exposure to Shaw's recording?"

Arthur put down his beer and stared out over Hal's right shoulder. "I was having dreams. Dreams of claustrophobia. Hannah thought I might be identifying with Shaw, locked up tight as he is. She talked me into doing something about it."

Hal bit back the next question: he had pried enough. But Arthur went on. "I had the memory erased. No one really knows yet whether that eliminates the playback effect. But I've only had one of the dreams since then." He paused, then sat up straighter. "And I had the prison make a recording of Shaw. If he ever does escape somehow, I can play it and help track him down. So I haven't made myself less useful."

Hal suppressed a smile. Only Arthur would feel guilty about freeing himself from the visitations of such a malignant ghost.

The doorbell rang. Arthur scooted back his chair and sprang up, a smile lighting his face. "That'll be Hannah." He walked out of the kitchen with a bounce to his step and let Hannah in. Hal heard a murmured exchange between them, and then Hannah's cheery call, "Ahoy, there, Friend of Boss!"

Arthur protested. "Hey, I'm not your boss!" Technically, of course, that was correct. The new Director (formerly the Deputy Director) had been unable to dissuade Arthur from resigning and setting up shop as a private investigator, but he had not gone so far as to take Hannah with him. Apparently Hannah's services were valuable enough for the Director to overlook the likelihood that Hannah would act as an inside resource for Arthur's firm. Eventually institutional pressures might put an end to that arrangement, and Arthur might well become Hannah's employer once again.

After an interval he deemed sufficient for an affectionate greeting, Hal emerged from the kitchen to find he had not waited long enough. He stood watching the happy couple for a moment, then shook his head in exaggerated indulgence. "Such goings-on! Well, I'll be heading out. Wynne and I have an appointment with her doctor. I'm going to learn how to breathe, so I can be a nuisance and second-guess her when the time comes."

Hannah rolled her eyes, then smiled at him. "Please give Wynne my best. And congratulations! Mazel tov!"

Hal tipped an imaginary hat. "Thanks, milady. Arthur — poker this Saturday?"

"You're on! Hannah's going to help me with my poker face, aren't you, Hannah?"

"I sure am!" Hannah seized Arthur's arm in a firm grasp. "You won't have a clue, Hal. No more amateur detective for you."

Hal nodded with more emphasis than strictly necessary. "That's more than all right with me." Then he waved at them both and made his way out.

* * *

"Wynne, honey, that's impossible. You know there's a gag order on this supposed side effect. We start offering memory erasure to our customers, and we'd be violating that order — not to mention planting the idea that our product somehow taints our customers' brains! If we're going to go out of business, I'd rather do it *without* ending up in the federal pen."

Wynne wracked her brains for pragmatic, unemotional arguments. "You don't have to highlight it. Just add it to the terms and conditions, as a sort of guarantee. Just say that if they're less than delighted with the results, they can get the dream erased."

Her agent smiled at her as at a precocious child attempting a grownup game. "You haven't mentioned the cost of erasure. So either you don't know it — or you know it's too high."

She clenched her teeth, then made herself relax. "I know the usual range — and for the occasional customer, you could handle it. You could always discontinue the option if it got too expensive."

"Tell you what. You write up a proposal and send it to me. I'll submit it to management. All right?"

There was little point in saying what they both knew, that this was a brush-off. Her proposal would go nowhere. She had already relinquished most of her leverage by restricting distribution of her dreams. She forced a smile, kept her goodbyes short, and left him behind.

* * *

The copywriter had known all along that the campaign was doomed. But the brass had persisted, and she had done her best with the assignment—for pride's sake and in the hope that the quality of the product might be remembered, even when it was inevitably discarded.

So she listened with apparent attention as her boss told her what anyone with minimal knowledge of current technology and culture should have known already.

"The promotion for artists is dead. The helmets can't keep them from forgetting their inspiration when they're interrupted or whatever. Testing showed that all the helmets could pick up was the creative "aha!" moment—not the idea behind it. It drove 'em crazy. We had three helmets damaged—destroyed, more like—by test subjects."

The copywriter had expected nothing from this meeting but the dubious satisfaction of a suppressed "I told them so." But sitting there, looking at the round soft face of her dimwit boss, she was struck with an "aha" moment of her own.

She almost asked permission to share her idea with him. But she thought better of it, just in time, and asked for permission to go on with her next assignment. (In fact, she had none, but it would never do to say as much.) She hurried back to her office, grabbed her private tablet, and clocked out for an early lunch.

The helmets captured emotions, the more intense the better. What better raw material for art than emotions themselves? Artists had always sought to inspire emotion—from the classic pity, fear, and catharsis of tragedy, to terror or bathos or lust. But now, they could cut through to the essence: design landscapes, melodies, chords, of emotions, dictating exactly what their audiences would feel. What power! No artist could resist it!

She just had to find the right partners—lucid dreamers, perhaps—with the right skills and the necessary blend of ambition and discretion.

A year from now, or two, or three at the most, she would be watching her boss grovel for her business. And he could just get in line.

CHAPTER 40

"SO THEY FOUND IT? In *Shaw's* house? Jesus!"

"They must have had cops swarming over the place like cockroaches. Found some other recordings, too—nasty ones. Dunno if we'll have anything to do with those."

"What about all those rumors?"

The second worker looked around furtively. "You just shut up about that! Anyone spreading 'em, anyone saying anything at all, is going to get tossed out on his ear, and with nothing—no accrued leave, no pension."

The first worker looked as if he had bit into something sour. "So they're supposed to study the death recording, all very scientific and thorough. And somehow ignore what anybody's learned about how recordings work."

"Do you make the rules? Do I make the rules? Just watch your mouth. Keep your head down, like."

* * *

"It's just routine. Just dotting the i's. We had already obtained your mother's consent—and please accept my sympathies on her passing."

The girl looked up from her folded hands. "Thank you. If it's just routine, why are you bothering me about it?"

The visitor's bland expression did not change. Had the girl imagined that moment of hesitation?

"I'm so sorry." The woman did not sound sorry. "But we want to have everything fully covered—every possible contingency. To avoid any misunderstandings later on."

"You have my mother's consent, you say. Consent to what? Or should I ask: to which? Which recording are you talking about?"

The visitor's eyelids fluttered. What sort of weasel-words had they slipped into what they wanted her to sign? They'd taken her for a fool, but she was on to them!

"Yes, I know he—" The girl closed her eyes and concentrated on breathing deeply until the nausea subsided. "I know that monster recorded my mother's—my mother. I know because he made me play it."

And she would never, never let anyone else intrude on that sacred moment. Or on her brother's. She had not experienced that recording, and she never would. She would find a way to stop them for studying it like a specimen in a jar!

She was left alone now; but she would protect what her family had left behind.

***

The judge ran her gaze up and down the line of lawyers, and then back again. Several of the more susceptible flinched as if at actual contact.

"I will not claim astonishment that we are assembled here again. It seemed likely enough that some further controversy would arise from the implementation of my prior order. However, there are a few of you who did not attend the previous hearing; and the motion before me claims that new facts, or new information concerning facts previously discussed, justifies or requires me to vacate the existing order. Upon urgent requests from various authorities, this hearing has been closed to the public, and its contents—as well as all pertinent court records—will remain confidential until I have an adequate opportunity to assess those authorities' concerns." A sniff, and an economical twitch of the eyebrows, suggested the fate of those restrictions once the judge had leisure to evaluate them.

"I'll hear from one of the motion's proponents. The rest of you may sit down."

A trim young woman, looking rather like a younger version of the judge, stood up straight and waited. When the muted scraping of chair legs on wood had ceased, she looked up at the judge and began.

"Your Honor, I represent the National Privacy Federation. We have joined with the Ecumenical Counsel, who appeared previously in this matter, to request a permanent injunction as to any experimentation on or dissemination of any recording that includes the experience of dying, including the recording recently recovered by police. I also represent the only surviving immediate family member of the subject of that recording, who has filed a separate motion addressing her brother's recording and any recording made of their mother.

"The recent revelations as to the scope of experience captured and transmitted in helmet recordings, and the involuntary identification with the subject—"

"A moment, counselor. The term 'revelation' suggests definite information, rather than rumor or speculation. What is the source of this information?"

The attorney lifted a sheaf of papers and put them down again. "The detailed internal police reports, including that of former Senior Homicide Detective Arthur Kellic, are attached to our motion."

"I've read them. They list various inferences to be drawn from recent events—though not all the inferences bear that label. I would go so far as to call many of those inferences reasonable, and some even compelling. Do you propose that we as a society pause indefinitely on that threshold, rather than attempting to verify these hypotheses?"

"Your Honor, the evidence already available indicates a serious risk to the psychological well-being of any human subject. Exposure to any helmet recording carries these risks, but where the playback may form an empathetic connection to a person already deceased, the likelihood of creating a grief complex is too great to be ignored. As indicated in the affidavit of Doctor—"

The judge shook her head. "I will save Project counsel the trouble of pointing out that no one, even the good doctor, is at this point in a position to offer expert testimony on the likely result of exposure to such recordings. Have you anything pertinent to offer, before I hear from those opposing these motions?"

The attorney cleared her throat. "As to the motion filed by the survivor: she asserts the privacy interest of the deceased. There is already substantial evidence that exposure to these recordings will transfer some, if an unpredictable, amount of information beyond what the person recorded experienced during the period of the recording itself. We thus have multiple intrusions: on one of the most personal of all human experiences, as well as multiple past experiences."

The judge gave a brisk nod. "Would any of opposing counsel care to respond on that specific point?"

The three attorneys for the Project put their heads together and muttered, two of them glancing repeatedly at the judge as the caucus continued. And indeed, its length appeared to be trying the judge's patience.

"Ladies and gentlemen, the longer it takes for you to come up with anything to say, the more I am inclined to rely on my tentative judgment—which is to grant the motion as to the two existing recordings. Now or never, people."

The elder of the three, the man with the whitest hair and most expensive suit, straightened up and faced the judge. "Your Honor, we already have the consent of the subject of the second recording, as to the study of the first. The logical inference is that she would have consented to the use of her own recording as well."

The judge snorted. "And that consent was obtained before the evidence as to the scope of these recordings became available. Feeble, counselor. Anything else?"

The one woman on the legal team took a small step forward. "This determination may be premature. The negotiations with the surviving family member are ongoing."

The judge fixed the attorney with a stern eye. "That assessment is perhaps inconsistent with the motion she has filed. But if an agreement is reached in the future and presented to me with all proper authentication, I will revise my ruling accordingly. I am enjoining any use of, and any duplication of, any recordings made of petitioner's family members, until such time as petitioner withdraws her objection, and I also order that all existing copies—including originals—of those recordings be turned over to her." The judge took a moderately deep breath before she continued. "As to the broader issue, I will now hear opposition to the motion."

The two Project attorneys whom the judge had already swatted down turned toward the third, who bowed almost imperceptibly in the judge's direction and then spoke. "As you suggested a moment ago, Your Honor, it is imperative that the possibilities raised by recent events be explored, rather than left unexamined. We must, as soon as possible, end the uncertainty as to whether the playback industry is disseminating personal information and creating unexpected emotional entanglements. Studying the recordings of the deceased avoids what would otherwise be inevitable if this effect is in fact demonstrated: namely, intrusion on the privacy of the living."

The judge pursed her lips for a moment. "The crucial point, it seems to me, is the permission of the person recorded. And the crucial issue to be investigated has nothing to do with that person's eventual fate. All of which I will consider during a short recess. Please remain on the premises." She stood up and exited through the back door of the courtroom before the attorneys had finished scrambling to their feet.

A few of them looked longingly toward the main door, but none seemed inclined to risk being found absent when the judge returned. Those on the same side huddled together in muted conversation, except for the young attorney for the

National Privacy Foundation, who walked restlessly up and down the center aisle.

No more than ten minutes had passed before the bailiff announced the judge's return. She took the bench, waited briefly for the attorneys to resettle themselves, and then addressed them all.

"Here is my ruling. Any testing of any kind on helmet recordings, effective immediately, may be conducted only on recordings procured with the informed consent of the one recorded. I will issue a written order within the week, stating the minimum details to be included in the consent form. You may study death recordings as per my previous order, if and only if you have obtained either the consent of the closest surviving family member or the pre-mortem consent of the individual recorded."

The movants' attorney raised her hand and received the judge's unspoken permission to speak. "Your Honor, we would ask that you reconsider allowing reliance on the permission of relatives. Given the uniquely personal nature—"

"No, counselor. I cannot agree that the way we die is more personal and private than the way we live. And while the consent of anyone other than the subject is, I agree, inferior to an extent, I will not obstruct the study of these recordings so far as to require researchers to eagerly await the demise of those who have granted permission. Aside from all other considerations, I have no wish to create problematic incentives."

* * *

Security chief Martin Prujack took a cautious sip of his beer and looked across the rough wooden table at the warden. Warden Heath had never before invited him—or anyone else at the prison, as far as he knew—to go out for a drink. The chief had learned, in his job, to distrust unexplained changes in routine. At least the warden was impatient enough to blurt out whatever he had in mind before much longer.

Sure enough, Heath gestured to the server with his empty shot glass, thumped it down on the table, and leaned in toward the chief. He muttered something, but a sudden shout from the bar area drowned him out. Martin glanced over, but the television was pointed in the wrong direction: he could not see what game was on, let alone who had scored.

The warden frowned and spoke a little louder, looking around furtively. "Something's coming down the pike. We need to be ready."

"Okay."

The server approached with the warden's drink. The warden waited for her to move away, then leaned as far across the table as his good-sized midsection would allow. He was almost whispering; Martin suppressed a frown and leaned forward in his turn, straining to hear.

"You know about all that funny business with the prisoners and the playbacks and the vics. Well, we were right. It's all being treated as top secret, and they're trying to keep the reporters away from it—but the effect is real. And there's a plan in the works to take care of it."

The warden paused again, as if there was anything useful the chief could say before he knew what the plan was. Martin filled the silence by draining his mug and looking around for the server. Before he could find her, the warden tapped impatiently on the table. "Listen! They're going to try to erase the prisoners' memories."

"What?"

"Not all their memories! Just whatever they remember from the playbacks."

Martin stared at the warden. "Are the doctors, or whoever, going to come into the prison? Where would we put them?

How long would they stay? Or would we have to get all those prisoners to and from hospitals somehow?"

"Well, you see why I wanted to tell you. You'll have to work out all that, come up with solid procedures...."

Great. Just great.

As for the idea itself —"And that's supposed to undo whatever else the playbacks did? What if it's something that just sort of piggybacked on the memories? How do they know it'll work?"

The warden snorted. "They don't. It's not exactly something you can get volunteers to test. But they're going to try it and see."

The longer Martin thought, the more problems popped up. "What about the lawyers? The defense bar is going to be all over this. Monkeying with memories? Jesus."

The warden fidgeted and looked down. "I'm not sure whether the lawyers will get a chance to interfere."

Now that was just crazy. They were planning to zap all those prisoners' brains—in secret—and expect to get away with it? Martin was going to end up doing private security at a home and garden store. And the warden was going to end up in a cell.

"Boss—can you give anyone any feedback about this plan? How soon is it all supposed to go down?"

The warden slumped back in his chair. "I don't know. I don't know what to do. I haven't even mentioned the worst part."

"Hold on. If there's something worse, I need another beer."

The warden ignored him. "The brides."

"Oh, shit."

"They're going to murder us. However it pans out, whether the prisoners go back to their old selves or whether we end up screwing around with their brains for nothing, the brides are going to march on the prison with pitchforks and torches. We're toast, chief. We're done for."

Martin stared at the warden, then silently arose and made his way to the bar. He caught the bartender's eye and presented his mug, silently, as if pleading for alms. He returned to their table, stood by his chair, and raised the mug toward the warden. "To our asses, boss. Let's drink as we kiss them goodbye."

Chapter 41

ONE HAD TO TAKE the unexpected gifts that life handed one. If Wynne had not found out that she was unwittingly turning her customers into followers, she would have gone on doing the same old thing, the familiar path becoming a rut. (So to speak.) She might not have noticed the online chatter about the new art form, let alone tracked down the young woman who was promoting it. She might have missed a medium ideally suited to her abilities, an unexplored territory in which she would be a pioneer.

The same abilities that let her craft her dreams would now enable her to control the nuances of emotion itself. She could look forward to years of exploring the aesthetic relationships between various feelings, and the effects of different transitions between them. Why, in years to come, beginning students might learn the equivalent of chord structures—structures that Wynne had created!

Of course, the same constraints of conscience would apply for the time being. But secrets never stayed secret for long. Once the effect of helmet playback became generally known, potential consumers, whether of dreams or of the new emotional journeys, would know the risks. They would have a choice. And as for the users' intrusion on Wynne's own privacy: that ship had sailed, long since. With all those who might have glimpsed bits of Wynne's thoughts and feelings already, she would not trouble herself about an increase in their number.

Surely this secrecy could not continue long. Of course, once the secret was out, the playback industry might disintegrate completely or even be outlawed. If that happened, she could still create. Hal, at least, would be eager to share her visions;

and if repeated playbacks strengthened the empathic effect, he would welcome that as well.

(She would not offer to share her product with Arthur. He was not the sort to want his emotions tugged about; and if repetition did intensify the effect, that would hardly be a kindness. Besides, she owed Hannah better.)

Maybe some day soon, the engineers that had made the playbacks possible would find a way to separate out the Effect and make it voluntary. Then she could dream for others again without fear of hijacking their emotions.

Though she would miss their love.

***

The last real reporter read through his notes with growing excitement. The story was coming together. It might even be time to alert his network of bloggers that he had something in store for them, something big.

The prisoners—that had been his first hint, his first break. A victims' support group had discovered that several of their members were getting disturbingly well-informed, even intimate, messages from the incarcerated criminals who had victimized them. And all those criminals had gotten the helmet.

And then there had been the on-again-off-again research into the accidentally created death recording, and more recently, a publicity blackout on the subject. His informants might not defy such an edict, but one or more of them would would let him know as soon as it was lifted. Indeed, he'd just received a tip that the gag order would be reversed within the week.

(One of the police detectives who had been in charge of the recording had resigned—right after helping capture a serial killer. What kind of sense did that make? Was it part of the puzzle?)

The reporter's intuition had led him next to the professional dreamers and their fan base. Without the other threads, he would have seen nothing remarkable about any artist having flocks of followers, but in context....

Then there was the reaction when he finally approached a few prosecutors and a vendor of dreams: instant, almost panicky stonewalling. And threats. But he was used to threats. He would hardly be doing his job if no one cared enough to threaten him. He had simply done additional research and added some items to his "insurance" file. If the threats escalated, he would inform the party in question of just how counterproductive trying to silence him could be.

Then, just the other day, one of his stable of sources had sent a nervous and cryptic message about something funny going on in one of the security agencies, that agents' loyalties were being undermined somehow. He was still working on how to follow up on that tip. Those fellows played rough.

Lighting an illicit cigarette and taking a deep drag, he pondered some possible headlines. "Helmets: the Hidden Dangers"? No, incomplete alliteration was worse than none. "Helmets: the Poisoned Promise"? A bit sensational for modern sensibilities.

"Helmets: Learning You from the Inside Out." Yes, that was more like it. The bloggers would run with it. He would crack this thing wide open.

Vive le journalisme!

* * *

Wynne had considered dreaming of the later stages of her pregnancy, or of the labor and delivery. On reflection, however, she was afraid that feeding herself such detailed images might make it harder to cope with the reality, should it prove different than her creations. But the impulse to dwell on and revel in her pregnancy would not be denied. In the end, she chose a different approach.

...She swam inside the backlit, golden fluid around her, weightless, learning to move, learning her limbs. What was this new toy, now so close and then farther away? She made it move, brought it toward her face. One little piece thrust toward her. It would fit in her mouth! She sucked her thumb, floating, tumbling, somersaulting, content.

Life was good. And more good things would happen, later....

* * *

The large, obviously heavy object, swathed in blankets and drapes, swung from the hook of the crane as it moved over the plaza toward its destination. To Hal it looked like a giant victory bell, tolling its triumph in tones too low for human ears.

The site of the former fountain had been cleared of debris and a new foundation built, complete with all the necessary plumbing. There was even an alarm system, installed despite Hal's opposition. He had wanted children to splash about, and reckless college kids to climb around illicitly at two in the morning, without the intrusion of sirens blaring; but he had grudgingly accepted a compromise. The alarm would be activated only at nightfall.

Hal stood arm in arm with Wynne in the spring sunshine, his parents beside him. He knew Arthur and Hannah were watching from somewhere back in the crowd. All around, spectators took innumerable pictures. Hal preferred to watch without the distraction of framing and filtering.

The sculpture swayed lower, lower, more and more slowly, and finally settled into place, rocking just a bit and then standing firm.

Now came the unwrapping, just as nerve-wracking if he let it be, with all the smaller, more delicate pieces—the reaching, flying spirits—to be released from their cocoons. A swarm of workers clambered about, using ladders and stools to reach the padded blankets. Spectators oo'ed and aah'ed as each graceful figure was revealed. Wynne leaned over, each time, and murmured in his ear, "Remember the day I posed for that one for two hours straight?... Remember what we did, right there on the studio floor, when that one was finished?..."

Through the outer branches, Hal could catch only glimpses of the worker unwrapping the innermost sculpture, the heart of the piece: an infant, curled close, its face hidden. When the water was turned on, it would be submerged, continually bathed, as if floating in the womb.

Hal turned back toward the outer edges of the sculpture. He had not told even Wynne what those identical abstract forms, one at every compass point, represented. Some might guess that they were meant to suggest a human figure, its arms spread wide in benediction or protection, but he might never reveal to whom they paid tribute: Arthur, guardian and defender, keeping watch.

It seemed to take hours, but finally the fountain stood as he hoped it would stand for many years to come. The first workers left and others took their places. Then, after even more waiting, they could hear the creaking of metal parts and the rush of water; and the arcs and waterfalls gushed forth to complete his vision.

The crowd moved forward, taking more pictures, reaching out to catch the spray or to toss the first coins. A man hoisted his little daughter on his shoulders to see above the milling people; his wife smiled and squeezed his arm. Hal looked toward Wynne and pointed. For a moment she looked distressed, as if the happy family triggered some sadder memory; but then she smiled back and stretched upward to kiss him.

Hal's father grabbed Hal's hand and shook it, then helped Hal's mother make her way through the crowd to reach Hal and kiss his cheek. In a moment Arthur and Hannah joined them. Arthur looked at Wynne, who was standing almost on tiptoe and seemed about to take flight toward the fountain. "Go on, get up there. We'll keep Hal's folks company."

Hal nodded his gratitude and put an arm around Wynne's shoulders, guiding her through the crush, turning her this way and that so that no one came in contact with her swelling belly. He led her to the spot through which one could best see the infant in the center. "There she is, love." Then he pointed upward. "And there you are, and there, looking down at her. And there, looking out at the world."

"Oh, Hal, it's so beautiful!" She reached out her hand to dabble in the water. He supported her as she leaned, then gathered her back and into his arms. As he kissed her, someone started to clap. Soon, all around the fountain, people were clapping and whistling.

Wynne broke free of the kiss and whispered to him, "Should you say something?"

Hal shook his head. "I've said it, here, for all to see." He looked around at all that they had wrought, at the water catching and spreading the sunlight. "Now let's go home."

They could not, in fact, leave immediately. There were reporters to satisfy, or to frustrate where they intruded too far. And then they had to see his parents home—the home they once again shared, with a live-in caretaker to help look after his mother.

When Hal and Wynne finally reached their house, they were both too tired to cook, assembling a hodge-podge of a supper from pantry and refrigerator. They soon gave up on any sort of evening activity. Hal drew a deep hot bath for Wynne, with the aromatic bath salts she loved and which her doctor had approved. He helped her in, then sat on the lid of the toilet and kept her company, neither of them feeling much need for conversation.

He levered her back out again, helped her dry the areas she found increasingly hard to reach, and slipped her nightgown over her head. Finally, they were ready for bed. He drew back the covers and helped Wynne clamber in, then handed her the sleep inducer. She settled it over her right ear and lay curled on her left side.

He turned off the light and joined her, curving around her, placing his arm carefully around her belly where her waist would have been. Wynne snuggled backward against him with a humming, purring sound of contentment.

Soon she would be asleep—in his arms.

THE END

ACKNOWLEDGMENTS

Once again, I heartily thank my beta readers, who this time included (in alphabetical order): Jill-Elizabeth Arent, Karen Banes, Danielle Evans, Lehsa Griebel, Steven Karel, David Leek, and Samantha Sabovitch.

My thanks to Alissa Wyle and Paul Hager (daughter and husband respectively) for responding with patience to innumerable requests for feedback on story elements, word choices, and book cover options.

ABOUT THE AUTHOR

KAREN A. WYLE was born a Connecticut Yankee, but eventually settled in Bloomington, Indiana, home of Indiana University. She now considers herself a Hoosier. Wyle's childhood ambition was to be the youngest ever published novelist. While writing her first novel at age ten, she was mortified to learn that some British upstart had beaten her to the goal at age nine.

Wyle is an appellate attorney, photographer, political junkie, and mother of two daughters. Her voice is the product of almost five decades of reading both literary and genre fiction. It is no doubt also influenced, although she hopes not fatally tainted, by her years of law practice. Her personal history has led her to focus on often-intertwined themes of family, communication, personal identity, the impossibility of controlling events, and the persistence of unfinished business.

Connect with
Karen A. Wyle Online

Learn more about Karen A. Wyle by looking her up
on:

Her website at
www.KarenAWyle.net

Twitter, where her handle is
@WordsmithWyle

Facebook, at
www.facebook.com/KarenAWyle

Her Goodreads profile at
www.goodreads.com/kawyle

Or her blog, Looking Around, at
looking-around.blogspot.com

Like the book? Please tell readers!
Online book reviews are enormously helpful—and
old-fashioned word of mouth is terrific as well!